劉毅「一口氣英語 ～～
北京發佈會

～～丂子稟

2018年4月13日上午，劉毅「一口氣極短句」北京發佈會圓滿成功，近200名來自全國各地的英語名師齊聚一堂，大家聆聽大師培訓，感受「一口氣英語」的獨特魅力。

劉毅老師熱情地與學員分享「一口氣英語」

劉毅老師親傳弟子第一名，百萬女神Windy老師當場展示這套方法，轟動全場，引起了老師們熱烈的掌聲！從四年前的濟南第一屆一口氣師訓的第一名，到如今眾人矚目的明星老師，

Windy老師的成長經歷，讓每一位在座的老師動容。

本次會議由劉毅老師「一口氣英語」推廣大使關海南主持，關校為「一口氣英語」在大陸的推廣和發展方面做出了突出的貢獻，同時他也是劉毅老師的學生兼董事長助理，主持現場激情四射，掌聲連連。

楊晨老師　　　　　　　　　　關海南校長

　　本次發佈會的成功舉辦，離不開「北京超常國際教育」董事長、「中高考批量滿分生產者」楊晨老師的精心組織，楊晨老師也在現場發表講話，述說和「一口氣英語」的獨特情緣。

這是一次有溫度的思想盛宴，英語圈智慧的交流。活動結束後，老師們仍然意猶未盡，大家排隊和劉毅老師合影、簽名，每位與會老師都獲得了劉毅老師贈送的厚厚的一口氣經典教材。

劉毅老師與「一口氣必考字彙極短句講座」學員合影

當天下午，來自北京教育培訓界的眾多大咖在楊晨老師的組織下，舉辦了「劉毅一口氣座談會」，共同就「一口氣英語」在海峽兩岸的傳承和推廣進行了深入探討，大家紛紛各抒己見，獻言獻策。

特別感謝座談會成員的支持（排名不分先後）

李國慶	華夏都市記者俱樂部主席
賈主任	全國青少年法制教育心理、指導中心主任
	教育部下一代基金會主任
田院長	中國小作家報總編
	中華少年國學院院長
方主席	中國中小學趣味數學教育聯盟主席
苗　總	名師橋教師資源分享平臺董事長
	北京育新苗教育創始人
安　總	中國教育仲介服務行業協會線上教育分會秘書長
	直播與雙師課堂協會會發起人
張　總	三好網教師幫秘書長
黃　總	閒問線上教育平臺董事長
	北京課後港教育平臺創使人
莊　校	莊則敬國學堂創始人
陳　總	北大新世紀教育集團總經理
一　哥	北京校長眾籌俱樂部執行總裁
蔡　箐	外文出版社編輯部主任
楊　晨	北京超常國際教育董事長

序 言

　　以前，人們學英文，是利用閱讀文章，造成了「啞巴英語」。其實，人類最早學說話，是從一個字開始。我們這項發明，就像小孩學語言一樣，從極短句開始。不過我們融入了必考字彙，每個單字均註明級數，第 1 級最簡單，第 6 級最困難，全部不超出常用 7000 字範圍。學完不僅單字增加，能說出美妙的語言，還能夠讓同學戰勝考試。從 Lesson 1 Persevere! Persist! Carry on! 以三句為一組，九句為一段開始背。背以前可以先看劉毅老師親授的「Lesson 1 教學實況影音」。

劉毅老師親授 Lesson 1
教學實況影音

　　每一回 9 句，背至 10 秒內，即變成直覺，終生不忘。剛開始有點困難，因為你的嘴部發音肌肉不習慣說英語，如：I'm sad. I feel bad. I'm unhappy about it. 中的 sad〔sæd〕、bad〔bæd〕、unhappy〔ʌnˈhæpɪ〕，a 唸 /æ/，中文裡沒有 /æ/ 的音，中文裡也沒有 /m/ 的音，所以會把 I'm 唸成 I'n。碰到 /æ/，嘴巴裂開，用力唸即可；碰到 m 在字尾，唸的時候嘴巴要閉上，就不會唸錯。只要先背完 Lesson 1 的 108 句，其他就簡單了。

　　每一課有 108 句，在最後總複習有 QR 碼，只要用手機掃描，就可以聽到美籍播音員的錄音，並且可以重複播放。全部 Lesson 1～Lesson 10，共 1,080 句的錄音 QR 碼，在本書的封底。

　　英文不使用就會忘記，背「一口氣必考字彙極短句」，有助於快速增加單字，背過的句子，說起來有信心，每一句都可以主動對外國人說。早上一起床，到公園裡空氣好的地方，一面走路、一面背，是最好的選擇。養成隨時隨地背的習慣，英文越來越好，非常有成就感。

　　背這本書是一種挑戰，一個 Lesson、一個 Lesson 地背下去，共 1,080 句，可以一口氣全部背完，如果能背到 12 至 15 分鐘內，便終生難忘。每一回、每一個 Lesson 都有劇情連貫，背的時候，要有耐心經過精心設計，你一定能背得下來，這是學好英文最快速的方法。

劉　毅

CONTENTS

CONTENTS

Lesson 1　I'm thankful.

1. Persevere!

看英文唸出中文	一 口 氣 說 九 句	看中文唸出英文
persevere[6] 〔ˌpɝsəˈvɪr〕v.	*Persevere!* 要堅忍！	堅忍
persist[5] 〔pɚˈsɪst〕v.	*Persist!* 要堅持！	堅持
carry on	*Carry on!* 繼續堅持下去！	繼續堅持下去
reliable[3] 〔rɪˈlaɪəbḷ〕adj.	Be *reliable*. 要可靠。	可靠的
responsible[2] 〔rɪˈspɑnsəbḷ〕adj.	Be *responsible*. 要負責任。	負責任的
count[1] 〔kaʊnt〕v.	Be someone to *count on*. 要做一個能夠被依賴的人。	數
quit[2] 〔kwɪt〕v.	Don't *quit*. 不要停止。	停止
discourage[4] 〔dɪsˈkɝɪdʒ〕v.	Don't get *discouraged*. 不要氣餒。	使氣餒
abandon[4] 〔əˈbændən〕v.	Don't *abandon* your goals.　不要放棄你的目標。	放棄

【背景說明 1】

　　這九個字、九句話經過巧妙安排，任何人都可以背下來，天天用得到，可以用來鼓勵你的朋友和同學。

兩個 per
開頭的
同義字 {
*Per*severe!
*Per*sist!
}
成語 ← *Carry on!*
唸一遍就背下來

兩個單
字都是
re 開頭 {
*Be re*liable.
*Be re*sponsible.
}
成語 ← Be someone to *count on.*
唸一遍就背下來

三個否定句 {
Don't quit.
Don't get discouraged.
Don't abandon your goals.
}
最多唸兩遍就背下來

　　一個字一個字地背，背到後面忘了前面；背了不使用，立刻就會忘記。我們要背一些可以主動說的話。傳簡訊時，可以用到這些話：*Persevere! Persist! Carry on!*（要堅忍！要堅持！要繼續堅持下去！）如果你今天背一個 persevere，幾個月以後再碰到一個 persist，怎麼記得住？即使暫時記住，也不知道怎麼用。*Carry on!* 的意思是「繼續堅持下去！」也可說成：Continue on!（繼續前進！）三個一起背，背了不忘記，多麼令人興奮！養成習慣，不停地唸，想像對某一個人說話，就更容易背了。

reliable 和 responsible 是同義字，都是 re 開頭的。***count on*** 是「依賴」(= *depend on* = *rely on*)。***Be someone to count on.*** 句子兩短一長，最好背，短句在前，長句在後。

Don't quit. 也可說成：Don't stop.（不要停止。）或 Don't give up.（不要放棄。）quit 是及物和不及物兩用動詞，如：Don't quit your job.（不要辭職。）也可接動名詞為受詞，如：I can't quit smoking.（我無法戒煙。）I can't quit watching television.（我無法停止看電視。）***Don't get discouraged.*** 中的 discourage 是「使氣餒」，如：Don't let them discourage you.（不要讓它們使你氣餒。）***Don't get discouraged.*** 也可說成：Don't be discouraged. 意思相同。

晚上睡覺前背這九句話，有助於睡眠，也可以激勵自己，做一個成功的人。

2. Look forward.

看英文唸出中文	一 口 氣 說 九 句	看中文唸出英文
end[1] 〔 ɛnd 〕 *n.*	It's not the **end**. 這不是結束。	結束
beginning[1] 〔 bɪ'gɪnɪŋ 〕 *n.*	Just the **beginning**. 只是開始。	開始
forward[2] 〔'fɔrwəd 〕 *adv.*	Look **forward**. 要向前看。	向前
hope[1] 〔 hop 〕 *n.*	Have **hope**. 要有希望。	希望
faith[3] 〔 feθ 〕 *n.*	Have **faith**. 要有信心。	信念；信心
courage[2] 〔'kɝɪdʒ 〕 *n.*	Have **courage**. 要有勇氣。	勇氣
determined[3] 〔 dɪ'tɝmɪnd 〕 *adj.*	Be **determined**. 要有決心。	有決心的
tide[3] 〔 taɪd 〕 *n.*	The **tide** will turn. 形勢會轉變。	潮流；形勢
one's **day**	*Your day* will come. 你會飛黃騰達。	（某人）飛黃騰達 的時候；全盛時期

Lesson 1

【背景說明 2】

　　當你看到朋友落魄、失意，你就可以跟他說：*It's not the end.* 也可以加長為：Don't worry. It's not the end. （別擔心。這不是結束。）It's not the end of the world. （這不是世界末日。）*Just the beginning.* 源自：It's just the beginning. （這只是剛開始。）（= *It's just the start.*）*Look forward.* 也可說成：Look ahead. （向前看。）可加長為：I encourage you to look forward. （我鼓勵你向前看。）

　　Have hope. 可說成：Be hopeful. （要有希望。）See the future. （要看未來。）*Be determined.* 可說成：Be persistent. （要堅持。）*The tide will turn.* 可說成：Things will change. （情況會改變。）可加長為：The tide will turn and better things will happen. （形勢會改變，會有好事發生。）Things will change for the better. （情況會變好。）（= *Things will be better.*）

　　Your day will come. 字面的意思是「你的日子會來到。」引申為「你會飛黃騰達；你會成功。」可加長為：Be patient. Your day will come. （要有耐心。你終將成功。）I promise you that your day will come. （我保證你會飛黃騰達。）有句英文諺語：Every dog has his day. （凡人皆有得日。）【詳見「英文諺語辭典」p.110】

3. Be able.

看英文唸出中文	一 口 氣 說 九 句	看中文唸出英文
able[1] (ˈebḷ) adj.	Be **able**. 要有能力。	有能力的
skillful[2] (ˈskɪlfəl) adj.	Be **skillful**. 要有專門技術。	有技術的
talent[2] (ˈtælənt) n.	Develop **talents**. 發揮你的天賦。	才能;天賦
valuable[3] (ˈvæljəbḷ) adj.	Be **valuable**. 要有價值。	有價值的
versatile[6] (ˈvɜsətḷ) adj.	Be **versatile**. 要多才多藝。	多才多藝的
flexibility[4] (ˌflɛksəˈbɪlətɪ) n.	Have **flexibility**. 要懂得變通。	彈性;靈活度
desire[2] (dɪˈzaɪr) v.	Be **desired**. 要被人需要。	想要
demand[4] (dɪˈmænd) n.	Be in **demand**. 要被人需要。	需求
employer[3] (ɪmˈplɔɪɚ) n.	Make **employers** seek you. 讓雇主來找你。	雇主

【背景説明 3】

天天都可用這九句話來激勵他人。*Be able.* 可説成：Have ability. (要有能力。) *Develop talents.* 可説成：Develop your talents. (要發揮你的天賦。) versatile 的意思是「多才多藝的」，也就是「什麼都會一些」。字典上有兩個發音：〔ˈvɜsətḷ, ˈvɜsə͵taɪl 〕，美國人多唸前者，英國人多唸後者。

flexibility 的主要意思是「彈性」，在這裡作「可變性；靈活度」解。如：My schedule has flexibility. (我的時間表有彈性。) *Have flexibility.* 也可説成：Be flexible. (要懂得變通。) desire 是「想要」，*Be desired.*「被別人想要。」即是「要被人需要。」意思和 *Be in demand.* 相同。這兩句話可以合在一起説：Be desired and be in demand. (要被人需要。)

每三回 27 句爲一個段落。接下來的三回，是回答前面的 27 句。

4. Great advice.

看英文唸出中文	一 口 氣 說 九 句	看中文唸出英文
advice [3] 〔 əd'vaɪs 〕 *n.*	Great *advice*. 很棒的建議。	勸告；建議
totally [1] 〔'totḷɪ 〕 *adv.*	I *totally* agree. 我完全同意。	完全地
right [1] 〔 raɪt 〕 *adj.*	You're so *right*. 你非常正確。	正確的
understand [1] 〔,ʌndɚ'stænd 〕 *v.*	I *understand*. 我了解。	了解；明白
comprehend [5] 〔,kɑmprɪ'hɛnd 〕 *v.*	I *comprehend*. 我了解。	理解；了解
loud and clear	I read you *loud and clear*. 我非常清楚你的意思。	非常清楚的
trust [2] 〔 trʌst 〕 *v.*	*Trust* me. 要信任我。	信任
promise [2] 〔'prɑmɪs 〕 *v.*	I *promise*. 我保證。	保證
disappoint [3] 〔,dɪsə'pɔɪnt 〕 *v.*	I won't *disappoint*. 我不會讓人失望。	使人失望

【背景説明 4】

　　這一課的 4, 5, 6 回是接著 1, 2, 3 回的劇情回答。當你聽到別人對你的忠告時，你可以説：*Great advice.*（= *That's great advice.*）可説成：Great suggestion.（很棒的建議。）（= *Good suggestion.*）

　　I read you loud and clear.（我非常清楚你的意思。）（= *I totally understand.*）read 在這裡是指「聽到…的聲音」，源自無線電用語：Do you read me?（你聽得到我的聲音嗎？）美國人也常説成：I hear you loud and clear.（你的意思我聽得很清楚。）loud and clear「又大聲又清楚」，引申爲「非常清楚的」。

　　I won't disappoint. 一般英文老師看到這句話，一定會認爲它錯，因爲 disappoint 在小字典、文法書上都是及物動

詞。人類近百年來，學英文太費功夫了，把單字分成及物和不及物動詞、名詞、形容詞、副詞等，想要走捷徑學英文，結果都學不好，包含美國人。

I won't disappoint. 中的 disappoint，是不及物動詞，作「使人失望」解。當然也可說成：*I won't disappoint you.*（我不會使你失望。）或 I won't let you down.（我不會使你失望。）文法規則永遠學不完，字典永遠查不完，編者認為最簡單的方法，就是背短句，句子越短越好。背了就要用，用多自然會。學一些簡單的文法，才能夠在句中找出主詞、動詞，有助於閱讀和書寫英語。

別人給你任何的建議或勸告，不要只說："Yes, sir." 要說："*Great advice. I totally agree. You're so right.*" 下次再說："*I understand. I comprehend. I read you loud and clear.*" 說話是一種藝術，用英文來回答，別人更佩服你。而且不是說一句，要記住，永遠一次說三句，把握每一次說英文的機會。

5. *Terribly sorry*.

看英文唸出中文	一 口 氣 説 九 句	看中文唸出英文
terribly[2] (ˈtɛrəblɪ) *adv.*	***Terribly*** sorry. 非常抱歉。	非常地
sincerely[3] (sɪnˈsɪrlɪ) *adv.*	I'm ***sincerely*** sorry. 我真的很抱歉。	真誠地
apologize[4] (əˈpɑləˌdʒaɪz) *v.*	I ***apologize***. 我道歉。	道歉
fault[2] (fɔlt) *n.*	It's my ***fault***. 是我的錯。	過錯
mistake[1] (məˈstek) *n.*	My ***mistake***. 我的錯。	錯誤
blame[3] (blem) *v.*	I'm to ***blame***. 我該受責備。	責備
pardon[2] (ˈpɑrdn̩) *v.*	***Pardon*** me. 原諒我。	原諒
forgive[2] (fɚˈgɪv) *v.*	***Forgive*** me. 原諒我。	原諒
regret[3] (rɪˈgrɛt) *v.*	I ***regret*** it. 我很後悔。	後悔

【背景說明 5】

　　不會說英文，反倒是好事，因為你可以學到比美國人好的英文。一般美國人常說：Sorry. So sorry. Very sorry. 我們可以利用 sorry，學到不少單字。*Terribly sorry. I'm sincerely sorry.* 你說起話來與眾不同，更好聽，更讓人佩服。也可以說：I'm extremely sorry.（我非常抱歉。）I'm genuinely sorry.（我真的很抱歉。）(= *I'm really sorry.*) I'm incredibly sorry.（我非常抱歉。）背「一口氣英語」可以改變你的個性，使你在世界上活得更快樂。常說 *Terribly sorry. I'm sincerely sorry. I apologize.* 每個人都喜歡你。道歉不花一毛錢，卻是給別人最大的禮物。

　　It's my fault. 也常說成：It's all my fault.（都是我的錯。）*My mistake.* 源自 It's my mistake.（是我的錯。）*I'm to blame.* 也可說成：I'm to be blamed.（我該受責備。）原則上，不定詞該用被動，就要用被動，但 to blame、to let（出租）、to do 當主詞補語時，常以主動形式表被動意思。【詳見「文法寶典」p.425】

　　Forgive me. 可以加強語氣說成：Please forgive me.（請原諒我。）*I regret it.* 在中文裡，「後悔」是不及物動詞，英文卻是及物動詞。

　　【比較】　中文：　我後悔。

　　　　　　英文：　I regret it.（正）

　　　　　　　　　　I regret.（誤）

regret 後面一定要接受詞，找不到受詞時，才接 it。如：I regret the decision.（我後悔這個決定。）

6. *I was mistaken*.

看英文唸出中文	一口氣說九句	看中文唸出英文
mistaken[1] (məˈstekən) *adj.*	I was ***mistaken***. 我錯了。	錯誤的
make a mistake	I ***made a mistake***. 我犯了錯。	犯錯
regretful[3] (rɪˈgrɛtfəl) *adj.*	I'm ***regretful***. 我很後悔。	後悔的； 遺憾的
sad[1] (sæd) *adj.*	I'm ***sad***. 我很傷心。	悲傷的
bad[1] (bæd) *adj.*	I feel ***bad***. 我覺得難過。	難過的
unhappy[1] (ʌnˈhæpɪ) *adj.*	I'm ***unhappy*** about it. 這件事我覺得很難過。	感到難過的
pity[3] (ˈpɪtɪ) *n.*	It's a ***pity***. 真遺憾。	可惜的事； 遺憾的事
shame[3] (ʃem) *n.*	It's a ***shame***. 真丟臉。	羞恥； 可惜的事
apology[4] (əˈpɑlədʒɪ) *n.*	Please accept my ***apology***. 請接受我的道歉。	道歉

Lesson 1

【背景説明 6】

　　道歉的話説得越多越好。除了前一回説 Terribly sorry. 以外，這一回學到 *I was mistaken.* 也可説成：I was wrong.（我錯了。）*I'm regretful.* 也可説成：It's regretful.（眞遺憾。）

　　對學英文的人來説，這三句話最棒：

> I'm *sad*.
> /æ/
> I feel *bad*.
> /æ/
> I'm *unhappy* about it.
> /æ/

中文裡沒有 /æ/ 的音，唸起來會吃力。可用這三句話來訓練自己讀 /æ/，祕訣是嘴巴裂開、張大，否則就會唸成 /ɛ/ 的音，會把 bad〔bæd〕唸成 bed〔bɛd〕*n.* 床。這三句話是經典，習慣説了之後，人人會喜歡你。道歉的英文不僅要對外國人説，也要跟中國人説。對不會説話的小孩，你對他説，他也聽得懂。

/ɛ/，中國人不會唸錯。

/æ/，中文無此音，嘴巴裂開張大即可。

　　It's a pity. 中的 pity，可當「可惜」或「遺憾」解，是當你很失望的時候説的。所以可以翻成「很可惜。」或「很遺憾。」也可説成：It's pitiful.（眞糟糕。）或 It's regretful.（眞遺憾。）*It's a shame.* 可説成：It's shameful.（眞丟臉。）

7. *Have a dream.*

看英文唸出中文	一 口 氣 說 九 句	看中文唸出英文
dream[1] 〔 drim 〕 *n.*	Have a ***dream***. 要有夢想。	夢想
plan out	***Plan*** it ***out***. 要擬定計劃。	擬定計劃
prepare[1] 〔 prɪˈpɛr 〕 *v.*	***Prepare*** well. 做好準備。	準備
focus[2] 〔ˈfokəs 〕 *v.*	***Focus!*** 要專注！	專注
concentrate[4] 〔ˈkɑnsn̩ˌtret 〕 *v.*	***Concentrate!*** 要專心！	專心
happen[1] 〔ˈhæpən 〕 *v.*	Make it ***happen***. 做就對了。	發生
achieve[3] 〔 əˈtʃiv 〕 *v.*	***Achieve*** it! 要達成它！	達成
accomplish[4] 〔 əˈkɑmplɪʃ 〕 *v.*	***Accomplish*** it! 要完成它！	完成
success[2] 〔 səkˈsɛs 〕 *n.*	***Success*** will follow you. 你一定會成功。	成功

【背景説明 7】

Have a dream. 可加長爲：You should have a dream.（你應該有個夢想。）類似的有：Have a goal.（要有目標。）Have a future plan.（要有未來的計劃。）*Plan it out.* 是 Plan it.（擬定計劃。）的加強語氣。可加長爲：You must plan it out well.（你必須好好地擬定計劃。）Plan it out very carefully.（要很小心地擬定計劃。）*Prepare well.* 可説成：Carefully prepare.（要小心準備。）可加長爲：Prepare well to accomplish it.（好好準備去完成它。）To succeed, you must prepare well.（想要成功，必須好好準備。）

Focus! 可加長爲：Focus on your goal!（專注於你的目標！）Focus on your task!（專注於你的任務！）*Concentrate!* 可加長爲：Concentrate on your job!（專心於你的工作！）You must totally concentrate on it.（你必須完全專注。）*Make it happen.* 這句話最常用來鼓勵別人，字面的意思是「使它發生。」也就是「做就對了。」一般人有夢想，但是都沒有採取行動，光説不練。此時，你就可以跟他説：*Go for it. Just do it. Make it happen. Take action.* 這四句話意思都相同。

Achieve it! 可加長爲：To succeed, you must achieve it.（要成功，你就必須達成它。）（= *Achieve it to succeed.*）也可説成：Attain it!（達成它！）Reach your goal!（要達成你的目標！）*Accomplish it!* 和 *Achieve it!* 意思相同。*Success will follow you.* 字面的意思是「成功會跟著你。」表示「你一定會成功。」（= *You will succeed for sure.*）類似的還有：Big money will follow you.（你一定會賺大錢。）Good fortune will follow you.（你一定會有好運。）

8. *You did it*.

看英文唸出中文	一 口 氣 說 九 句	看中文唸出英文
do[1] 〔 du 〕*v.*	You *did* it. 你辦到了。	做
make[1] 〔 mek 〕*v.*	You *made* it. 你成功了。	做;製造
well[1] 〔 wɛl 〕*adv.*	*Well* done. 做得好。	良好地
applaud[5] 〔 ə'plɔd 〕*v.*	I *applaud* you. 我為你鼓掌。	鼓掌;為…鼓掌
praise[2] 〔 prez 〕*v.*	I *praise* you. 我稱讚你。	稱讚
compliment[5] 〔'kɑmpləmənt 〕*n.*	My *compliments*. 我讚美你。	稱讚
wish[1] 〔 wɪʃ 〕*n.*	Best *wishes*. 祝你萬事如意。	祝福
moment[1] 〔'momənt 〕*n.*	Enjoy the *moment*. 好好享受這一刻。	時刻
proud[2] 〔 praʊd 〕*adj.*	So *proud* of you. 我非常以你為榮。	驕傲的;感到光榮的

【背景說明8】

　　每天都不要忘記稱讚別人。看到別人成功，你就可以說：*You did it. You made it. Well done.* 這三句美妙的話。稱讚的話說得越多越好。*Well done.* 也可說成 Good job. (做得好！) make it 是「成功；辦到」【詳見「一口氣背會話」p.575】。*Well done.* 不要寫成 Well-done. 「(牛排) 全熟的」。

　　My compliments. 是慣用句，源自 You have my compliments. (我向你致意。) 可說成：My compliments to you. (我向你致意。)【詳見「一口氣背會話」p.1343】如果在餐廳要稱讚主廚，或在朋友家吃飯，要稱讚女主人，就可以說：My compliments to the chef. (我向主廚致意。) 句中 compliments 須用複數。有些名詞一定要用複數形式，如 wishes (祝福)、congratulations (恭喜)、regards (問候)、greetings (問候) 等。【詳見「文法寶典」p.84】

　　慣用句 *Best wishes.* 也可說成：Best wishes to you. (祝你萬事如意。) 和 I wish you all the best. 意思相同。*So proud of you.* 源自 I'm so proud of you. (我非常以你為榮。) 和 You make me proud. 意思相同。也可加強語氣說成：We are all so proud of you. (我們都非常以你為榮。)

9. *Amazing!*

看英文唸出中文	一 口 氣 說 九 句	看中文唸出英文
amazing[3] (ə'mezɪŋ) *adj.*	*Amazing!* 真棒！	令人驚訝的
astonishing[5] (ə'stɑnɪʃɪŋ) *adj.*	*Astonishing!* 真令人驚訝！	令人驚訝的
awesome[6] ('ɔsəm) *adj.*	*Awesome!* 真棒！	很棒的
impressive[3] (ɪm'prɛsɪv) *adj.*	*Impressive!* 真令人佩服！	令人印象深刻的
incredible[6] (ɪn'krɛdəbḷ) *adj.*	*Incredible!* 真令人難以置信！	令人難以置信的
unbelievable[2] (ˌʌnbə'livəbḷ) *adj.*	*Unbelievable!* 真令人難以置信！	令人難以置信的
remarkable[4] (rɪ'mɑrkəbḷ) *adj.*	*Remarkable!* 真是不同凡響！	出色的
outstanding[4] ('aʊt'stændɪŋ) *adj.*	So *outstanding!* 真棒！	傑出的
tremendous[4] (trɪ'mɛndəs) *adj.*	Truly *tremendous!* 真了不起！	巨大的；了不起的

Lesson 1

【背景説明9】

　　這九個字經過精心安排，前三個字 amazing-astonishing-awesome 都是 a 開頭，ama*zing* 和 astoni*shing* 字尾是 ing，唸一遍就可以記得。impressive-incredible-unbelievable，前兩個字都是 i 開頭，後兩個字都是 ble 結尾，如此説起來順，又容易背，而且 incredible 和 unbelievable 是同義字。第三組 remarkable-outstanding-tremendous 中的 remark*able*，接上面的 unbeliev*able*，字尾是 able。*So outstanding!* 兩個字一個 o 結尾，一個 o 開頭，*Truly tremendous!* 都是 t 開頭。特別注意，Truly 不要拼成 *Truely*（誤）。

　　當你看到一個很美麗的景色，或聽到一件了不起的事情，都可説這九句話。*Amazing!* 是 It's amazing! 的省略，也可説成：So amazing!（真棒！；真好！；真了不起！）*Astonishing!* 可説成：So astonishing!（真令人驚訝！）*Awesome!* 可説成：Truly awesome!（真的很棒！）

　　Impressive! 可説成：So impressive!（非常令人佩服！）*Incredible!* 可説成：Just incredible!（真令人難以置信！）unbelievable 和 incredible 是同義字，都作「令人難以置信的」解。

　　remarkable 的主要意思是「引人注意的」，在這裡作「出色的；不同凡響的」解。*So outstanding!* 可説成：It's outstanding!（真棒！）或只説 Outstanding!（真棒！）（= *Excellent!*）【詳見 Collins English Thesaurus p.494】tremendous 的主要意思是「巨大的」，在這裡作「真棒；真了不起；真好」解。

10. Be positive.

看英文唸出中文	一 口 氣 說 九 句	看中文唸出英文
positive[2] 〔ˈpɑzətɪv〕 *adj.*	Be *positive*. 要正向思考。	正面的；樂觀的
optimistic[3] 〔ˌɑptəˈmɪstɪk〕 *adj.*	Be *optimistic*. 要樂觀。	樂觀的
appreciative[3] 〔əˈpriʃɪˌetɪv〕 *adj.*	Be *appreciative*. 要心存感激。	感激的
care[1] 〔kɛr〕 *v.*	*Care*. 要關心。	關心；在乎
share[2] 〔ʃɛr〕 *v.*	*Share*. 要分享。	分享
inspire[4] 〔ɪnˈspaɪr〕 *v.*	*Inspire* and lead. 要激勵並領導別人。	激勵
encourage[2] 〔ɪnˈkɝɪdʒ〕 *v.*	*Encourage*. 要鼓勵。	鼓勵
enthusiastic[5] 〔ɪnˌθjuzɪˈæstɪk〕 *v.*	Be *enthusiastic*. 要熱心。	熱心的
attitude[3] 〔ˈætəˌtjud〕 *n.*	*Attitude* is everything. 態度是一切；態度最重要。	態度

【背景説明 10】

　　我們每天都可以勸周圍的朋友：*Be positive. Be optimistic. Be appreciative.* 編排的方式是由短到長，positive 和 optimistic 又是同義字。這三句話一起背，比單背一個字簡單，背了又能使用，多麼划得來。

　　Care. 的意思是「要關心。」要關心周圍的人（*Care about others. Care about people.*），也就是要有好心腸。（*Be kind. Be kind-hearted.*）*Share.* 源自 Share with others.（要和他人分享。）Share what you have with people.（和人分享自己的東西。）也就是 Give what you have.（給別人你擁有的東西。）*Inspire and lead.* 可説成：Try to inspire and lead people.（努力去激勵和領導人們。）（= *You must inspire and lead others.*）

　　Encourage. 可説成：Encourage others to be positive.（鼓勵他人正向思考。）（= *Encourage people to be hopeful.*）*Be enthusiastic.* 可説成：Be eager.（要有熱忱。）Be energetic.（要充滿活力。）*Attitude is everything.* 可加長為：A positive attitude is everything in life.（正面的態度在人生中是最重要的。）A good attitude is most important.（良好的態度非常重要。）Being positive is essential.（正向思考很重要。）

11. *Many thanks*.

看英文唸出中文	一 口 氣 說 九 句	看中文唸出英文
thanks[1] 〔 θæŋks 〕*n. pl.*	Many *thanks*. 多謝。	感謝
appreciate[3] 〔 ə'priʃɪˌet 〕*v.*	I *appreciate* it. 我很感激。	感激
owe[3] 〔 o 〕*v.*	I *owe* you big. 我欠你很大的人情。	欠
kind[1] 〔 kaɪnd 〕*adj.*	You're *kind*. 你人眞好。	親切的；仁慈的
considerate[5] 〔 kən'sɪdərɪt 〕*adj.*	You're *considerate*. 你很體貼。	體貼的
best[1] 〔 bɛst 〕*adj.*	You're the very *best*. 你就是最棒的。	最好的
heap[3] 〔 hip 〕*n.*	Thanks a *heap*. 非常感謝。	一堆
million[2] 〔'mɪljən 〕*n.*	Thanks a *million*. 多謝。	百萬
bundle[2] 〔'bʌndḷ 〕*n.*	Thanks a *bundle*. 多謝。	一把；一捆

【背景説明 11】

美國人喜歡説、也喜歡聽 I owe you. 之類的話。

1. I owe you. (我感謝你。)

2. I owe you one. (我欠你一次人情。)

3. I owe you a big one. (我欠你一個大人情。)

4. I owe you big. (我欠你很多人情。)

5. I owe you big-time. (我欠你很多人情。)

6. I owe you a lot. (我欠你很多。)

7. I owe you a favor. (我欠你一次人情。)

8. I owe you a big favor. (我欠你一個大人情。)

9. I owe you a huge favor. (我虧欠你太多。)

表示感謝的話，詳見「演講式英語」p.300。

You're the very best. 中的 the very，修飾最高級形容詞
【詳見「文法寶典」p.207】，語氣比 You're the best. (你最棒。)
強。可再加強語氣，説成：You're the best of the best. (你是
超棒的。)【詳見「一口氣背會話」p.19】

Thanks a heap. 可加長爲：Thanks a heap for what you
did. (非常感謝你所做的一切。) From my heart, thanks a
heap. (我眞心感謝你。) I want to say thanks a heap. (我想說
非常感謝你。) *Thanks a million.* 可加長爲：Thanks a million
for your kindness. (非常感謝你的好意。) Thanks a million
for what you did. (非常感謝你所做的一切。) *Thanks a bundle.*
可加長爲：Thanks a bundle for helping me. (非常感謝你幫助
我。) Thanks a bundle for your kindness. (非常感謝你的好意。)

12. I'm thankful.

看英文唸出中文	一口氣說九句	看中文唸出英文
thankful[3] 〔'θæŋkfəl〕*adj.*	I'm **thankful**. 我很感謝。	感謝的
grateful[4] 〔'gretfəl〕*adj.*	I'm **grateful**. 我很感激。	感激的
obliged[6] 〔ə'blaɪdʒd〕*adj.*	Much **obliged**. 非常感激。	感激的
indebted 〔ɪn'dɛtɪd〕*adj.*	I'm **indebted**. 我很感激。	感激的
debt[2] 〔dɛt〕*n.*	I'm in your **debt**. 我很感激你。	債務
appreciated[3] 〔ə'priʃɪ,etɪd〕*adj.*	Much **appreciated**. 非常感激。	感激的
pleased[1] 〔plizd〕*adj.*	I'm so **pleased**. 我很高興。	高興的
day[1] 〔de〕*n.*	You made my **day**. 你使我非常高興。	一天；一日
gratitude[4] 〔'grætə,tjud〕*n.*	I'm full of **gratitude**. 我心中充滿感激。	感激

【背景説明 12】

　　感激的話説越多越好，而且每次要説不一樣的話，來表示感謝。要養成對中國人説英文的習慣。

Much obliged. 源自 I'm much obliged. (我非常感激。) 雖然 obliged 已經變成形容詞，還是不能用 very 來修飾。*Very obliged.* (誤) 可以説：Very tired. (很疲倦。) Very excited. (非常興奮。) 語言千變萬化，不是每個句子都可以歸納成文法，背短句是最簡單的方法。

I'm indebted. 字面的意思是「我是負債的。」引申爲「我很感激。」*Much appreciated.* 不能説成：*Very appreciated.* (誤) 但可説成：Very appreciative. (非常感激。)

I'm so pleased. 可説成：I'm quite pleased. (我非常高興。) (= *I'm very pleased.*) *You made my day.* 字面的意思是「你製造了我的一天。」引申爲「你使我非常高興。」(= *You made me happy.*) 或「你使我今天很高興。」(= *You made me happy today.*) 可加長爲：I want to let you know *you made my day*. (我想讓你知道，你使我非常高興。) *I'm full of gratitude.* 可加長爲：I'm full of gratitude to you. (我對你充滿感激。) 或 I'm full of gratitude for what you did. (我對你所做的一切充滿感激。)

Lesson 1　總複習

1.～3. 激勵

1. *Persevere!*
   Persist!
   Carry on!

   Be *reliable*.
   Be *responsible*.
   Be someone to *count on*.

   Don't *quit*.
   Don't get *discouraged*.
   Don't *abandon* your goals.

2. It's not the *end*.
   Just the *beginning*.
   Look *forward*.

   Have *hope*.
   Have *faith*.
   Have *courage*.

   Be *determined*.
   The *tide* will turn.
   Your day will come.

3. Be *able*.
   Be *skillful*.
   Develop *talents*.

   Be *valuable*.
   Be *versatile*.
   Have *flexibility*.

   Be *desired*.
   Be in *demand*.
   Make *employers* seek you.

4.～6. 贊同＋道歉【回答1～3】

4. Great *advice*.
   I *totally* agree.
   You're so *right*.

   I *understand*.
   I *comprehend*.
   I read you *loud and clear*.

   Trust me.
   I *promise*.
   I won't *disappoint*.

5. *Terribly* sorry.
   I'm *sincerely* sorry.
   I *apologize*.

   It's my *fault*.
   My *mistake*.
   I'm to *blame*.

   Pardon me.
   Forgive me.
   I *regret* it.

6. I was *mistaken*.
   I *made a mistake*.
   I'm *regretful*.

   I'm *sad*.
   I feel *bad*.
   I'm *unhappy* about it.

   It's a *pity*.
   It's a *shame*.
   Please accept my *apology*.

7.~9. 激勵＋稱讚

7. Have a *dream*.
Plan it *out*.
Prepare well.

Focus!
Concentrate!
Make it *happen*.

Achieve it!
Accomplish it!
Success will follow you.

8. You *did* it.
You *made* it.
Well done.

I *applaud* you.
I *praise* you.
My *compliments*.

Best *wishes*.
Enjoy the *moment*.
So *proud* of you.

9. *Amazing!*
Astonishing!
Awesome!

Impressive!
Incredible!
Unbelievable!

Remarkable!
So *outstanding!*
Truly *tremendous!*

10. 激勵；11., 12. 感謝激勵

10. Be *positive*.
Be *optimistic*.
Be *appreciative*.

Care.
Share.
Inspire and lead.

Encourage.
Be *enthusiastic*.
Attitude is everything.

11. Many *thanks*.
I *appreciate* it.
I *owe* you big.

You're *kind*.
You're *considerate*.
You're the very *best*.

Thanks a *heap*.
Thanks a *million*.
Thanks a *bundle*.

12. I'm *thankful*.
I'm *grateful*.
Much *obliged*.

I'm *indebted*.
I'm in your *debt*.
Much *appreciated*.

I'm so *pleased*.
You made my *day*.
I'm full of *gratitude*.

Lesson 2　Be a good citizen.

1. Core National Values

看英文唸出中文	一口氣說九句	看中文唸出英文
prosperity[4] (prɑs'pɛrətɪ) *n.*	*Prosperity.* 富強。	繁榮
democracy[3] (də'mɑkrəsɪ) *n.*	*Democracy.* 民主。	民主
dedication[6] (,dɛdə'keʃən) *n.*	*Dedication.* 敬業。	敬業；專心
integrity[6] (ɪn'tɛgrətɪ) *n.*	*Integrity.* 誠信。	誠信；正直
civility[6] (sə'vɪlətɪ) *n.*	*Civility.* 文明。	文明
equality[4] (ɪ'kwɑlətɪ) *n.*	*Equality.* 平等。	平等
freedom[2] ('fridəm) *n.*	*Freedom* and *friendship.* 自由與友善。	自由
justice[3] ('dʒʌstɪs) *n.*	*Justice* and *harmony.* 公正與和諧。	公正
patriotism[6] ('petrɪə,tɪzəm) *n.*	*Patriotism* and *rule of law.* 愛國與法治。	愛國心

Lesson 2

【背景説明 1】

　　到大陸旅遊，到處看到「富強」
（prosperity）、「民主」(democracy)、
「文明」(civility)、「和諧」(harmony)
等標語。外國遊客會問你，那是什麼意

思？你就可以説：They are the core national values.（它們是國家
的核心價值。）中文不容易背下來，但英文編排之後，就容易背了。

<table>
<tr><td rowspan="3">開頭都是 De</td><td>Prosperity.（富強。）</td></tr>
<tr><td><u>De</u>mocracy.（民主。）</td></tr>
<tr><td><u>De</u>dication.（敬業。）</td></tr>
</table>

<table>
<tr><td rowspan="3">字首是 ICE (冰)，
方便記憶</td><td>Integr<u>ity</u>.（誠信。）</td><td rowspan="3">字尾是 ity，
重音在倒數
第三音節上</td></tr>
<tr><td>Civil<u>ity</u>.（文明。）</td></tr>
<tr><td>Equal<u>ity</u>.（平等。）</td></tr>
</table>

civility 和 civilization（文明）不同，civility 是指「行為的文
明」，即「禮貌」；civilization 是指「文明社會；文明國家」。

　　　　　Freedom and *friendship*.（自由與友善。）
　　　　　【都是 fr 開頭】
　　　　　Justice and *harmony*.（公正與和諧。）
　　　　　【有了「公正」才會「和諧」】
　　　　　Patriotism and *rule of law*.（愛國與法治。）
　　　　　【「愛國」就要遵守「法治」，把較長的 rule of
　　　　　law 放在最後，才容易背】

背完以後，看到這些標語，都能用英文説出來，心情會非常愉快。

2. *The Best Personality* (*I*)

看英文唸出中文	一 口 氣 説 九 句	看中文唸出英文
honest[2] (ˈɑnɪst) *adj.*	Be ***honest***. 要誠實。	誠實的
humorous[3] (ˈhjumərəs) *adj.*	***Humorous***. 幽默。	幽默的
generous[2] (ˈdʒɛnərəs) *adj.*	***Generous***. 慷慨。	慷慨的
easygoing (ˈiziˌgoɪŋ) *adj.*	***Easygoing***. 隨遇而安。	隨遇而安的
energetic[3] (ˌɛnɚˈdʒɛtɪk) *adj.*	***Energetic***. 充滿活力。	充滿活力的
cheerful[3] (ˈtʃɪrfəl) *adj.*	***Cheerful***. 高高興興的。	高興的
diligent[3] (ˈdɪlədʒənt) *adj.*	***Diligent***. 勤勉。	勤勉的
intelligent[4] (ɪnˈtɛlədʒənt) *adj.*	***Intelligent***. 聰明。	聰明的
trustworthy (ˈtrʌstˌwɝðɪ) *adj.*	***Trustworthy***. 值得信任。	值得信任的

Lesson 2

【背景説明 2】

Be honest. 可説成：Always be honest. (一定要誠實。) 也可説成：Honesty is best. (誠實最好。) *Humorous.* 可説成：Be humorous. (要幽默。) *Generous.* 可説成：Be generous. (要慷慨。) (= *Be a generous person.*) Be a person who is generous. (做一個慷慨的人。)

Easygoing. 可説成：Be easygoing. (要隨遇而安。) (= *Be an easygoing person.*) Be calm. (要冷靜。) Be relaxed. (要放鬆。) *Energetic.* 可説成：Be energetic. (要充滿活力。) (= *Be an energetic person.*) Have energy. (要有活力。) *Cheerful.* 可説成：Be cheerful. (要高高興興的。) (= *Be a cheerful person.*) cheerful 可作「快樂的；令人愉快的」解。

Diligent. 可説成：Be diligent. (要勤勉。) (= *Be a diligent person.*) Be hardworking. (要努力工作。) Be industrious. (要勤勉。) *Intelligent.* 可説成：Be intelligent. (要聰明。) (= *Be an intelligent person.*) Be smart. (要聰明。) (= *Be wise.*) *Trustworthy.* 可説成：Be trustworthy. (要值得信任。) (= *Be a trustworthy person.*) Be a person people trust. (要做一個讓人信任的人。)

> 背誦技巧：Honest. 和 Humorous. 都是 H 開頭，Humorous. 和 Generous. 是 rous 結尾，前三句唸一遍就記得。第二組 Easygoing. 和 Energetic. 都是 E 開頭，「隨遇而安」、「精力充沛」，更要「高高興興的」(Cheerful.)。第三組 Diligent. 和 Intelligent. 字尾都是 ligent，Trustworthy. 是複合字，字長放到最後。

3. *The Best Personality* (*II*)

看英文唸出中文	一口氣説九句	看中文唸出英文
friendly[2] (ˈfrɛndlɪ) *adj.*	Be *friendly*. 要友善。	友善的
funny[1] (ˈfʌnɪ) *adj.*	*Funny*. 風趣。	有趣的
active[2] (ˈæktɪv) *adj.*	*Active*. 活躍。	活躍的
moral[3] (ˈmɔrəl) *adj.*	*Moral*. 有道德感。	道德的
modest[4] (ˈmɑdɪst) *adj.*	*Modest*. 謙虛。	謙虛的
polite[2] (pəˈlaɪt) *adj.*	*Polite*. 有禮貌。	有禮貌的
sincere[3] (sɪnˈsɪr) *adj.*	*Sincere*. 眞誠。	眞誠的
sensitive[3] (ˈsɛnsətɪv) *adj.*	*Sensitive*. 體貼。	敏感的；體貼的
compassionate[5] (kəmˈpæʃənɪt) *adj.*	*Compassionate*. 有同情心。	同情的

Lesson 2

Lesson 2

【背景說明3】

Be friendly. 可說成：Be a friendly person.（做一個友善的人。）Be kind.（要對人友善。）Be a friend to others.（對別人伸出友誼之手。）*Funny.* 可說成：Be funny.（要風趣。）Tell funny stories.（說有趣的故事。）*Active.* 可說成：Be active.（要活躍。）Be lively.（要活潑。）Be full of life.（要充滿生命力。）Be an active person.（做一個活躍的人。）前兩句中的 friendly 和 Funny. 都是 f 開頭。一個人 friendly 和 funny，自然會 active。

Moral. 可說成：Be moral.（要有道德。）(= *Be a moral person.*) Have morality.（要有道德。）*Modest.* 可說成：Be modest.（要謙虛。）(= *Be a modest person.*) Have modesty.（要謙虛。）還可說成：Be humble.（要謙虛。）*Polite.* 可說成：Be polite.（要有禮貌。）(= *Be a polite person.*) *Moral.* 和 *Modest.* 字首都是 Mo，*Polite.* 的 P 和 M 一樣，都是嘴唇音，三個排在一起，就好背了。

Sincere. 可說成：Be sincere.（要真誠。）(= *Be a sincere person.*) Be true.（要真誠。）Always be true.（一定要真誠。）*Sensitive.* 可說成：Be sensitive.（要體貼。）(= *Be a sensitive person.*) sensitive 的主要意思是「敏感的」，在英文裡，「敏感」就意謂「體貼」。還可說成：Be aware of others' feelings.（要知道別人的感受。）*Compassionate.* 可說成：Be compassionate.（要有同情心。）(= *Be a compassionate person.*) Care about others.（要關心別人。）Show compassion.（要表現出同情。）Sincere. 和 Sensitive. 都是 S 開頭；把最難唸的 Compassionate. 放在最後，才不會影響背誦。

4. *Bad Personality*

看英文唸出中文	一口氣說九句	看中文唸出英文
greedy[2]	Don't be *greedy*.	貪心的
(ˋgridɪ) *adj.*	不要貪心。	
jealous[3]	*Jealous*.	嫉妒的
(ˋdʒɛləs) *adj.*	嫉妒。	
lazy[1]	*Lazy*.	懶惰的
(ˋlezɪ) *adj.*	懶惰。	
dishonest[2]	*Dishonest*.	不誠實的
(dɪsˋɑnɪst) *adj.*	不誠實。	
disloyal[4]	*Disloyal*.	不忠實的
(dɪsˋlɔɪəl) *adj.*	不忠實。	
disrespectful[4]	*Disrespectful*.	不尊敬的
(ˌdɪsrɪˋspɛktfəl) *adj.*	不尊敬。	
selfish[1]	*Selfish*.	自私的
(ˋsɛlfɪʃ) *adj.*	自私。	
impatient[2]	*Impatient*.	不耐煩的
(ɪmˋpeʃənt) *adj.*	不耐煩。	
immoral[3]	*Immoral*.	不道德的
(ɪˋmɔrəl) *adj.*	不道德。	

Lesson 2

【背景説明4】

這九個字是不好的個性，可用來警惕自己，並勸導別人。

Don't be *greedy*. （不要貪心。）
Don't be *jealous*. （不要嫉妒。）
Never be *lazy*. （絕對不要懶惰。）

Don't be *dishonest*. （不要不誠實。）
Don't be *disloyal*. （不要不忠實。）
Never be *disrespectful*. （絕對不要不尊敬。）

Don't be *selfish*. （不要自私。）
Don't be *impatient*. （不要不耐煩。）
Bad people are *immoral*. （壞人都是不道德的。）

Lesson 2

　　美國人和中國人一樣，也常在背後說別人的壞話。如某人太貪心了，你就可以跟朋友說：He's *greedy*. （他很貪心。）（= He's a greedy guy.）Don't be *jealous*. 可説成：Never be jealous of others. （絕不要嫉妒別人。）Don't be *lazy*. 還可説成：Lazy people waste time. （懶惰的人浪費時間。）Don't be *dishonest*. 可説成：Tell the truth. Don't be dishonest. （要說實話。不要不誠實。）Don't be *disloyal*. 可説成：Don't be disloyal to your country. （不要對你的國家不忠實。）Don't be *disrespectful*. 可説成：Never be disrespectful to your parents. （絕不要對你的父母不尊敬。）看到一個自私的行為，可説：What a *selfish* act! （多麼自私的行為！）Don't be *impatient*. 可説成：Try not to be impatient. （儘量不要不耐煩。）可勸別人説：Never, ever be *immoral*. （永遠不要不道德。）

5. *The Secret of Success*

看英文唸出中文	一 口 氣 説 九 句	看中文唸出英文
study [1]	*Study*.	讀書
(ˈstʌdɪ) *v.*	要讀書。	
struggle [2]	*Struggle*.	掙扎；奮鬥
(ˈstrʌgl̩) *v.*	要奮鬥。	
sacrifice [4]	*Sacrifice*.	犧牲
(ˈsækrəˌfaɪs) *v.*	要犧牲。	
suffer [3]	*Suffer*.	受苦
(ˈsʌfə) *v.*	要受苦。	
sweat [3]	*Sweat*.	流汗；努力工作
(swɛt) *v.*	要努力工作。	
survive [2]	*Survive*.	存活
(səˈvaɪv) *v.*	要會求生存。	
sunny [2]	Be *sunny*.	晴朗的；
(ˈsʌnɪ) *adj.*	要開朗。	開朗的
straightforward [5]	Be *straightforward*.	直率的
(ˌstret'fɔrwəd) *adj.*	要直率。	
successful [2]	You'll be *successful*.	成功的
(səkˈsɛsfəl) *adj.*	你會成功的。	

Lesson 2

【背景説明 5】

這九個字都是 s 開頭，是成功的祕訣。*Study.* 可加強語氣說成：Study hard.（要用功讀書。）Study often.（要常常讀書。）Study all the time.（要一直讀書。）*Struggle.* 可説成：You must struggle.（你必須奮鬥。）Be willing to struggle.（要願意奮鬥。）*Sacrifice.* 可説成：You must sacrifice.（你必須犧牲。）Be willing to sacrifice.（要願意犧牲。）Sacrifice time.（要犧牲時間。）Sacrifice to succeed.（要爲了成功而犧牲。）

Suffer. 可説成：Suffer to succeed.（要爲了成功而受苦。）Sometimes you must suffer.（有時你必須受苦。）Suffering is necessary.（受苦是必須的。）*Sweat.* 可説成：Sweat to succeed.（爲了成功而努力工作。）You must sweat.（你必須努力工作。）You must work hard to succeed.（要成功，你必須努力工作。）sweat 的主要意思是「流汗」，在此作「努力工作」解。*Survive.* 可説成：Be a survivor.（要會求生存。）Don't quit.（不要放棄。）（= *Don't give up.*）Don't stop.（不要停止。）Stick it out.（要堅持到底。）

Be sunny. 可説成：Have a sunny personality.（要有開朗的個性。）Have a sunny disposition.（要有開朗的性情。）*Be straightforward.* 可説成：Be a straightforward person.（做一個直率的人。）Be direct.（要直接。）Be to the point.（要切中要點。）Don't beat around the bush.（不要拐彎抹角。）*You'll be successful.* 可説成：You will succeed.（你會成功。）You will be a success.（你會是個成功者。）Victory will be yours.（勝利將屬於你。）

6. *Be a neat person*.

看英文唸出中文	一 口 氣 說 九 句	看中文唸出英文
neat[2] 〔 nit 〕 *adj.*	Be *neat*. 要整齊清潔。	整潔的
tidy[3] 〔'taɪdɪ 〕 *adj.*	*Tidy*. 要整齊。	整齊的
clean[1] 〔 klin 〕 *adj.*	*Clean*. 要愛乾淨。	愛乾淨的
orderly[6] 〔'ɔrdəlɪ 〕 *adj.*	*Orderly*. 要有秩序。	有秩序的
exact[2] 〔 ɪg'zækt 〕 *adj.*	*Exact*. 要一絲不苟。	精確的
precise[4] 〔 prɪ'saɪs 〕 *adj.*	*Precise*. 要嚴謹。	精確的;嚴謹的
organized[2] 〔'ɔrgən͵aɪzd 〕 *adj.*	*Organized*. 要有條理。	有條理的
methodical[2] 〔 mə'θɑdɪkl̩ 〕 *adj.*	*Methodical*. 要井井有條。	井井有條的
systematic[4] 〔͵sɪstə'mætɪk 〕 *adj.*	*Systematic*. 要有系統。	有系統的

Lesson 2

7. *Things I Like*

看英文唸出中文	一口氣說九句	看中文唸出英文

meet[1]
〔 mit 〕*v.*

*I like **meeting** people.*
我喜歡認識人。

認識

talk[1]
〔 tɔk 〕*v.*

***Talking** to people.*
和人談話。

談話

make friends

***Making friends**.*
交朋友。

交朋友

---

chocolate[2]
〔'tʃɔkəlɪt 〕*n.*

***Chocolate**.*
巧克力。

巧克力

ice cream

***Ice cream**.*
冰淇淋。

冰淇淋

papaya[2]
〔 pə'paɪə 〕*n.*

***Papaya** milk.*
木瓜牛奶。

木瓜

---

hike[3]
〔 haɪk 〕*v.*

***Hiking**.*
健行。

健行

leisure[3]
〔'liʒɚ 〕*adj.*

***Leisure** travel.*
休閒旅遊。

休閒的

ocean[1]
〔'oʃən 〕*n.*

*The sound of the **ocean**.*
大海的聲音。

海洋

【背景說明 6】

Be neat. 可説成：Be a neat person.（做一個整潔的人。）*Tidy.* 可説成：Be tidy.（要整齊。）（= *Be a tidy person.*）*Clean.* 可説成：Be clean.（要愛乾淨。）（= *Be a clean person.*）*Orderly.* 可説成：Be orderly.（要有秩序。）（= *Be an orderly person.*）*Exact.* 可説成：Be exact.（要一絲不苟。）*Precise.* 可説成：Be precise.（要嚴謹。）（= *Be a precise person.*）Be clear, not unclear.（做事要清清楚楚，不要不清不楚。）*Organized.* 可説成：Be organized.（要有條理。）（= *Be an organized person.*）*Methodical.* 可説成：Be methodical.（要井井有條。）（= *Be a methodical person.*）Arrange things well.（把事情安排妥當。）*Systematic.* 可説成：Be systematic.（要有系統。）Be a systematic person.（做一個有系統的人。）Do things step by step.（按部就班做事。）Act in an orderly way.（行為要有條理。）neat（整潔的）是 tidy（整齊的）+ clean（清潔）；要有秩序（orderly）就必須 exact 和 precise。orderly 和 organized、methodical、systematic 是同義字。

【背景說明 7】

I like meeting people. 可説成：I enjoy meeting people.（我喜歡認識人。）Meeting people is fun.（認識人很有趣。）（= *Meeting people is interesting.*）*Talking to people.* 可説成：I like talking to people.（我喜歡和人談話。）*Making friends.* 可説成：Making friends is enjoyable.（交朋友令人愉快。）*Hiking.* 可説成：Hiking is healthy.（健行有益健康。）I love to hike.（我喜歡健行。）*Leisure travel.* 可説成：To travel for leisure is best.（休閒旅遊最好。）My family loves leisure travel.（我的家人喜歡休閒旅遊。）*The sound of the ocean.* 可説成：I love the sound of the ocean.（我喜歡大海的聲音。）The sound of the ocean is so peaceful.（大海的聲音非常平靜。）

Lesson 2

8. *Things I Dislike*

Lesson 2

看英文唸出中文	一 口 氣 說 九 句	看中文唸出英文
laziness[1] (ˈlezɪnɪs) *n.*	I dislike *laziness*. 我不喜歡懶惰。	懶惰
theft[6] (θɛft) *n.*	*Theft*. 偷竊。	偷竊
rude[2] (rud) *adj.*	*Rude* behavior. 粗魯的行為。	粗魯的
pollution[4] (pəˈluʃən) *n.*	*Pollution*. 污染。	污染
violence[3] (ˈvaɪələns) *n.*	*Violence*. 暴力。	暴力
innocent[3] (ˈɪnəsṇt) *n.*	Hurting *innocents*. 傷害無辜的人。	無辜的人
liar[3] (ˈlaɪɚ) *n.*	*Liars*. 說謊的人。	說謊者
criminal[3] (ˈkrɪmənḷ) *n.*	*Criminals*. 罪犯。	罪犯
corrupt[5] (kəˈrʌpt) *adj.*	*Corrupt* people. 貪污的人。	貪污的

9. *Jaywalking is unlawful.*

看英文唸出中文	一口氣說九句	看中文唸出英文
jaywalk[5] 〔ˈdʒeˌwɔk〕 *v.*	*Jaywalking* is unlawful. 擅自穿越馬路是非法的。	擅自穿越馬路
risky[3] 〔ˈrɪskɪ〕 *adj.*	It's *risky*. 很危險。	危險的
hit[1] 〔hɪt〕 *v.*	You could get *hit*. 你可能會被撞到。	撞
stupid[1] 〔ˈstjupɪd〕 *adj.*	Don't be *stupid*. 不要愚蠢。	愚蠢的
dumb[2] 〔dʌm〕 *adj.*	*Dumb*. 不要愚蠢。	啞的；愚蠢的
idiot[5] 〔ˈɪdɪət〕 *n.*	An *idiot*. 不要當個白癡。	白癡
crime[2] 〔kraɪm〕 *n.*	It's a *crime*. 這是犯罪。	犯罪
action[1] 〔ˈækʃən〕 *n.*	An illegal *action*. 是一種違法的行爲。	行爲
punishable[2] 〔ˈpʌnɪʃəbḷ〕 *adj.*	*Punishable* by the law. 該受法律處罰。	可處罰的

Lesson 2

【背景說明 8】

I dislike laziness. 可說成：I detest laziness.（我非常討厭懶惰。）Laziness is awful.（懶惰很糟糕。）*Theft.* 可說成：Theft is illegal.（偷竊是犯法的。）Theft is a sin.（偷竊是一種罪惡。）To steal is awful.（偷竊很糟糕。）*Rude behavior.* 可說成：Never be rude.（絕不要粗魯。）Avoid rude people.（避開粗魯的人。）

Pollution. 可說成：Fight against pollution.（要對抗污染。）Pollution kills people.（污染會使人致命。）*Violence.* 可說成：Avoid violence.（要避免暴力。）Violence is never right.（暴力絕對不正確。）*Hurting innocents.* 可說成：Avoid hurting innocents.（避免傷害無辜的人。）

Liars. 可說成：Avoid liars.（要避開說謊者。）Liars are terrible.（說謊者很可怕。）*Criminals.* 可說成：Avoid criminals.（要避開罪犯。）(= *Stay away from criminals.*) Criminals are awful.（罪犯很可怕。）*Corrupt people.* 可說成：I hate corrupt people.（我討厭貪污的人。）Avoid corrupt people.（要避開貪污的人。）

【背景說明 9】

Jaywalking is unlawful. 可說成：Don't jaywalk.（不要擅自穿越馬路。）jay 是「快樂的」，walk 是「走路」，jaywalk 字面的意思是「快樂的走路」，引申為「擅自穿越馬路」，可體會到美語的幽默。

It's risky. 可加長為：It's a risky thing to do. （做這件事很危險。）還可說成：It's not safe. （不安全。）*You could get hit.* 可加長為：You could get hit by a car. （你可能會被車子撞到。）You could get injured. （你可能會受傷。）could 是假設法助動詞，表示說話者認為你不會被撞到。因此，用 could 較客氣。

【比較】 下面兩句意思相同，語氣不同。
You could get hit.【較客氣】
You can get hit. 【較直接】

Don't be stupid. 可說成：Don't be a stupid person. （不要愚蠢。）Don't do stupid things. （不要做愚蠢的事。）*Dumb.* 可說成：Don't be dumb. （不要愚蠢。）Don't be a dumb person. （不要當傻子。）Don't do dumb things. （不要做愚蠢的事。）dumb 的主要意思是「啞的」，在此作「愚蠢的」解。
An idiot. 可說成：Don't be an idiot. （不要當個白痴。）Don't be like an idiot. （不要像白痴一樣。）Don't do idiotic things. （不要做傻事。）

It's a crime. 可說成：It's illegal. （這是違法的。）It's wrong. （這是錯的。）*An illegal action.* 可說成：It's an illegal activity. （這是違法的活動。）*Punishable by the law.* 源自 It's punishable by the law. （這該受法律的處罰。）還可說成：You could be punished. （你可能會受處罰。）You could be fined. （你可能會被罰款。）The police might arrest you. （警察可能會逮捕你。）

Lesson 2

10. It's dangerous.

看英文唸出中文	一 口 氣 說 九 句	看中文唸出英文
dangerous [2] ('dendʒərəs) *adj.*	It's **dangerous**. 很危險。	危險的
unsafe [1] (ʌn'sef) *adj.*	**Unsafe**. 不安全。	不安全的
risk [3] (rɪsk) *n.*	A **risk**. 很危險。	危險
wary [5] ('wɛrɪ) *adj.*	Be **wary**. 要謹慎。	謹慎的
on guard	Be **on guard**. 要警戒。	警戒著
careless [1] ('kɛrlɪs) *adj.*	Don't be **careless**. 不要粗心大意。	粗心的
heads-up ('hɛdz,ʌp) *adj.*	**Heads-up**. 要機警。	機警的
keep an eye out	**Keep an eye out**. 要密切注意。	密切注意
warn [3] (wɔrn) *v.*	I'm **warning** you. 我是在警告你。	警告

【背景説明 10】

It's dangerous. 可加長爲：It's a dangerous activity.（這是危險的活動。）*Unsafe.* 可説成：It's unsafe.（不安全。）It's an unsafe thing to do.（做這件事不安全。）*A risk.* 可説成：It's a risk.（很危險。）也可説成：It's risky.（很危險。）It's too risky.（太危險。）It's not safe to do.（這樣做不安全。）

Be wary. 可説成：Be careful.（要小心。）Be cautious.（要謹慎。）Use caution.（要謹慎。）*Be on guard.* 可説成：Be alert.（要有警覺。）Pay attention.（要注意。）*Don't be careless.* 可説成：Don't take a risk.（不要冒險。）Always be careful.（一定要小心。）

Heads-up. 源自 Heads up.（把頭抬起來。）(= *Get your heads up.* ）已經是慣用語，即使只對一個人説，也用 Heads up. 而 heads-up 字面的意思是「頭抬起來的」，引申爲「機警的」。*Heads-up.* 可加長爲 Always heads-up.（一定要有警覺。）(= *Always be alert.*) *Keep an eye out.* 字面的意思是「要一隻眼睛一直看外面。」表示「要密切注意。」可加強語氣説成：Always keep an eye out.（一定要密切注意。）*I'm warning you.* 可説成：Heed my warning.（注意我的警告。）

Heads-up.
Keep an eye out.
I'm warning you.

Thanks.

11. Spitting.

看英文唸出中文	一口氣説九句	看中文唸出英文
spit [3] 〔 spɪt 〕 v.	*Spitting.* 吐痰。	吐痰
litter [3] 〔 'lɪtə 〕 v.	*Littering.* 亂丟垃圾。	亂丟垃圾
unacceptable [3] 〔 ͵ʌnək'sɛptəbḷ 〕 adj.	*Unacceptable.* 是無法接受的。	無法接受的
unpleasant [2] 〔 ʌn'plɛzn̩t 〕 adj.	*Unpleasant.* 令人不愉快。	令人不愉快的
uncivilized [6] 〔 ʌn'sɪvḷ͵aɪzd 〕 adj.	*Uncivilized.* 不文明。	不文明的
unsanitary [6] 〔 ʌn'sænə͵tɛrɪ 〕 adj.	*Unsanitary.* 不衛生。	不衛生的
disgusting [4] 〔 dɪs'gʌstɪŋ 〕 adj.	*Disgusting.* 很噁心。	噁心的
sickening [1] 〔 'sɪkənɪŋ 〕 adj.	*Sickening.* 很噁心。	噁心的
offensive [4] 〔 ə'fɛnsɪv 〕 adj.	*Offensive.* 會冒犯人。	冒犯的

Lesson 2

【背景説明 11】

Spitting. 的原形是 spit（吐痰），不可説成：*Don't spit.*（誤），這是中式英文，英文應該説成：Don't spit in public.（不要當眾吐痰。）也就是中文的「不要隨地吐痰。」也可説成：No spitting.（禁止吐痰。）Spitting is dirty.（吐痰很髒。）Spitting is not allowed.（吐痰是不被允許的。）*Littering.* 的原形是 litter（亂丟東西；亂丟垃圾），可和 little 比較，便可背下來了。在美國，隨地吐痰和亂丟垃圾是同一個罪名。(If you get caught spitting, you will be charged with littering.) *Unacceptable.* 可説成：It's unacceptable.（是令人無法接受的。）Simply unacceptable.（完全令人無法接受。）That's unacceptable.（那令人無法接受。）We don't allow that.（我們不允許那樣。）

Unpleasant. 可説成：It's unpleasant.（令人不愉快。）(= *It's not pleasant.*) 可加強語氣説成：It's quite unpleasant.（令人相當不愉快。）*Uncivilized.* 可説成：It's uncivilized.（不文明。）(= *It's not civilized.*) 可加強語氣説成：It's completely uncivilized.（完全不文明。）*Unsanitary.* 可説成：It's unsanitary.（不衛生。）(= *It's not sanitary.*) It's very unsanitary.（非常不衛生。）

Disgusting. 可説成：It's disgusting.（很噁心。）It's very disgusting.（非常噁心。）(= *It's quite disgusting.*) *Sickening.* 可説成：It's sickening.（很噁心。）It's so sickening.（真是噁心。）It sickens me.（這使我覺得噁心。）*Offensive.* 可説成：Offensive to everyone.（會冒犯所有的人。）It's offensive to everyone.（會冒犯所有的人。）It's offensive.（這會令人不愉快。）It offends me.（這會冒犯我。）

12. *Don't drink and drive.*

看英文唸出中文	一口氣說九句	看中文唸出英文
drink[1] 〔 drɪŋk 〕 *v.*	Don't *drink* and drive. 不要酒醉駕車。	喝酒
drunk[3] 〔 drʌŋk 〕 *adj.*	Don't drive *drunk*. 不要酒醉駕車。	酒醉的
against[1] 〔 ə'gɛnst 〕 *prep.*	It's *against* the law. 這是違法的。	違反
forbid[4] 〔 fɚ'bɪd 〕 *v.*	*Forbidden.* 是被禁止的。	禁止
prohibit[6] 〔 prə'hɪbɪt 〕 *v.*	*Prohibited.* 是被禁止的。	禁止
allow[1] 〔 ə'laʊ 〕 *v.*	Not *allowed.* 是不被允許的。	允許
harm[3] 〔 hɑrm 〕 *v.*	Don't *harm* others. 不要傷害別人。	傷害
considerate[5] 〔 kən'sɪdərɪt 〕 *adj.*	Be *considerate.* 要體貼。	體貼的
citizen[2] 〔 'sɪtəzn̩ 〕 *n.*	Be a good *citizen.* 要當個好公民。	公民

【背景説明 12】

drink and drive 本來的意思是「一面喝酒，一面開車」，但這種情況很少，其實是源自 drink and then drive（酒後駕車）(= *drink first, then drive*)。*Don't drink and drive.* 的意思是「不要酒醉駕車。」可說成：Drunk driving is dangerous.（酒醉駕車很危險。）Please don't drink

Don't drink and drive.

Wise words.
（很有智慧的話。）

and drive.（請不要酒醉駕車。）*Don't drive drunk.* 源自：Don't drive while you're drunk.（喝醉時不要開車。）要把 drive drunk（酒醉駕車）看成成語。*It's against the law.* 可說成：It's unlawful.（是非法的。）It's illegal.（是不合法的。）(= *It's not legal.*)

Forbidden. 可說成：It's forbidden.（是被禁止的。）It's forbidden to do it.（禁止這麼做。）*Prohibited.* 可說成：It's prohibited.（是被禁止的。）It's prohibited to do it.（禁止這麼做。）*Not allowed.* 可說成：It's not allowed.（這是不被允許的。）(= *You can't do it.*)

Don't harm others. 可說成：Don't do harm to others.（不要傷害別人。）*Be considerate.* 可說成：Be considerate of others.（要對別人體貼。）Show consideration.（要表現出體貼。）*Be a good citizen.* 可說成：Be a responsible citizen.（要做一個負責任的公民。）

Lesson 2 總複習

1.～3. 愛國＋修身

1. *Prosperity.*
   Democracy.
   Dedication.

   Integrity.
   Civility.
   Equality.

   Freedom and *friendship.*
   Justice and *harmony.*
   Patriotism and *rule of law.*

2. Be *honest.*
   Humorous.
   Generous.

   Easygoing.
   Energetic.
   Cheerful.

   Diligent.
   Intelligent.
   Trustworthy.

3. Be *friendly.*
   Funny.
   Active.

   Moral.
   Modest.
   Polite.

   Sincere.
   Sensitive.
   Compassionate.

4.～6. 修身＋激勵

4. Don't be *greedy.*
   Jealous.
   Lazy.

   Dishonest.
   Disloyal.
   Disrespectful.

   Selfish.
   Impatient.
   Immoral.

5. *Study.*
   Struggle.
   Sacrifice.

   Suffer.
   Sweat.
   Survive.

   Be *sunny.*
   Be *straightforward.*
   You'll be *successful.*

6. Be *neat.*
   Tidy.
   Clean.

   Orderly.
   Exact.
   Precise.

   Organized.
   Methodical.
   Systematic.

7.～9. 個人好惡＋勸導

7. I like *meeting* people.
Talking to people.
Making friends.

Chocolate.
Ice cream.
Papaya milk.

Hiking.
Leisure travel.
The sound of the *ocean*.

8. I dislike *laziness*.
Theft.
Rude behavior.

Pollution.
Violence.
Hurting *innocents*.

Liars.
Criminals.
Corrupt people.

9. *Jaywalking* is unlawful.
It's *risky*.
You could get *hit*.

Don't be *stupid*.
Dumb.
An *idiot*.

It's a *crime*.
An illegal *action*.
Punishable by the law.

10.～12. 勸導

10. It's *dangerous*.
Unsafe.
A *risk*.

Be *wary*.
Be *on guard*.
Don't be *careless*.

Heads-up.
Keep an eye out.
I'm *warning* you.

11. *Spitting*.
Littering.
Unacceptable.

Unpleasant.
Uncivilized.
Unsanitary.

Disgusting.
Sickening.
Offensive.

12. Don't *drink* and drive.
Don't drive *drunk*.
It's *against* the law.

Forbidden.
Prohibited.
Not *allowed*.

Don't *harm* others.
Be *considerate*.
Be a good *citizen*.

Lesson 2

Lesson 3　Simply unforgettable!

1. Let's go out!

看英文唸出中文	一 口 氣 說 九 句	看中文唸出英文
out[1] 〔 aʊt 〕 *adv.*	Let's go *out*! 我們出去吧！	向外
escape[3] 〔 ə'skep 〕 *v.*	*Escape* the house. 逃離這間房子。	逃離
fun[1] 〔 fʌn 〕 *n.*	Have some *fun*. 去好好玩一下。	樂趣
windowshop[3] 〔'wɪndo͵ʃɑp 〕 *v.*	*Windowshop*. 去逛街。	逛街
movie[1] 〔'muvɪ 〕 *n.*	Watch a *movie*. 去看場電影。	電影
market[1] 〔'mɑrkɪt 〕 *n.*	Walk the *market*. 去市場走走。	市場
snack[2] 〔 snæk 〕 *n.*	Eat *snacks*. 吃小吃。	點心；小吃
treat[5,2] 〔 trit 〕 *n.*	Enjoy *treats*. 享受美食。	招待；樂事
live it up	*Live it up*. 盡情享受人生。	盡情享受人生

Lesson 3

2. *Hurry*.

看英文唸出中文	一口氣説九句	看中文唸出英文
hurry[2] 〔ˋhɝɪ〕 v.	*Hurry*. 趕快。	趕快
waste[1] 〔west〕 v.	We're *wasting* time. 我們在浪費時間。	浪費
daylight 〔ˋde͵laɪt〕 n.	We're burning *daylight*. 我們在浪費時間。	日光；白天
hustle 〔ˋhʌsl̩〕 v.	*Hustle*. 趕快。	趕快
speed[2] 〔spid〕 v.	*Speed* it up. 加快速度。	加速
shake[1] 〔ʃek〕 v.	*Shake* a leg. 趕快。	搖動
quick[1] 〔kwɪk〕 adj.	Be *quick*. 要快一點。	快的
haste[4] 〔hest〕 n.	Make *haste*. 趕快。	匆忙
carpe diem 〔͵kɑrpɪˋdiəm〕	*Carpe diem*. 把握時間。	把握時間

Lesson 3

【背景說明 1】

Let's go out! 可說成：Let's leave!（走吧！）*Escape the house.* 是幽默用語，可說成：Let's leave the house.（我們離開這個房子吧。）Let's get out.（我們出去吧。）可加強語氣說成：Let's get out of the house.（我們離開這間房子吧。）*Have some fun.* 可說成：Have fun.（去好好玩一下。）Have a good time.（玩得愉快。）(= *Enjoy ourselves.*)

Windowshop. 字面的意思是「看櫥窗購物。」由於一般人逛街都看櫥窗，引申為「逛街」。可說成：Let's windowshop.（我們去逛街吧。）(= *Let's go windowshopping.*) *Watch a movie.* 可說成：See a movie.（去看電影。）(= *Catch a movie.*) Let's watch a movie.（我們去看電影吧。）*Walk the market.* 中的 walk，通常是不及物動詞，在這裡是及物動詞，作「走遍；走過」解。也可說成：Walk around the market.（到市場走走。）(= *Walk in the market.*)

Eat snacks. 可說成：Let's eat snacks.（我們去吃點小吃吧。）Have some snacks.（吃點小吃吧。）(= *Let's have some snacks.*)

Enjoy treats. 可說成：Let's enjoy treats.（我們吃美食吧。）(= *Let's have some treats.*) treat 的主要意思是「招待」，通常別人招待的東西，都是最好的，平常吃不到的東西（something you don't get every day），只要是喜歡的食物，都可稱作 treat，如臭豆腐、某種餅乾、糖果等，在這裡引申為「美食」。凡是好的事物，都可說 treat，如：What a treat to see you.（看到你真好。）You deserve a treat.（你應該得到好的回報。）(= *You deserve something for doing a good job.*) Seeing a movie could be a treat.（看場電影可能會是件快樂的事。）

　　Live it up. 是慣用語，字面的意思是「好好過生活。」引申為「盡情享受人生。」(= *Enjoy life to the full.*) *Live it up.* 中的 it，相當於 life，up 是加強語氣。這個成語美國人常說，說了以後，大家都會很興奮，表示我們要去狂歡了。Life is short. Let's *live it up.*（人生苦短。我們盡情享受人生吧。）I don't have much time, so I'm going to *live it up*.（我時間不多，所以我要好好玩一下。）

【背景説明 2】

　　Hurry. 可説成：Hurry up.（趕快。）Quickly.（快點。）We must hurry.（我們必須趕快。）

We're burning daylight. 常用在當白天趕路時，趁有日光的時候趕快走。字面的意思是「我們在燃燒日光。」引申為「我們在浪費時間；我們沒有時間了。」這句話也可説成：We're running out of time.（我們快沒時間了。）We're taking too long.（我們花太多時間。）We're going too slowly.（我們走得太慢。）

　　Hustle. 可加強語氣説成：Hustle up.（趕快。）Go faster.（走快一點。）*Speed it up.* 中的 speed，主要的意思是「速度」，字面的意思是「把它的速度往上調。」引申為「加快速度。」可説成：Pick up the pace.（加快腳步。）*Shake a leg.* 字面的意思是「搖動一隻腿。」引申為「趕快。」

　　Carpe diem. 是拉丁文，美國人現在也在使用，carpe 的意思是 seize（抓住），diem 的意思是 time（時間），字面的意思是「抓住時間。」即「把握時間；把握時機。」可説成：Seize the moment.（把握時機。）(= *Seize the day.*) Use time wisely.（聰明地使用時間。）Don't waste time.（不要浪費時間。）

3. *Show up*.

看英文唸出中文	一 口 氣 説 九 句	看中文唸出英文
show¹ 〔 ʃo 〕 *v.*	***Show* up.** 要出現。	顯露
face¹ 〔 fes 〕 *n.*	**Show your *face*.** 要露面。	臉
care¹ 〔 kɛr 〕 *v.*	**Show you *care*.** 要表示你很在乎。	在乎
attend² 〔 əˈtɛnd 〕 *v.*	***Attend*.** 要參加。	參加
appear¹ 〔 əˈpɪr 〕 *v.*	***Appear*.** 要出現。	出現
appearance² 〔 əˈpɪrəns 〕 *n.*	**Make an *appearance*.** 要出席。	出現
present² 〔ˈprɛznt 〕 *adj.*	**Be *present*.** 要在場。	在場的
count¹ 〔 kaʊnt 〕 *v.*	**That's what *counts*.** 那很重要。	重要
battle² 〔ˈbætl̩ 〕 *n.*	**That's half the *battle*.** 那是成功的一半。	戰役

Lesson 3

4. *Eat pure*.

看英文唸出中文	一口氣說九句	看中文唸出英文
pure[3] 〔 pjʊr 〕 *adj.*	Eat *pure*. 吃純粹的食物。	純粹的
natural[2] 〔'nætʃərəl 〕 *adj.*	Eat *natural*. 吃天然的食物。	天然的
artificial[4] 〔ˌɑrtə'fɪʃəl 〕 *adj.*	Avoid *artificial*. 避免人工的食品。	人工的
fruit[1] 〔 frut 〕 *n.*	*Fruit* is good. 水果很好。	水果
vegetable[1] 〔'vɛdʒtəbl̩ 〕 *n.*	*Vegetables* are better. 蔬菜更好。	蔬菜
grain[3] 〔 gren 〕 *n.*	*Grains* are best. 穀物最棒。	穀物
variety[3] 〔 və'raɪətɪ 〕 *n.*	Eat a *variety*. 吃各式各樣的食物。	各式各樣
regular[2] 〔'rɛgjələ 〕 *adj.*	*Regular* meals. 規律地用餐。	規律的
salt[1] 〔 sɔlt 〕 *n.*	Less fat, sugar and *salt*. 少油、少糖、少鹽。	鹽

Lesson 3

【背景説明 3】

Show up. 可加強語氣説成：Just show up. (出現就對了。)
Showing up is important. (出席很重要。) *Attend.* 可加強語氣説
成：Always try to attend. (一定要儘量出席。) Attend events.
(參加活動。) (= *Attend activities.*) *Appear.* 可説成：Appear
there. (在那裡出現。) Try to appear. (儘量出現。) Appear and
participate. (出現並參與。) *That's what counts.* 中的 count，主
要的意思是「數；計算」，在這裡作「重要」解。可説成：That's
what is important. (那很重要。) *That's half the battle.* 字面的意
思是「那是一半的戰爭。」引申為「那是成功的一半。」可説成：
Half the work is done. (一半的工作已經完成。)

【背景説明 4】

Eat pure. 可説成：Eat pure foods. (吃純粹的食物。) Eat
100% pure foods. (吃百分之百純粹的食物。) *Avoid artificial.*
可説成：Avoid artificial foods. (避免吃人工食品。) Don't eat
food with chemicals in it. (不要吃含有化學物質的食物。)
Vegetables are better. 可加強語氣説成：Vegetables are even
better. (蔬菜更好。) *Grains are best.* 可説成：Whole grain
foods are best. (全穀類的食物最好。) Grains are the best food
source. (穀類是最好的食物來源。) *Eat a variety.* 中的 variety 是
vary (變化；不同) 的名詞，作「各式各樣的東西」解。可説成：
Eat a variety of foods. (要吃各式各樣的食物。) *Regular meals.*
可説成：Eat at regular times. (要在規律的時間用餐。) (= *Have
meals at regular times.*) Eat at the same times daily. (每天都要在
同樣的時間吃飯。)

5. *Delicious*.

看英文唸出中文	一口氣說九句	看中文唸出英文
delicious[2] 〔 dɪˈlɪʃəs 〕 *adj.*	***Delicious*.** 很好吃。	美味的
delightful[4] 〔 dɪˈlaɪtfəl 〕 *adj.*	***Delightful*.** 很令人愉快。	令人愉快的
mouth-watering 〔ˌmaʊθˈwɔtərɪŋ 〕 *adj.*	***Mouth-watering*.** 令人垂涎三尺。	令人垂涎的
tasty[2] 〔ˈtestɪ 〕 *adj.*	***Tasty*.** 很好吃。	美味的
yummy[1] 〔ˈjʌmɪ 〕 *adj.*	***Yummy*.** 很好吃。	好吃的
heavenly[5] 〔ˈhɛvənlɪ 〕 *adj.*	***Heavenly*.** 太棒了。	天堂的
flavorful[3] 〔ˈflevəfəl 〕 *adj.*	***Flavorful*.** 味道很香。	味道香的
exquisite[6] 〔ˈɛkskwɪzɪt 〕 *adj.*	***Exquisite*.** 很精緻。	精緻的
lick[2] 〔 lɪk 〕 *v.*	Finger-*licking* good. 令人吮指回味的好吃。	舔

Lesson 3

【背景説明 5】

Delicious. 可說成：This tastes delicious.（這個嚐起來很好吃。）It's simply delicious.（這個非常好吃。）I think it's delicious.（我認為很好吃。）*Delightful*. 可說成：It's delightful.（眞令人愉快。）I'm happy.（我很高興。）I like it.（我喜歡這個。）It's good.（很好吃。）*Mouth-watering*. 可說成：It's mouth-watering.（令人流口水。）It tastes excellent.（嚐起來非常好。）中文的「流口水」，通常是還沒吃以前，美國人說的 *Mouth-watering*. 在餐前或用餐時都會說，也可寫成：Mouthwatering.

Tasty. 可說成：It's very tasty.（很好吃。）It tastes fantastic.（嚐起來很棒。）*Yummy*. 可加強語氣說成：It's really yummy.（眞的很好吃。）It tastes yummy.（嚐起來很好吃。）*Heavenly*. 字面的意思是「天堂的。」引申為「絕佳的；很棒的。」常用來形容食物。可說成：It tastes heavenly.（很可口。）It's out of this world.（這是世界上找不到的。）

Exquisite. 可說成：It's exquisite.（非常精緻。）It's excellent.（非常棒。）*Flavorful*. 可說成：It's flavorful.（味道很香。）flavor 是「味道」，flavorful 是「有香味的；美味的；可口的」。可說成：It's so flavorful.（味道很香。）（= *It's very flavorful.*）*Finger-licking good*. 可說成：It's finger-licking good.（令人吮指回味的好吃。）*Finger-licking good*. 源自肯德雞的廣告標語，炸雞吃完後，還舔舔手指，現在已用於日常生活中，表示「很好吃。」

6. *Full?*

看英文唸出中文	一口氣説九句	看中文唸出英文
full[1]	*Full?*	吃飽的
〔 fʊl 〕 *adj.*	吃飽了嗎?	
enough[1]	*Enough?*	足夠的
〔 ə'nʌf 〕 *adj.*	夠了嗎?	
more[1]	*More?*	更多的人或物
〔 mor 〕 *pron.*	還要更多嗎?	
waste[1]	No *waste*.	浪費
〔 west 〕 *n.*	不要浪費。	
scraps[5]	No *scraps*.	碎片
〔 skræps 〕 *n. pl.*	不要有剩菜。	
leftovers	No *leftovers*.	剩飯
〔ˌlɛft'ovɚz 〕 *n. pl.*	不要有剩飯。	
help[1]	*Help* yourself.	自行取用
〔 hɛlp 〕 *v.*	自己拿。	
plate[2]	Clear your *plate*.	盤子
〔 plet 〕 *n.*	把盤子裡的東西吃光。	
worth[2]	Get your money's	價值
〔 wɝθ 〕 *n.*	*worth*. 要吃得夠本。	

Lesson 3

【背景説明 6】

Full? 源自：Are you full?（你吃飽了嗎？）*Enough?*
源自 Have you eaten enough?（你吃夠了嗎？）*More?* 可
説成：Want more?（還要嗎？）Care for more?（還要一些
嗎？）Like some more?（喜歡再來一點嗎？）

No waste. 可説成：No wasting food.（不要浪費食
物。）Please don't waste food.（請不要浪費食物。）
No scraps. 是幽默話，句中的 scrap，主要意思是「碎片」，
在此作「剩餘的食物」解。*No leftovers.* 可説成：Leave
no leftovers.（不要留下剩飯。）Eat everything.（全部吃
下去。）Leave no food on your plate.（盤子上不要留下
食物。）

Help yourself. 可以客氣地説：Please help yourself.
（請隨意取用。）Eat whatever you want.（想吃什麼就吃
什麼。）*Clear your plate.* 字面的意思是「把你的盤子清
乾淨。」意思是「把你盤子裡的東西全部吃完。」

Get your money's worth. 字面的意思是「得到你所
花的錢的價值。」在這裡引申爲「要吃得夠本。」get *one's*
money's worth 這個成語的意思是「花錢花得合算」，如：
I really enjoyed the movie. I got my money's worth.
（我很喜歡這部電影。錢花得很合算。）

7. *How about this weather?*

看英文唸出中文	一 口 氣 説 九 句	看中文唸出英文
weather[1] (ˈwɛðɚ) *n.*	How about this *weather?* 你覺得這個天氣如何？	天氣
change[2] (tʃendʒ) *v.*	Always *changing*. 總是在改變。	改變
unpredictable[4] (ˌʌnprɪˈdɪktəbl̩) *adj.*	*Unpredictable*, huh? 無法預測，不是嗎？	無法預測的
leave[1] (liv) *v.*	Take it or *leave* it. 接不接受由你決定。	留下
hate[1] (het) *v.*	Love it or *hate* it. 你可以喜歡它或討厭它。	討厭
dull[2] (dʌl) *adj.*	It's never *dull*. 絕不會無聊。	無聊的
complain[2] (kəmˈplen) *v.*	Can't *complain*. 我不能抱怨。	抱怨
worse[1] (wɝs) *adj.*	Could be *worse*. 原本可能更糟。	更糟的
nature[1] (ˈnetʃɚ) *n.*	That's Mother *Nature*. 大自然就是這樣。	大自然

Lesson 3

【背景説明 7】

How about this weather? 源自：*How do you feel about this weather?* 這是書寫英語，美國人不説。這句話講完之後，可以接著説：What do you think?（你覺得怎麼樣？）美國人不説：*What about this weather?*（誤）説 What do you think about this weather?（你覺得這個天氣如何？）*Always changing.* 源自 The weather is always changing. 用現在進行式，表示説話者認爲不好的事。*Unpredictable, huh?* huh〔hʌ〕*int.* 哈！；哼！；什麼【表示驚奇、輕視或疑問等】huh 的翻譯要看前後句意來決定，例如：Pretty crazy, huh?（很瘋狂，不是嗎？）【huh = don't you agree】【詳見「一口氣背會話」p.890】這句話源自：It's unpredictable, huh? 也可説成：Pretty interesting, huh?（很有趣，不是嗎？）

Take it or leave it. 字面的意思是「接受或留著不動。」也就是「要就接受，否則拉倒；接不接受，由你決定。」可説成：Accept or refuse.（接受或拒絕。）Approve or disapprove.（贊成或反對。）*Love it or hate it.* 源自：You can love it or hate it.（你可以喜歡它或討厭它。）*It's never dull.* 可説成：It's never boring.（它絕不會無聊。）、It's never the same.（絕不會一樣。），或 It's exciting.（它令人興奮。）

Can't complain. 源自 I can't complain.（我不能抱怨。）也可説成：I'm satisfied.（我很滿意。）*Could be worse.* 源自 It could be worse.（原本可能更糟。）*That's Mother Nature.* Mother Nature 是「（孕育萬物的）大自然」，要大寫。

8. *My daily routine*.

看英文唸出中文	一口氣說九句	看中文唸出英文
routine³ 〔 ru'tin 〕*n.*	My daily *routine*. 我的日常事務。	例行公事
move¹ 〔 muv 〕*v.*	Always *moving*. 我總是很活躍。	移動
dynamic⁴ 〔 daɪ'næmɪk 〕*adj.*	Very *dynamic*. 非常有活力。	充滿活力的
wake² 〔 wek 〕*v.*	*Wake* up. 起床。	醒來
wash¹ 〔 wɑʃ 〕*v.*	*Wash* up. 洗臉。	洗
hurry² 〔 'hɝɪ 〕*v.*	*Hurry* to school. 趕快去上學。	趕快
attend² 〔 ə'tɛnd 〕*v.*	*Attend* classes. 上課。	上（課）
homework¹ 〔 'hom,wɝk 〕*n.*	Do *homework*. 做功課。	功課
bed¹ 〔 bɛd 〕*n.*	Go to *bed*. 上床睡覺。	床

9. *Asking Directions*

看英文唸出中文	一口氣說九句	看中文唸出英文
excuse[2] 〔 ɪkˈskjuz 〕*v.*	***Excuse* me.** 對不起。	原諒
pardon[2] 〔ˈpɑrdn̩ 〕*v.*	Please ***pardon* me.** 請原諒我。	原諒
bother[2] 〔ˈbɑðɚ 〕*v.*	Sorry to ***bother* you.** 抱歉打擾你。	打擾
information[4] 〔ˌɪnfɚˈmeʃən 〕*n.*	I need ***information*.** 我需要一些資訊。	資訊
directions[2] 〔 dəˈrɛkʃənz 〕*n. pl.*	I need ***directions*.** 我需要方向指引。	方向指引
mind[1] 〔 maɪnd 〕*v.*	Do you ***mind*?** 你介意嗎？	介意
ATM[4] 〔ˈeˈtiˈɛm 〕*n.*	Where's an ***ATM*?** 哪裡有自動提款機？	自動提款機
nearby[2] 〔ˈnɪrˈbaɪ 〕*adv.*	Is there one ***nearby*?** 附近有嗎？	在附近
away[1] 〔 əˈwe 〕*adv.*	How far ***away*?** 有多遠？	離開

* ***ATM*** *n.* 自動提款機 (= *automated teller machine*)

Lesson 3

10. Awesome apartment!

看英文唸出中文	一 口 氣 說 九 句	看中文唸出英文
place[1] (ples) *n.*	Nice *place*! 好漂亮的家！	地方
residence[5] (ˊrɛzədəns) *n.*	Cool *residence*! 好酷的住宅！	住宅
apartment[2] (əˊpɑrtmənt) *n.*	Awesome *apartment*! 好棒的公寓！	公寓
furnish[4] (ˊfɝnɪʃ) *v.*	Well *furnished*. 傢俱齊全。	裝置傢俱
furniture[3] (ˊfɝnɪtʃɚ) *n.*	Tasteful *furniture*. 有品味的傢俱。	傢俱
modern[2] (ˊmɑdɚn) *adj.*	*Modern* kitchen. 現代化的廚房。	現代化的
appliance[4] (əˊplaɪəns) *n.*	Many *appliances*. 許多的家電用品。	家電用品
bathroom[1] (ˊbæθˌrum) *n.*	Tidy *bathroom*. 整齊的浴室。	浴室
relaxing[3] (rɪˊlæksɪŋ) *adj.*	Feels *relaxing*. 令人覺得很放鬆。	令人放鬆的

Lesson 3

【背景説明 8】

My daily routine. 也可説成：This is my daily routine.（這是我的日常事務。）(= *This is my daily schedule.*) This is what I usually do.（這是我通常會做的事。）*Always moving.* 書寫英語是：I'm always moving.（我總是很活躍。）(= *I'm always active.*) *Very dynamic.* 源自 I'm very dynamic.（我非常有活力。）可説成：I'm very busy.（我非常忙碌。）*Wake up.* 可加長爲：I wake up early.（我很早起床。）I get up at dawn.（我天亮就起床。）I rise at six a.m.（我早上六點起床。）*Hurry to school.* 源自 I hurry to school.（我趕快去上學。）可説成：I get ready for school.（我準備好要上學。）*Attend classes.* 可説成：I attend classes all day.（我整天上課。）I go to school.（我去上學。）I'm in school all day.（我整天在學校。）*Do homework.* 源自 I do my homework.（我做功課。）*Go to bed.* 可説成：I go to bed late.（我很晚才上床睡覺。）

【背景説明 9】

Excuse me. 客氣的説法是：Please excuse me.（請原諒我。）Please excuse my interrupting.（請原諒我打斷你。）*Please pardon me.* 也可只説 Pardon me.（對不起。）Pardon my interruption.（原諒我打斷你。）向陌生人問路，開頭的時候説：*Excuse me. Pardon me.* 最有禮貌。*Sorry to bother you.* 可説成：Sorry to disturb you.（抱歉打擾你。）*Do you mind?* 可説成：Do you mind talking to me?（你介不介意和我説話？）Do you mind helping me?（你介不介意幫助我？）Do you mind if I ask you a question?（你介不介意我問你一個問題？）

How far away? 源自 How far away is it?（有多遠？）還可説：From here, is it far?（離這裡遠不遠？）How close is it?（有多近？）

【背景説明 10】

Nice place! 可説成：You have a nice place!（你有好漂亮的家！）This is a nice place!（這是個漂亮的家！）What a nice place!（這個地方真漂亮！）place 的主要意思是「地方」，在此作「家；住處」解。*Cool residence!* 源自 This is a cool residence!（這是個很酷的住宅！）*Awesome apartment!* 可説成：You have an awesome apartment!（你有好棒的公寓！）

Well furnished. 源自 It's well furnished.（它傢俱俱齊全。）可説成：You have nice furniture.（你有很好的傢俱。）*Modern kitchen.* 可説成：The kitchen is new.（廚房很新。）It has a modern kitchen.（它有現代化的廚房。）

Many appliances. 源自 You have many appliances.（你有很多家電用品。）*Tidy bathroom.* 可説成：This is a tidy bathroom.（這是個整齊的浴室。）*Feels relaxing.* 源自 It feels relaxing.（它令人覺得很放鬆。）feel 在這裡是特殊用法，作「使人感覺」解，如：The breeze feels good.（微風使人感覺很舒服。）The sun feels nice.（陽光使人感覺很好。）The wind feels cold.（這陣風使人覺得冷。）

11. *Nice property!*

看英文唸出中文	一 口 氣 説 九 句	看中文唸出英文
lovely [2] 〔ˈlʌvlɪ 〕 *adj.*	*Lovely* home! 可愛的家！	可愛的
beautiful [1] 〔ˈbjutəfəl 〕 *adj.*	*Beautiful* house! 漂亮的房子！	美麗的
property [3] 〔ˈprɑpɚtɪ 〕 *n.*	Nice *property*! 很好的房產！	房地產
lawn [3] 〔 lɔn 〕 *n.*	Pretty *lawn*. 漂亮的草地。	草地
spacious [6] 〔ˈspeʃəs 〕 *adj.*	*Spacious* yard. 寬敞的院子。	寬敞的
garden [1] 〔ˈgɑrdn̩ 〕 *n.*	Excellent *garden*. 很棒的花園。	花園
flower [1] 〔ˈflauɚ 〕 *n.*	Many *flowers*. 有許多花。	花
grass [1] 〔 græs 〕 *n.*	Green *grass*. 有綠色的草。	草
bush [3] 〔 buʃ 〕 *n.*	Lots of *bushes* and trees. 有很多灌木叢和樹。	灌木叢

Lesson 3

12. *Magnificent!*

看英文唸出中文	一 口 氣 説 九 句	看中文唸出英文
magnificent[4] 〔 mæg'nɪfəsn̩t 〕*adj.*	*Magnificent!* 很壯麗！	壯麗的
majestic[5] 〔 mə'dʒɛstɪk 〕*adj.*	*Majestic!* 很雄偉！	雄偉的
marvelous[3] 〔'mɑrvl̩əs 〕*adj.*	How *marvelous!* 真棒！	很棒的
grand[1] 〔 grænd 〕*adj.*	*Grand!* 很雄偉！	雄偉的
glorious[4] 〔'glorɪəs 〕*adj.*	*Glorious!* 很壯麗！	光輝的
impressive[3] 〔 ɪm'prɛsɪv 〕*adj.*	Very *impressive!* 令人印象非常深刻！	令人印象深刻的
uplifting 〔 ʌp'lɪftɪŋ 〕*adj.*	*Uplifting!* 令人振奮！	令人振奮的
inspiring[4] 〔 ɪn'spaɪrɪŋ 〕*adj.*	*Inspiring!* 能激勵人心！	激勵人心的
unforgettable[1] 〔ˌʌnfɚ'gɛtəbl̩ 〕*adj.*	Simply *unforgettable!* 真令人難忘！	令人難忘的

Lesson 3

【背景説明 11】

拜訪朋友的家，就可説這九句話。

Lovely home! 可説成：What a lovely home!（多麼可愛的家！）
Beautiful house! 可説成：It's a beautiful house!（它是漂亮的房子！）
Pretty lawn. 可説成：A pretty lawn.（漂亮的草地。）或 It's a
pretty lawn.（好漂亮的草地。）You have a pretty lawn.（你有漂亮
的草地。）I love your lawn.（我喜歡你的草地。）*Many flowers.* 可
説成：There are many kinds of flowers.（有許多種花。）You have
many flowers.（你有很多花。）The yard has many flowers.（院子
裡有很多花。）*Green grass.* 可加強語氣説成：Beautiful green grass.
（漂亮的綠色草地。）The grass is really green.（這草地真的很綠。）

【背景説明 12】

這九個字巧妙安排，magnificent-majestic-marvelous 都是 m
開頭，grand-glorious-impressive，前兩個是 g 開頭，uplifting-
inspiring-unforgettable，前兩個字是 ing 結尾。看到一棟很雄偉的
建築物，就可以説：*Magnificent!* 或 It's magnificent!（真是壯麗！）
It's truly magnificent!（真的很壯觀！）前三句是兩短一長，容易
背。*Grand!* 可加強語氣説成：How grand!（多麼雄偉！）*Glorious!*
字面的意思是「很光輝的！」在此作「很壯麗！」解。*Inspiring!* 可説
成：It's inspiring!（它能激勵人心！）It inspires me!（它激勵了我！）
It makes me feel great.（它使我覺得很舒服。）*Simply unforgettable!*
中的 simply 有很多意思：① 僅僅；只不過 ② 簡單地；清楚地 ③ 完全
地；非常；的確 ④ 簡樸地；樸素地，在這裡作「非常」（= *very*）解。這
句話源自 This is simply unforgettable!（這真是令人難忘！）（ = *It's
unforgettable!*）

Lesson 3 總複習

1.～3. 出去參加活動

1. Let's go *out*!
   Escape the house.
   Have some *fun*.

   Windowshop.
   Watch a *movie*.
   Walk the *market*.

   Eat *snacks*.
   Enjoy *treats*.
   Live it up.

2. *Hurry*.
   We're *wasting* time.
   We're burning *daylight*.

   Hustle.
   Speed it up.
   Shake a leg.

   Be *quick*.
   Make *haste*.
   Carpe diem.

3. *Show* up.
   Show your *face*.
   Show you *care*.

   Attend.
   Appear.
   Make an *appearance*.

   Be *present*.
   That's what *counts*.
   That's half the *battle*.

4.～6. 和朋友用餐時說

4. Eat *pure*.
   Eat *natural*.
   Avoid *artificial*.

   Fruit is good.
   Vegetables are better.
   Grains are best.

   Eat a *variety*.
   Regular meals.
   Less fat, sugar and *salt*.

5. *Delicious*.
   Delightful.
   Mouth-watering.

   Tasty.
   Yummy.
   Heavenly.

   Flavorful.
   Exquisite.
   Finger-*licking* good.

6. *Full?*
   Enough?
   More?

   No *waste*.
   No *scraps*.
   No *leftovers*.

   Help yourself.
   Clear your *plate*.
   Get your money's *worth*.

Lesson 3

7., 8. 個人好惡；9. 勸告

10. 加強；11., 12. 勸告

7. How about this *weather*?
   Always *changing*.
   Unpredictable, huh?

   Take it or *leave* it.
   Love it or *hate* it.
   It's never *dull*.

   Can't *complain*.
   Could be *worse*.
   That's Mother *Nature*.

8. My daily *routine*.
   Always *moving*.
   Very *dynamic*.

   Wake up.
   Wash up.
   Hurry to school.

   Attend classes.
   Do *homework*.
   Go to *bed*.

9. *Excuse* me.
   Please *pardon* me.
   Sorry to *bother* you.

   I need *information*.
   I need *directions*.
   Do you *mind*?

   Where's an *ATM*?
   Is there one *nearby*?
   How far *away*?

10. Nice *place*!
    Cool *residence*!
    Awesome *apartment*!

    Well *furnished*.
    Tasteful *furniture*.
    Modern kitchen.

    Many *appliances*.
    Tidy *bathroom*.
    Feels *relaxing*.

11. *Lovely* home!
    Beautiful house!
    Nice *property*!

    Pretty *lawn*.
    Spacious yard.
    Excellent *garden*.

    Many *flowers*.
    Green *grass*.
    Lots of *bushes* and trees.

12. *Magnificent*!
    Majestic!
    How *marvelous*!

    Grand!
    Glorious!
    Very *impressive*!

    Uplifting!
    Inspiring!
    Simply *unforgettable*!

Lesson 3

Lesson 4　　Ready to go?

1. Weather Forecast

看英文唸出中文	一口氣説九句	看中文唸出英文
weather[1] ('wεðɚ) *n.*	How's the ***weather***? 天氣如何？	天氣
forecast[4] ('for,kæst) *n.*	What's the ***forecast***? 氣象預報如何？	預報
temperature[2] ('tεmprətʃɚ) *n.*	The ***temperature***? 溫度怎麼樣？	溫度
rise[1] (raɪz) *v.*	***Rising?*** 上升？	上升
fall[1] (fɔl) *v.*	***Falling?*** 下降？	下降
steady[3] ('stεdɪ) *adj.*	***Steady?*** 穩定？	穩定的
wave[2] (wev) *n.*	Heat ***wave***? 有熱浪嗎？	波浪
front[1] (frʌnt) *n.*	Cold ***front***? 有冷鋒嗎？	前面；鋒面
rainy[2] ('renɪ) *adj.*	Sunny or ***rainy***? 晴天還是雨天？	下雨的

2. *It's hot as hell.*

看英文唸出中文	一口氣說九句	看中文唸出英文
hell[3] 〔hɛl〕 *n.*	It's hot as *hell*. 天氣非常熱。	地獄
oven[2] 〔'ʌvən〕 *n.*	Like an *oven*. 像烤箱一樣。	烤箱
sauna 〔'saʊnə〕 *v.*	Like a *sauna*. 像三溫暖一樣。	三溫暖；桑拿
boiling[2] 〔'bɔɪlɪŋ〕 *adj.*	*Boiling*. 非常炎熱。	炎熱的
sizzling 〔'sɪzḷɪŋ〕 *adj.*	*Sizzling*. 非常炎熱。	非常炎熱的
humid[2] 〔'hjumɪd〕 *adj.*	*Humid*. 很潮濕。	潮濕的
sweat[3] 〔swɛt〕 *v.*	I'm *sweating*. 我正在流汗。	流汗
perspire 〔pɚ'spaɪr〕 *v.*	*Perspiring*. 我正在流汗。	流汗
dripping[3] 〔'drɪpɪŋ〕 *adj.*	*Dripping* wet. 濕透了。	濕透的

Lesson 4

【背景説明 1】

What's the forecast? 中的 <u>fore</u>:<u>cast</u> 丟在前面，就表示「預
     before ¦ throw
測；預報」。*The temperature?* 源自：What will the temperature
be?（溫度會幾度？）(= *What is the temperature going to be?*)

Rising? 可説成：Is it rising?（會上升嗎？）*Falling?* 可説
成：Is it falling?（會下降嗎？）*Steady?* 可説成：Will it be
steady?（會穩定嗎？）Will the temperature remain steady?
（氣溫會保持穩定嗎？）

Heat wave? 可説成：Is a heat wave coming?（是不是有熱
浪要來？）Are we going to have a heat wave?（我們是不是會
有熱浪？）*Cold front?* 可説成：Is a cold front moving in?（是
不是有冷鋒要來？）Are we going to have a cold front?（我們
會有冷鋒嗎？）Will we have a cold front?（我們會有冷鋒嗎？）
Sunny or rainy? 可説成：Will it be sunny or rainy?（會是晴天
還是雨天？）也可説成：Rainy or sunny?（雨天還是晴天？）

【背景説明 2】

It's hot as hell. 中的 as hell，字面的意思是「像地獄一樣」，
引申為「非常」。可説成：It's hot as hell outside.（外面天氣
非常熱。）It's extremely hot outside.（外面天氣非常熱。）
Like an oven. 可説成：It feels like an oven.（天氣使人覺得像
烤箱一樣。）It's so hot outside, it feels like an oven.（外面天

氣很熱，使人覺得像烤箱。）*Like a sauna*. 可說成：It feels like a sauna outside.（外面感覺像三溫暖一樣。）It's so hot out, it is like a sauna.（外面天氣很熱，就像是三溫暖。）

Boiling. 可說成：It's boiling outside.（外面非常炎熱。）The weather is boiling outside.（外面的天氣非常炎熱。）boil 的意思是「沸騰」，boiling 引申為「炎熱的」（= *extremely hot*）。*Sizzling*. 可說成：It's sizzling outside.（外面熱得令人發昏。）It's so hot, it feels like it's sizzling outside.（天氣很熱，外面使人覺得非常炎熱。）sizzle 的意思是「（食物在油炸時）發出滋滋聲」，sizzling 引申為「非常炎熱的」（= *very hot*）。*Humid*. 可說成：It's so humid out.（外面非常潮濕。）It's really humid out today.（今天外面真的很潮濕。）

I'm sweating. 可說成：I'm sweating like crazy.（我汗流浹背。）（= *I'm sweating all over.*）It's so hot that I'm sweating a lot.（天氣很熱，我流汗流很多。）*Perspiring*. 可說成：I'm perspiring.（我正在流汗。）It's so hot that I'm really perspiring.（天氣很熱，我真的在流汗。）The temperature is so high that I'm perspiring a lot.（氣溫很高，我流很多汗。）*Dripping wet*. 可說成：Soaking wet.（濕透了。）drip 的意思是「滴」，dripping 是形容詞，作「濕淋淋的；濕透的」解，dripping wet 當成慣用語來看，作「濕透的」解。I'm dripping wet.（我濕透了。）I'm sweating so much that I'm dripping wet.（我流很多汗，我濕透了。）It's so hot that I'm dripping wet with sweat.（天氣很熱，我汗流浹背。）

3. *It's freezing!*

看英文唸出中文	一口氣說九句	看中文唸出英文
freezing³ 〔'frizɪŋ 〕 *adj.*	It's *freezing!* 超冷!	冷凍的
chilly³ 〔'tʃɪlɪ 〕 *adj.*	*Chilly!* 很冷!	寒冷的
bitter² 〔'bɪtɚ 〕 *adj.,adv.*	*Bitter* cold! 刺骨的寒冷!	苦的;刺骨地
numb 〔 nʌm 〕 *adj.*	*Numb* fingers. 手指麻木了。	麻木的
frozen³ 〔'frozn̩ 〕 *adj.*	*Frozen* toes. 腳趾凍僵了。	結冰的
chilled³ 〔 tʃɪld 〕 *adj.*	*Chilled* to the bone. 冷到骨頭裡。	冷凍的
shiver⁵ 〔'ʃɪvɚ 〕 *v.*	I'm *shivering*. 我在發抖。	發抖
chatter⁵ 〔'tʃætɚ 〕 *v.*	My teeth are *chattering*. 我的牙齒冷得咯咯作響。	咯咯作響
warm up	I need to *warm up*. 我需要變溫暖。	變溫暖

Lesson 4

【背景説明 3】

　　It's freezing! 可説成：It's freezing outside!（外面超冷！）
It's so cold that it feels like it's freezing.（天氣很冷，使人感
覺像快要結冰。）freeze 的意思是「結冰」，freezing 字面的意
思是「快結冰的」，引申爲「冷凍的；極冷的」。*Chilly!* 可説
成：It's chilly outside!（外面很冷！）It feels chilly out
today.（今天外面感覺很冷。）It's a chilly day.（天氣很冷。）
Bitter cold! 可説成：It's bitter cold out today.（今天外面刺骨
的寒冷。）It feels bitter cold today.（今天冷死了。）bitter 是
形容詞，在此做副詞，用以加強語氣。類似的有：dead tired
（非常累）、sound asleep（熟睡）、a real good time（好時光）、
awful sick（病得很重）。【詳見「文法寶典」p.193】

　　Numb fingers. 可説成：I have numb fingers.（我的手指
麻木了。）My fingers feel numb.（我的手指感覺麻木。）
Frozen toes. 可説成：I have frozen toes.（我的腳趾凍僵了。）
(= *My toes feel frozen.*) *Chilled to the bone.* 可説成：I feel
chilled to the bone.（我覺得冷到骨頭裡。）I feel cold from
head to toe.（我從頭到腳都覺得冷。）

　　I'm shivering. 可説成：I'm freezing.（我很冷。）(= *I'm
so cold.*) *My teeth are chattering.* 中的 chatter，主要的意思
是「喋喋不休」和「咯咯作響」，這句話字面的意思「我的牙齒
咯咯作響。」引申爲「我很冷。」

4. Ready to go? (I)

看英文唸出中文	一口氣說九句	看中文唸出英文
ready[1] (ˈrɛdɪ) *adj.*	***Ready*** to go? 準備好要走了嗎？	準備好的
prepared[1] (prɪˈpɛrd) *adj.*	You ***prepared***? 你準備好了嗎？	準備好的
everything[1] (ˈɛvrɪθɪŋ) *pron.*	Have ***everything***? 所有的東西都帶了嗎？	一切事物
stuff[3] (stʌf) *n.*	Got your ***stuff***? 你的東西拿了嗎？	東西
double-check (ˌdʌbl̩ˈtʃɛk) *v.*	***Double-check***. 再檢查一次。	再檢查
leave[1] (liv) *v.*	Don't ***leave*** anything. 不要留下任何東西。	留下
phone[2] (fon) *n.*	Got your ***phone***? 電話帶了嗎？	電話
charger[2] (ˈtʃardʒɚ) *v.*	Got your ***charger***? 充電器帶了嗎？	充電器
money[1] (ˈmʌnɪ) *n.*	Have ***money*** on you? 你身上有錢嗎？	錢

【背景說明4】

Ready to go? 可説成:Are you ready to go?(你準備好要走了嗎?)*You prepared?* 可説成:Are you prepared to leave?(你準備好要走了嗎?)*Have everything?* 可説成:Do you have everything?(你所有的東西都帶了嗎?)Do you have everything you will need?(你需要的東西都帶了嗎?)

Got your stuff? 可説成:Have you got all your stuff?(你所有的東西都拿了嗎?)Got all your things?(你所有的東西都帶了嗎?)*Double-check.* 可説成:Please double-check your things.(請再檢查一次你的東西。)在字典上,double-check 翻成「複核;仔細檢查」,其實應該是「再檢查一次」(= *check again* = *check twice*)。*Don't leave anything.* 可説成:Don't forget anything.(不要忘記任何東西。)Don't leave anything behind.(不要留下任何東西在後面。)(= *Don't forget anything.*)Don't forget to bring anything.(不要忘記帶任何東西。)

Got your phone? 可説成:Have you got your phone?(你的電話帶了嗎?)*Got your charger?* 可説成:Have you got your charger?(你的充電器帶了嗎?)(= *Have you got your phone charger?*)*Have money on you?* 可説成:Have money with you?(你身上有錢嗎?)Do you have money on you?(你身上有錢嗎?)

5. *Ready to go? (II)*

看英文唸出中文	一 口 氣 說 九 句	看中文唸出英文
wallet² (ˈwɑlɪt) *n.*	Have your *wallet*? 你的皮夾帶了嗎？	皮夾
credit³ (ˈkrɛdɪt) *n.*	*Credit* card? 信用卡呢？	信用
metro² (ˈmɛtro) *n.*	*Metro* card? 捷運卡呢？	地下鐵
comfortable² (ˈkʌmfɚtəbḷ) *adj.*	*Comfortable* shoes? 有舒服的鞋子嗎？	舒服的
extra² (ˈɛkstrə) *adj.*	An *extra* jacket? 有多帶一件夾克嗎？	額外的
temperature² (ˈtɛmprətʃɚ) *n.*	What's the *temperature*? 溫度幾度？	溫度
tissue³ (ˈtɪʃu) *n.*	Have *tissues*? 有帶面紙嗎？	面紙
hat¹ (hæt) *n.*	Need a *hat*? 需要帽子嗎？	帽子
bathroom¹ (ˈbæθˌrum) *n.*	Use the *bathroom*? 上過廁所了嗎？	廁所

Lesson 4

【背景説明 5】

Have your wallet? 可説成：Do you have your wallet with you?（你的皮夾帶了嗎？）(= *Have your wallet with you?*) *Credit card?* 可説成：Do you have a credit card?（你有帶信用卡嗎？）(= *Are you bringing your credit card?*) *Metro card?* 可説成：Do you have your metro card?（你有捷運卡嗎？）(= *Did you bring your metro card?*)

Comfortable shoes? 可説成：Do you have comfortable shoes on?（你有穿舒服的鞋子嗎？）(= *Are you wearing comfortable shoes?*) *An extra jacket?* 可説成：Do you have an extra jacket?（你有沒有多帶一件夾克？）(= *Are you bringing an extra jacket?*) *What's the temperature?* 可説成：What's the temperature outside?（外面的溫度幾度？）

Have tissues? 可説成：Do you have tissues?（你有帶面紙嗎？）(= *Are you bringing tissues?*) tissue 可當「面紙」或廁所的「衛生紙」，如果是一整捲的，稱作 toilet paper。

tissue

toilet paper

Need a hat? 可説成：Do you need a hat?（你需要帽子嗎？）Will you bring a hat?（你會帶帽子嗎？）*Use the bathroom?* 可説成：Did you use the bathroom?（你上過廁所了嗎？）美國人也常説：Do you want to use the bathroom before we go?（我們去之前，你想去上廁所嗎？）

6. *Be outgoing.*

看英文唸出中文	一 口 氣 説 九 句	看中文唸出英文
outgoing[5] 〔'aʊt,goɪŋ〕*adj.*	Be *outgoing*. 要外向。	外向的
communicate[3] 〔kə'mjunə,ket〕*v.*	*Communicate* better. 要溝通得更好。	溝通
risk[3] 〔rɪsk〕*n.*	Take a *risk*. 要冒險。	風險
contact[2] 〔'kɑntækt〕*n.*	Make eye *contact*. 要做目光接觸。	接觸
nod[2] 〔nɑd〕*v.*	*Nod* and smile. 點頭並微笑。	點頭
greet[2] 〔grit〕*v.*	Go meet and *greet*. 去認識並打招呼。	打招呼
approach[3] 〔ə'protʃ〕*v.*	*Approach* people. 要與人接近。	接近
interact[4] 〔,ɪntɚ'ækt〕*v.*	*Interact* more. 要有更多的互動。	互動
network[3] 〔'nɛt,wɝk〕*n.*	Build a *network*. 要建立人際網路。	網路

Lesson 4

【背景説明 6】

Be outgoing. 可説成：Try to be outgoing. (要儘量外向。) Be an outgoing person. (做個外向的人。) *Communicate better.* 可説成：Try to communicate better. (要努力和別人溝通得更好。) *Take a risk.* 可説成：You must take a risk when meeting people. (認識人的時候，你必須要冒險。) Try and take a risk. (儘量冒險。) Take a chance and meet people. (要碰碰運氣，去認識人。)

Make eye contact. 可説成：Always make eye contact. (一定要做目光接觸。) 即用目光向對方表示善意。It is polite to make eye contact. (做目光接觸是禮貌的行為。) *Nod and smile.* 可説成：When greeting someone, nod your head and smile. (和人打招呼時，你要點頭並微笑。) When saying hello, nod your head and smile. (打招呼時，要點頭並微笑。) When shaking hands, nod your head and smile. (握手時，要點頭並微笑。) *Go meet and greet.* 可説成：Go out and meet and greet people. (出去外面認識人，並打招呼。) Go around the room and meet and greet people. (在房間裡走動，認識人，並打招呼。)

Approach people. 可説成：Try to approach people. (努力與人接近。) It's smart to try and approach people. (努力和人接近是聰明之舉。) *Interact more.* 可説成：You should interact more. (你應該要有更多的互動。) Interact more to learn more. (有更多的互動才會學到更多。) *Build a network.* 可説成：Build a network of friends. (要建立朋友的人際網路。) To build a network of friends is important. (建立一個朋友的人際網路很重要。)

7. *Download apps*.

看英文唸出中文	一口氣説九句	看中文唸出英文
download [4] 〔'daʊnˌlod 〕*v.*	***Download*** apps. 下載應用程式。	下載
application [4] 〔ˌæpləˈkeʃən 〕*n.*	***Applications***. 應用程式。	應用程式
software [4] 〔'sɔftˌwɛr 〕*n.*	They're ***software***. 它們是軟體。	軟體
Web [3] 〔 wɛb 〕*n.*	Surf the ***Web***. 上網。	網際網路
online 〔ˌɑnˈlaɪn 〕*adv.*	Shop ***online***. 在線上購物。	在線上
browse [5] 〔 braʊz 〕*v.*	***Browse*** the Internet. 瀏覽網頁。	瀏覽
e-mail [4] 〔'iˌmel 〕*n.*	***E-mail*** or LINE. 電子郵件或 LINE。	電子郵件
WeChat 〔'wiˌtʃæt 〕*n.*	***WeChat*** or Facebook. 微信或臉書。	微信
connected [3] 〔 kəˈnɛktɪd 〕*adj.*	Be ***connected***. 要能連線。	能接通的

【背景說明 7】

Download apps. 可說成：I often download apps.（我常下載應用程式。）I like to download useful apps.（我喜歡下載有用的應用程式。）apps 是 applications 的簡稱。*Applications*. 可說成：Download applications.（下載應用程式。）Applications are programs.（應用程式就是程式。）*They're software*. 可說成：They're software programs.（它們是軟體程式。）They're software that runs your computer.（它們是能讓你電腦運作的軟體。）

Surf the Web. 可說成：You can surf the worldwide web.（你可以上網。）網址的 www 就是指 worldwide web。

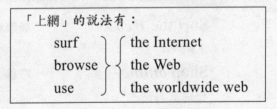

```
「上網」的說法有：
surf  ⎫  ⎧ the Internet
browse ⎬ ⎨ the Web
use   ⎭  ⎩ the worldwide web
```

Shop online. 可說成：You can shop online.（你可以在線上購物。）(= *You can purchase online. = You can buy things online.*)

E-mail or LINE. 可說成：You can use e-mail or LINE applications.（你可以使用電子郵件或 LINE 應用程式。）*WeChat or Facebook*. 可說成：You can use WeChat or Facebook.（你可以使用微信或臉書。）台灣大多用 LINE 或 Facebook，大陸多用微信。*Be connected*. 可說成：Always be connected.（一定要能連線。）You can be connected 24/7.（你可全年無休地連線。）Download the right app, and you will be connected.（如果下載正確的應用程式，你就可以連線了。）

8. *Smartphone*

看英文唸出中文	一口氣說九句	看中文唸出英文
everywhere [1] 〔'ɛvrɪ,hwɛr〕 *adv.*	It's *everywhere*. 它到處都有。	到處
everything [1] 〔'ɛvrɪθɪŋ〕 *pron.*	It's *everything*. 它能做所有的事。	一切事物
own [1] 〔on〕 *v.*	Everyone *owns* one. 每個人都擁有一支。	擁有
mobile [3] 〔'mobḷ〕 *adj.*	It's *mobile*. 它是可移動的。	可移動的
hand-held 〔'hænd,hɛld〕 *adj.*	*Hand-held*. 是手持的。	手持的
mini-computer 〔,mɪnɪkəm'pjutɚ〕 *n.*	A *mini-computer*. 是迷你電腦。	迷你電腦
function [2] 〔'fʌŋkʃən〕 *n.*	It has many *functions*. 它有很多功能。	功能
hi-tech 〔,haɪ'tɛk〕 *adj.*	It's very *hi-tech*. 它非常高科技。	高科技的
smartphone 〔'smɑrt,fon〕 *n.*	It's the *smartphone*. 它就是智慧型手機。	智慧型手機

Lesson 4

【背景説明 8】

It's everywhere. 可説成：It's everywhere you go.（不管你去哪裡都有。）It's all over.（到處都有。）It's in every place.（每個地方都有。）*It's everything.* 可説成：It's able to do everything.（它每件事都可以做。）It has many applications.（它有很多用途。）*Everyone owns one.* 可説成：Nowadays, everyone owns one.（現在每個人都擁有一支。）Everyone has one.（每個人都有一支。）

It's mobile. 可説成：The smartphone is mobile.（智慧型手機是可移動的。）You can carry it anywhere.（你可以帶它到任何地方。）It can go with you anywhere.（它可以跟你到任何地方。）*Hand-held.* 可説成：The smartphone is hand-held.（智慧型手機是手持的。）It's a hand-held device.（它是手持的器具。）*A mini-computer.* 可説成：It's like a mini-computer.（它像是一台迷你電腦。）The smartphone is actually a mini-computer.（智慧型手機其實是一台迷你電腦。）

It has many functions. 可説成：It can do many things.（它能做很多事。）It is multifunctional.（它是多功能的。）The smartphone has many functions.（智慧型手機有很多功能。）*It's very hi-tech.* 可説成：It has advanced technology.（它有先進的科技。）hi-tech 源自 high-technology（高科技的）。*It's the smartphone.* 可説成：It's called the smartphone.（它被稱爲智慧型手機。）

9. *Total cost?*

看英文唸出中文	一口氣說九句	看中文唸出英文
total[1] 〔'totl̩〕adj.	***Total*** cost? 總價是多少？	全部的
price[1] 〔praɪs〕n.	The ***price?*** 價格是多少？	價格
tax[3] 〔tæks〕n.	Including ***tax?*** 有含稅嗎？	稅
on sale	***On sale?*** 有特價嗎？	特價；拍賣
discount[3] 〔'dɪskaʊnt〕n.	Any ***discounts?*** 有打折嗎？	折扣
cheap[2] 〔tʃip〕adj.	Make it ***cheaper!*** 便宜一點吧！	便宜的
credit card	***Credit card*** OK? 信用卡可以嗎？	信用卡
plastic[3] 〔'plæstɪk〕adj.	A ***plastic*** bag. 要一個塑膠袋。	塑膠的
receipt[3] 〔rɪ'sit〕n.	My ***receipt?*** 我的收據呢？	收據

Lesson 4

【背景説明 9】

　　Total cost? 可説成：What's the total cost?（總價是多少？）*The price?* 可説成：What's the price?（價格是多少？）How much is it?（多少錢？）*Including tax?* 可説成：Does this include tax?（這有含稅嗎？）或 Does this price include tax?（這個價格有含稅嗎？）不能只説 *Include tax?*（誤）including（包括）已經成為純粹的介系詞，including tax 是「含稅」，not including tax 是「不含稅」，已經變成成語，如 The price is one hundred dollars, not including tax.（價錢是 100 元，不含稅。）

　　On sale? 可説成：Is it on sale?（有特價嗎？）*Any discounts?* 可説成：Do you have any special discounts?（你們有沒有任何特別的折扣？）*Make it cheaper!* 可説成：Can you make it cheaper?（你能便宜一點嗎？）Can you reduce the price?（你能降價嗎？）（= *Can you lower the price?*）

　　Credit card OK? 可説成：Is a credit card OK?（信用卡可以嗎？）*A plastic bag.* 可説成：I'd like a plastic bag.（我要一個塑膠袋。）Please put it in a plastic bag.（請把它放在塑膠袋裡面。）*My receipt?* 可説成：Where's my receipt?（我的收據在哪裡？）Is this my receipt?（這是不是我的收據？）

10. *Try to improve.*

看英文唸出中文	一 口 氣 說 九 句	看中文唸出英文
improve[2] 〔ɪm'pruv〕v.	Try to *improve*. 要努力改善。	改善
adventure[3] 〔əd'vɛntʃɚ〕n.	Seek *adventure*. 要尋求冒險。	冒險
strive[4] 〔straɪv〕v.	*Strive* to get better. 要努力變得更好。	努力
expand[4] 〔ɪk'spænd〕v.	*Expand* your skills. 要擴大你的技能。	擴大
enhance[6] 〔ɪn'hæns〕v.	*Enhance* your ability. 要增加你的能力。	增加
potential[5] 〔pə'tɛnʃəl〕n.	Achieve your *potential*. 要發揮你的潛力。	潛力
grow[1] 〔gro〕v.	Keep *growing*. 要持續成長。	成長
continue[1] 〔kən'tɪnju〕v.	*Continue* learning. 要繼續學習。	繼續
finish[1] 〔'fɪnɪʃ〕n.	There's no *finish* line. 沒有終點線。	結束

Lesson 4

【背景説明 10】

Try to improve. 可說成：Try to improve yourself. (要努力改善自己。) Always try to improve. (一定要努力改善。) *Seek adventure.* 可說成：Try to seek adventure in your life. (在人生中要努力尋求冒險。) *Strive to get better.* 可說成：Always strive to get better. (一定要努力變得更好。) Try to become a better person. (努力成爲一個更好的人。)

Expand your skills. 可說成：Increase your skills. (增加你的技能。) To improve, you must expand your skills. (爲了使自己改善，你必須擴大你的技能。) *Enhance your ability.* 可說成：Make efforts to enhance your ability. (努力增加你的能力。) *Achieve your potential.* 可說成：Try to achieve your potential. (努力發揮你的潛力。)

Keep growing. 可說成：You must keep growing and improving. (你必須持續成長與改善。) *Continue learning.* 可說成：Continue learning more and more. (要繼續學習越來越多的東西。) Always continue learning in life. (人生中一定要繼續學習。) *There's no finish line.* 可說成：Remember that, there's no finish line in life. (記住，人生沒有終點線。)

11. Sure. (I)

看英文唸出中文	一口氣說九句	看中文唸出英文
sure[1] 〔 ʃʊr 〕 adj.	*Sure.* 我確定。	確定的
certain[1] 〔 'sɝtn̩ 〕 adj.	*Certain.* 我確定。	確定的
positive[2] 〔 'pɑzətɪv 〕 adj.	*Positive.* 我確定。	肯定的；確信的
doubt[2] 〔 daʊt 〕 n.	No *doubt.* 毫無疑問。	疑問
question[1] 〔 'kwɛstʃən 〕 n.	No *question.* 沒有問題。	問題
percent[4] 〔 pɚ'sɛnt 〕 n.	One hundred *percent.* 百分之百確定。	百分之…
confident[3] 〔 'kɑnfədənt 〕 adj.	*Confident.* 我有信心。	有信心的
convinced[4] 〔 kən'vɪnst 〕 adj.	*Convinced.* 我確信。	確信的
confirm[2] 〔 kən'fɝm 〕 v.	I can *confirm* it. 我可以確定。	證實；確定

Lesson 4

【背景説明 11】

Sure. 可説成：I'm sure.（我確定。）I'm 100% sure.（我百分之百確定。）I'm absolutely sure.（我完全確定。）I'm sure about it.（我確定這件事。）I'm pretty sure.（我非常確定。）*Certain.* 可説成：I'm certain.（我確定。）(= *I'm certain about it.*) *Positive.* 可説成：I'm positive.（我確定。）I'm absolutely positive.（我完全確定。）(= *I'm sure.* = *I'm certain.*)

No doubt. 可説成：There is no doubt.（毫無疑問。）(= *There is no doubt about it.*) I have no doubt.（我毫無疑問。）*No question.* 可説成：There is no question.（沒有問題。）(= *I have no question about it.*) *One hundred percent.* 可説成：I am one hundred percent sure.（我百分之百確定。）

Confident. 可説成：I'm confident.（我有信心。）I'm very confident about it.（關於這件事，我很有信心。）*Convinced.* 可説成：I'm convinced.（我相信。）(= *I'm sure.*) *I can confirm it.* 可説成：I can confirm that it is true.（我可以確定它是真的。）

背了這九句以後，當別人問你：Are you sure? Are you certain? 時，你就不會只説：I'm sure. 了，今天説：*Sure.* 明天説：*Certain.* 後天説：*Positive.* 你説的英文隨著單字的增加，而變得更精彩了。

12. *Sure.* (*II*)

看英文唸出中文	一口氣說九句	看中文唸出英文
clear[1] (klɪr) *adj.*	*Clear.* 很明顯。	清楚的；明顯的
obvious[3] ('ɑbvɪəs) *adj.*	*Obvious.* 很明顯。	明顯的
guarantee[4] (,gærən'ti) *v.*	It's *guaranteed*. 可以保證。	保證
absolutely[4] ('æbsə,lutlɪ) *adv.*	*Absolutely.* 絕對是。	絕對
surely[1] ('ʃʊrlɪ) *adv.*	*Surely.* 確實是。	確實地
bet[2] (bɛt) *v.*	*Bet* on it. 當然是。	打賭
deny[2] (dɪ'naɪ) *v.*	Can't *deny* it. 無可否認。	否認
dispute[4] (dɪ'spjut) *v.*	Can't *dispute* it. 無可爭論。	爭論
definitely[4] ('dɛfənɪtlɪ) *adv.*	*Definitely.* 很確定。	確定地

Lesson 4

【背景說明 12】

Clear. 可說成：It's clear. (很明顯。) It's very clear. (非常明顯。) I am clear about it. (對於這件事情我很清楚。) It's clear-cut. (很明確。) It's crystal clear. (一清二楚。) *Obvious.* 可說成：It's obvious. (很明顯。) It's obvious to everyone. (大家都清楚。)(= *There is no doubt about it.*) *It's guaranteed.* 可說成：It's guaranteed one hundred percent. (百分之百保證。)

Absolutely. 可說成：I'm absolutely sure. (我完全確定。) 回答別人的話，可說 Sure. 或 *Surely.* 都表「當然。」現在 Sure. 較常用，surely 多用在句中。如：You will surely succeed. (你一定會成功。)(= *You are sure to succeed.*) *Bet on it.* 源自 You can bet on it. 字面的意思是「你可以在上面打賭。」引申為「當然。」(= *You bet.* = *Of course.*)

Can't deny it. 和 *Can't dispute it.* 的主詞，可用任何人，

$$\left.\begin{array}{l} \text{I} \\ \text{You} \\ \text{We} \\ \text{She} \\ \text{He} \\ \text{They} \end{array}\right\} \text{can't} \left\{\begin{array}{l} \text{deny} \\ \text{dispute} \end{array}\right\} \text{it.}$$

也可說成：It's a fact. (這是個事實。) It's true. (這是真的。) There's no denying it. (不可能否認這件事。) *Definitely.* 可說成：I'm definitely sure. (我非常確定。)(= *Absolutely.* = *For sure.*)

Lesson 4　總複習

1.～3. 談論天氣

1. How's the *weather*?
   What's the *forecast*?
   The *temperature*?

   Rising?
   Falling?
   Steady?

   Heat *wave*?
   Cold *front*?
   Sunny or *rainy*?

2. It's hot *as hell*.
   Like an *oven*.
   Like a *sauna*.

   Boiling.
   Sizzling.
   Humid.

   I'm *sweating*.
   Perspiring.
   Dripping wet.

3. It's *freezing!*
   Chilly!
   Bitter cold!

   Numb fingers.
   Frozen toes.
   Chilled to the bone.

   I'm *shivering*.
   My teeth are *chattering*.
   I need to *warm up*.

4.～6. 準備出發

4. *Ready* to go?
   You *prepared*?
   Have *everything*?

   Got your *stuff*?
   Double-check.
   Don't *leave* anything.

   Got your *phone*?
   Got your *charger*?
   Have *money* on you?

5. Have your *wallet*?
   Credit card?
   Metro card?

   Comfortable shoes?
   An *extra* jacket?
   What's the *temperature*?

   Have *tissues*?
   Need a *hat*?
   Use the *bathroom*?

6. Be *outgoing*.
   Communicate better.
   Take a *risk*.

   Make eye *contact*.
   Nod and smile.
   Go meet and *greet*.

   Approach people.
   Interact more.
   Build a *network*.

Lesson 4

7. , 8. 談論手機；9. 購物

7. *Download* apps.
   Applications.
   They're *software*.

   Surf the *Web*.
   Shop *online*.
   Browse the Internet.

   E-mail or LINE.
   WeChat or Facebook.
   Be *connected*.

8. It's *everywhere*.
   It's *everything*.
   Everyone *owns* one.

   It's *mobile*.
   Hand-held.
   A *mini-computer*.

   It has many *functions*.
   It's very *hi-tech*.
   It's the *smartphone*.

9. *Total* cost?
   The *price*?
   Including *tax*?

   On sale?
   Any *discounts*?
   Make it *cheaper*!

   Credit card OK?
   A *plastic* bag.
   My *receipt*?

10. 激勵；11. , 12. 表示贊同

10. Try to *improve*.
    Seek *adventure*.
    Strive to get better.

    Expand your skills.
    Enhance your ability.
    Achieve your *potential*.

    Keep *growing*.
    Continue learning.
    There's no *finish* line.

11. *Sure*.
    Certain.
    Positive.

    No *doubt*.
    No *question*.
    One hundred *percent*.

    Confident.
    Convinced.
    I can *confirm* it.

12. *Clear*.
    Obvious.
    It's *guaranteed*.

    Absolutely.
    Surely.
    Bet on it.

    Can't *deny* it.
    Can't *dispute* it.
    Definitely.

Lesson 5　　Need help?

1. You failed.

看英文唸出中文	一 口 氣 説 九 句	看中文唸出英文
fail [2] 〔 fel 〕 *v.*	You *failed*. 你失敗了。	失敗
drop [2] 〔 drɑp 〕 *v.*	You *dropped* the ball. 你失敗了。	使掉落
let down	You *let* me *down*. 你讓我失望。	使失望
acquire [4] 〔 ə'kwaɪr 〕 *v.*	You *acquired* nothing. 你什麼都沒獲得。	獲得
complete [2] 〔 kəm'plit 〕 *v.*	You *completed* nothing. 你什麼都沒完成。	完成
come up short	You *came up short*. 你功虧一簣。	功虧一簣
start [1] 〔 stɑrt 〕 *v.*	*Start* again. 重新開始。	開始
try [1] 〔 traɪ 〕 *v.*	*Try* again. 再試一次。	嘗試
attempt [3] 〔 ə'tɛmpt 〕 *n.*	Make another *attempt*. 再嘗試一次。	企圖；嘗試

【背景説明 1】

You failed. 可説成：It seems you failed.（你好像失敗了。）You have failed.（你已經失敗了。）You failed to do it.（你沒做到。）*You dropped the ball.* 源自打球時，你沒有把球抓好，引申為「你失敗了；你失職了。」*drop the ball* 失敗；失職（＝*fail to do something that you are responsible for doing*）可説成：You made a mistake.（你犯了錯。）*You let me down.* 可説成：You have let me down.（你讓我失望了。）I'm sorry to say, you have let me down.（我很遺憾的説，你讓我失望了。）

You acquired nothing. 可説成：You have acquired nothing.（你什麼都沒獲得。）*You completed nothing.* 可説成：You have completed nothing.（你什麼都沒完成。）In my opinion, you have completed nothing.（我認為你什麼都沒完成。）*You came up short.* 中的 come up 作「結果是」解，short 是「不足的」，come up short 字面的意思是「結果是不足的」，引申為「功虧一簣」（＝*fall short*）。例如：You needed to score 60 points, but you only scored 59. *You came up short.*（你需要得 60 分，但你只得到 59 分。你功虧一簣。）

Start again. 可説成：Begin again.（重新開始。）Do it over.（再做一次。）*Try again.* 可説成：Please try again.（請再試一次。）Try to do it again.（試著再做一次。）I think you should try it again.（我認為你應該再試一次。）*Make another attempt.* 可説成：Make another try.（再試一次。）You should make another attempt.（你應該再嘗試一次。）

2. I'm frustrated.

看英文唸出中文	一 口 氣 説 九 句	看中文唸出英文
frustrated[3] (ˈfrʌstretɪd) *adj.*	I'm *frustrated*. 我受到挫折。	受挫的
disappointed[3] (ˌdɪsəˈpɔɪntɪd) *adj.*	*Disappointed*. 很失望。	失望的
displeased[6] (dɪsˈplizd) *adj.*	*Displeased*. 很不高興。	不高興的
depressed[4] (dɪˈprɛst) *adj.*	*Depressed*. 很沮喪。	沮喪的
discouraged[4] (dɪsˈkɝɪdʒd) *adj.*	*Discouraged*. 很氣餒。	氣餒的
dismayed[6] (dɪsˈmed) *adj.*	*Dismayed*. 很不安。	不安的
defeated[4] (dɪˈfitɪd) *adj.*	I feel *defeated*. 我覺得挫敗。	挫敗的
failure[2] (ˈfeljɚ) *n.*	Like a *failure*. 像是個失敗的人。	失敗；失敗的人
setback[6] (ˈsɛtˌbæk) *n.*	It's a *setback*. 這是個挫折。	挫折

Lesson 5

【背景說明 2】

　　I'm frustrated. 可說成：I'm very frustrated.（我很受挫折。）
I'm feeling frustrated.（我覺得受到挫折。）I'm frustrated about it.
（我對這件事情很沮喪。）*Disappointed.* 可說成：I'm disappointed.
（我很失望。）I'm disappointed in myself.（我對自己很失望。）
I'm disappointed it happened.（發生這件事我很失望。）*Displeased.*
可說成：I'm displeased.（我很不高興。）I'm displeased about it.
（我對這件事很不高興。）(= *I'm not pleased about it.*)

　　Depressed. 可說成：I feel depressed.（我覺得沮喪。）I'm
so depressed.（我非常沮喪。）I'm depressed about it.（我對這件
事感到沮喪。）*Discouraged.* 可說成：I'm discouraged.（我很氣
餒。）I feel so discouraged.（我感到非常氣餒。）*Dismayed.* 可說
成：I'm dismayed.（我很不安。）I feel so dismayed.（我覺得很
不安。）I feel so dismayed about it.（我對這件事感到非常不安。）

　　I feel defeated. 可說成：After what happened, I feel
defeated.（發生這一切之後，我覺得很挫敗。）I feel like a loser.
（我覺得像是個輸家。）*Like a failure.* 可說成：I feel like a failure.
（我覺得像是個失敗者。）It makes me feel like a failure.（它讓我
覺得像個失敗者。）*It's a setback.* 可說成：It's a real setback.（這
真的是挫折。）To me, it's a setback.（對我來說，這是個挫折。）

　　前三句：*I'm frustrated. Disappointed. Displeased.* 三個字
都是 ed 結尾，後兩個是 Dis 開頭。*Depressed. Discouraged.*
Dismayed. 字首都是 D，字尾都是 ed，有助於記憶。

3. *Need help?*

看英文唸出中文	一口氣說九句	看中文唸出英文
help[1] 〔 hɛlp 〕 *n.*	Need *help*? 需要幫忙嗎？	幫忙
assist[3] 〔 ə'sɪst 〕 *v.*	Can I *assist*? 我可以協助嗎？	幫助
service[1] 〔 'sɝvɪs 〕 *n.*	Be of *service*? 我能為你效勞嗎？	服務；效勞
trouble[1] 〔 'trʌbḷ 〕 *n.*	*Trouble?* 有麻煩嗎？	麻煩
problem[1] 〔 'prɑbləm 〕 *n.*	*Problem?* 有問題嗎？	問題
worried[1] 〔 'wɝɪd 〕 *adj.*	*Worried?* 擔心嗎？	擔心的
hesitate[3] 〔 'hɛzə,tet 〕 *v.*	Don't *hesitate*. 不要猶豫。	猶豫
polite[2] 〔 pə'laɪt 〕 *adj.*	Don't be *polite*. 不要客氣。	有禮貌的；客氣的
available[3] 〔 ə'veləbḷ 〕 *adj.*	I'm *available*. 我有空。	可獲得的；有空的

Lesson 5

【背景說明 3】

Need help? 可說成：Do you need any help?（你需不需要任何幫助？）Need some help?（需要一些幫助嗎？）Need any help?（需要任何幫助嗎？）Can I help you?（我能幫助你嗎？）May I help you?（我可以幫助你嗎？）*Can I assist?* 可說成：Can I assist you?（我能幫助你嗎？）Can I assist you in any way?（有什麼我能幫助的嗎？）Can I be of assistance?（我能協助嗎？）*Be of service?* 可說成：May I be of service?（我能為你效勞嗎？）May I be of service to you?（我能為你效勞嗎？）

Trouble? 可說成：Any trouble?（有任何麻煩嗎？）Are you in any trouble?（你有任何麻煩嗎？）Are you OK?（你還好嗎？）Is everything OK?（一切都還好嗎？）*Problem?* 可說成：Any problem?（有任何問題嗎？）Do you have any problems?（你有任何問題嗎？）*Worried?* 可說成：Are you worried?（你在擔心嗎？）Are you worried about something?（你在擔心什麼事嗎？）

Don't hesitate. 可說成：Don't hesitate to ask.（想問就問，不要猶豫。）Don't hesitate to ask for help.（不要猶豫請求幫忙。）Please don't hesitate.（請不要猶豫。）*Don't be polite.* 可說成：Don't be too polite.（不要太客氣。）Just ask for help, don't be polite.（儘管請求幫忙，不要客氣。）*I'm available.* 可說成：I'm available for you.（你找我，我都有空。）I'm available 24/7.（我任何時候都有空。）（= *I'm available anytime.*）I'm always available for you. I'm here if you need me.（你找我我都有空。如果你需要的話，我就在這裡。）

4. Be direct.

看英文唸出中文	一 口 氣 説 九 句	看中文唸出英文
direct[1] (dəˈrɛkt) *adj.*	Be *direct*. 要直接。	直接的
truthful[3] (ˈtruθfəl) *adj.*	*Truthful*. 要眞實。	眞實的
point[1] (pɔɪnt) *n.*	To the *point*. 要切中要點。	點;要點
open[1] (ˈopən) *adj.*	*Open*. 要坦誠。	公開的
frank[2] (fræŋk) *adj.*	*Frank*. 要坦白。	坦白的
specific[3] (spɪˈsɪfɪk) *adj.*	*Specific*. 要明確。	特定的;明確的
explicit[6] (ɪkˈsplɪsɪt) *adj.*	*Explicit*. 要明確。	明確的
genuine[4] (ˈdʒɛnjʊɪn) *n.*	*Genuine*. 要眞心眞意。	眞正的
bush[3] (buʃ) *n.*	Don't beat around the *bush*. 不要拐彎抹角。	灌木叢

【背景說明4】

　　Be direct. 可說成：Try to be direct.（儘量直接一點。）Be direct with people.（和人說話要直接。）In conversation, be direct.（在會話時，要直接。）*Truthful.* 可說成：Be truthful.（要真實。）Be truthful to others.（對別人要真實。）Be truthful at all times.（要永遠真實。）*To the point.* 可說成：Be to the point.（要切中要點。）Be honest and to the point.（要誠實，並且說話要說重點。）

> Be direct.
> Truthful.
> To the point.

> I totally agree.

　　Open. 的主要意思是「公開的」，這裡指把想法公開，即「坦誠的」。可說成：Be open.（要坦誠。）Speak openly.（說話要坦誠。）*Frank.* 可說成：Be frank.（要坦白。）Speak frankly.（要坦白說。）*Specific.* 可說成：Please be more specific.（請說得更明確一點。）Try to be specific.（儘量說得明確一點。）

　　Explicit. 是 explain 的形容詞，可說成：Be explicit.（要明確。）Be very explicit.（要非常明確。）當你聽不懂別人講的話時，就可說：Would you be more explicit?（你能不能說得更清楚一點？）*Genuine.* 可說成：Be genuine.（要真心真意。）Be a genuine person. Don't be phony.（要真心真意。不要虛假。）*Don't beat around the bush.* 可說成：Don't beat around the bush with anyone.（不要和任何人拐彎抹角。）

5. *Don't be shy*.

看英文唸出中文	一口氣說九句	看中文唸出英文
shy [1] 〔 ʃaɪ 〕*adj.*	Don't be *shy*. 不要害羞。	害羞的
quiet [1] 〔'kwaɪət 〕*adj.*	Don't be *quiet*. 不要太安靜。	安靜的
timid [4] 〔'tɪmɪd 〕*adj.*	You're too *timid*. 你太膽小了。	膽小的
scared [1] 〔 skɛrd 〕*adj.*	Don't be *scared*. 不要害怕。	害怕的
nervous [3] 〔'nɝvəs 〕*adj.*	Don't be *nervous*. 不要緊張。	緊張的
conquer [4] 〔'kɑŋkɚ 〕*v.*	*Conquer* fear. 要克服恐懼。	征服；克服
embarrassed [4] 〔 ɪm'bærəst 〕*adj.*	Don't be *embarrassed*. 不要尷尬。	尷尬的
awkward [4] 〔'ɔkwəd 〕*adj.*	Don't be *awkward*. 不要不自在。	不自在的
brave [1] 〔 brev 〕*adj.*	Be *brave*. 要勇敢。	勇敢的

Lesson 5

【背景説明 5】

Don't be shy. 可説成：Please don't be shy.（請不要害羞。）Don't be shy with others.（和別人在一起不要害羞。）Don't be shy with me.（和我在一起不要害羞。）*Don't be quiet.* 可説成：Please don't be too quiet.（請不要太安靜。）*You're too timid.* 可説成：I think you're too timid.（我認為你太膽小了。）They say you're too timid.（大家都説你太膽小了。）

Don't be scared.
Don't be nervous.
Conquer fear.

Great advice.

Don't be scared. 可説成：Don't be afraid.（不要害怕。）(= *Don't fear it.*) *Don't be nervous.* 可説成：Don't be nervous about it.（對於這件事不要緊張。）Don't be uptight.（不要緊張。）Please just relax.（請放輕鬆就好。）*Conquer fear.* 可説成：Try to conquer fear.（要努力克服恐懼。）Conquer your fear.（要克服你的恐懼。）Overcome your fear.（要克服你的恐懼。）

Don't be embarrassed. 可説成：Don't be embarrassed about it.（對於這件事，不要不好意思。）Don't feel embarrassed.（不要覺得尷尬。）It's nothing to be embarrassed about.（這沒什麼好尷尬的。）*Don't be awkward.* 可説成：Don't feel awkward.（不要感到不自在。）*Be brave.* 可説成：In life, be brave.（在生活中要勇敢。）(= *Be fearless.*)

這九句話的排列，全部是兩個否定，一個肯定。前三個是：<u>*Don't be shy. Don't be quiet. You're too timid.*</u> 中間三個是：<u>*Don't be scared. Don't be nervous. Conquer fear.*</u> 背起來十分容易。

6. *Speak up!*

看英文唸出中文	一口氣說九句	看中文唸出英文
speak[1] 〔 spik 〕*v.*	***Speak* up!** 要大聲說出來！	說
voice[1] 〔 vɔɪs 〕*v.*	***Voice* your opinion.** 表達自己的意見。	表達
hear[1] 〔 hɪr 〕*v.*	**Be *heard*.** 你的話要被人聽見。	聽到
smart[1] 〔 smɑrt 〕*adj.*	**You're *smart*.** 你很聰明。	聰明的
intelligent[4] 〔 ɪnˈtɛlədʒənt 〕*adj.*	**You're *intelligent*.** 你很聰明。	聰明的
share[2] 〔 ʃɛr 〕*v.*	***Share* your ideas.** 要分享你的想法。	分享
bright[1] 〔 braɪt 〕*adj.*	**You're *bright*.** 你很聰明。	聰明的
on the ball	**You're *on the ball*.** 你很有能力。	很警覺；很有能力
offer[2] 〔ˈɔfɚ 〕*v.*	**You have so much to *offer*.** 你有很多東西可以提供他人。	提供

【背景説明 6】

Speak up! 可説成：It's important to speak up. (大聲說出來很重要。) Speak up for what you believe in. (說出你的信仰。) Always speak up! (一定要大聲說出來！) *Voice your opinion.* 可説成：Please voice your opinion. (請表達你的意見。) Tell people how you feel. (告訴大家你的感覺。) voice 的主要意思是「聲音」，當動詞時，作「表達」解。*Be heard.* 可説成：Make yourself be heard. (讓你自己的話被人聽見。) (= *Make yourself heard.*) Let others hear your opinion. (讓別人聽到你的意見。)

You're smart. 可説成：I think you're very smart. (我認爲你非常聰明。) Everybody knows you're smart. (每個人都知道你很聰明。) *You're intelligent.* 可説成：You're very intelligent. (你非常聰明。) (= *You're an intelligent person.*) *Share your ideas.* 可説成：Always share your ideas. (一定要分享你的想法。) Speak up and share your ideas. (要大聲說出來，分享你的想法。)

You're bright. 可説成：You're a bright person. (你是個聰明的人。) *You're on the ball.* 源自踢足球時，球在運動員的腳下，此時一定是「你很警覺。」(= *You're alert.*) 而且「你是很有能力的。」(= *You're not stupid.*) 可説成：You're always on the ball. (你總是很有能力。) *You have so much to offer.* 可説成：You have much to contribute. (你有很多東西可以貢獻。) You have lots of skills. (你有很多技能。) You can help many people. (你可以幫助很多人。) You have great abilities. (你很有能力。)

7. I'm broke.

看英文唸出中文	一口氣說九句	看中文唸出英文
broke [4] 〔brok〕*adj.*	I'm *broke*. 我沒錢。	沒錢的
money [1] 〔'mʌnɪ〕*n.*	Out of *money*. 沒有錢。	錢
cash [2] 〔kæʃ〕*n.*	No *cash*. 沒有現金。	現金
be hard up	I'm *hard up*. 我缺錢。	缺錢
penniless [3] 〔'pɛnɪlɪs〕*adj.*	I'm *penniless*. 我身無分文。	身無分文的
clean out	I'm *cleaned out*. 我把錢用光了。	用光…的錢
borrow [2] 〔'baro〕*v.*	May I *borrow* a few bucks? 我可以借幾塊美元嗎？	借
lend [2] 〔lɛnd〕*v.*	Could you *lend* me some cash? 你可以借我一些現金嗎？	借（出）
loan [4] 〔lon〕*n.*	How about a *loan*? 貨款給我如何？	貸款

【背景説明 7】

I'm broke. 句中的 broke，既是 break 的過去式，也是形容詞「沒錢的」，在此不能説成：*I'm broken.*（誤）。I'm broken. 的意思是「我心碎了。」（= *I'm heartbroken.*）這句話也可説成：I'm totally broke.（我一毛錢都沒有。）I have no money.（我沒錢。）*Out of money.* 可説成：I'm out of money.（我沒錢。）Today I'm out of money.（我今天沒錢。）*No cash.* 可説成：I have no cash.（我沒有現金。）I am out of cash.（我沒有現金。）

I'm hard up. 可説成：I'm hard up for money.（我缺錢。）I really need money.（我真的需要錢。）be hard up 的意思是「缺錢」（= *be short of cash*）。*I'm penniless.* 可加強語氣説成：I'm completely penniless.（我完全身無分文。）（= *I'm totally penniless.*）*I'm cleaned out.* 句中的 clean out 意思是「用光⋯的錢」（= *use all of your money*）。例如：This will clean me out.（這樣會用光我所有的錢。）*I'm cleaned out.* 可説成：I'm totally cleaned out.（我把錢全部用光了。）I've spent all my money.（我的錢全用光了。）

May I borrow a few bucks? 可説成：May I borrow a few bucks from you?（我可以向你借幾塊美元嗎？）Can I borrow some cash?（我可以借一些現金嗎？）

Could you lend me some cash? 可説成：Could you please lend me some cash? (能不能請你借我一些現金？) Can you lend me some money? (你可以借我一些錢嗎？)

> 【比較1】 Can you lend me some cash? 【一般語氣】
> *Could you lend me some cash?* 【較客氣】
> should, would, could, might 是假設法助動詞，説話者認爲不該做，所以較客氣。
>
> 【比較2】 { borrow + 受詞
> { lend + 間接受詞 + 直接受詞
>
> Can I *borrow* some cash? 【borrow 是完全及物動詞】
> Can you *lend* <u>me</u> <u>some cash</u>? 【lend 是授與
> 　　　　　　　間受　　直受
> 動詞，有兩個受詞】

How about a loan? 可説成：How about giving me a loan? (貸款給我如何？) (= *How do you feel about giving me a loan?*) Can I have a loan? (我可以貸款嗎？) Could you loan me some cash? (你可以借我一些錢嗎？)

How about a loan?

No problem. How much do you need?

8. *Symptoms of illness*.

看英文唸出中文	一 口 氣 説 九 句	看中文唸出英文
dizzy[2] (′dɪzɪ) *adj.*	*Dizzy*. 頭暈。	頭暈的
tired[1] (taɪrd) *adj.*	*Tired*. 疲倦。	疲倦的
weak[1] (wik) *adj.*	*Weak*. 虛弱。	虛弱的
fever[2] (′fivɚ) *n.*	*Fever*. 發燒	發燒
headache (′hɛd͵ek) *n.*	*Headache*. 頭痛。	頭痛
sore[3] (sor) *adj.*	*Sore* throat. 喉嚨痛。	疼痛的
pain[2] (pen) *n.*	In *pain*. 很痛苦。	疼痛；痛苦
hurt[1] (hɝt) *v.*	*Hurting* from head to toe. 全身都在痛。	痛
symptom[6] (′sɪmptəm) *n.*	*Symptoms* of illness. 都是生病的症狀。	症狀

【背景說明 8】

Dizzy. 可説成：I feel dizzy.（我覺得頭暈。）(= *I feel lightheaded.*) *Tired.* 可説成：I'm very tired.（我很疲倦。）Today I feel tired.（今天我覺得很疲倦。）*Weak.* 可説成：I feel weak.（我覺得很虛弱。）I feel sleepy.（我覺得很想睡覺。）

> 【比較】I feel weak.【一般語氣】
> I'm feeling weak.【語氣較強】
> 【詳見「文法寶典」p.342】

Fever. 可説成：I have a fever.（我發燒了。）(= *I have a temperature.*) *Headache.* 可説成：I have a headache.（我頭痛。）My head aches.（我頭痛。）I have a bad headache.（我頭非常痛。）*Sore throat.* 可説成：I have a sore throat.（我喉嚨痛。）My throat is sore.（我喉嚨痛。）(= *My throat hurts.*)

In pain. 可説成：I'm in pain.（我很痛苦。）My body hurts.（我的身體很痛。）(= *My body aches.*) *Hurting from head to toe.* 可説成：I'm hurting from head to toe.（我全身都在痛。）My whole body hurts.（我全身都痛。）(= *I have pain everywhere.*) *Symptoms of illness.* 可説成：Those are symptoms of illness.（那些都是生病的症狀。）

9. *First Aid Before Seeing a Doctor*

看英文唸出中文	一口氣說九句	看中文唸出英文
aid [2] 〔 ed 〕 *n.*	First *aid*. 急救。	援助
water [1] 〔'wɔtɚ 〕 *n.*	Drink *water*. 喝水。	水
coffee [1] 〔'kɔfɪ 〕 *n.*	Have *coffee*. 喝咖啡。	咖啡
massage [5] 〔 mə'sɑʒ 〕 *n.*	*Massage*. 按摩。	按摩
coining [2] 〔'kɔɪnɪŋ 〕 *n.*	*Coining*. 刮痧。	刮痧
cupping [1] 〔'kʌpɪŋ 〕 *n.*	*Cupping*. 拔罐。	拔罐
rest [1] 〔 rɛst 〕 *n.*	Take a *rest*. 休息一下。	休息
medicine [2] 〔'mɛdəsn̩ 〕 *n.*	Take *medicine*. 吃藥。	藥
physician [4] 〔 fə'zɪʃən 〕 *n.*	See a *physician*. 看醫生。	醫生

【背景説明9】

這一回九句，告訴你快要生病的時候，該如何處理。首先要 *Drink water. Have coffee. Massage. Coining. Cupping. Take a rest.* 再不行的時候，就 *Take medicine.* 都不行的時候，就 *See a physician.*

First aid. 字面的意思是「第一個援助。」引申為「急救；緊急治療。」(= *Emergency treatment.*) 可説成：I know first aid. (我知道如何急救。)

急救箱

You should know basic first aid. (你應該知道基本的急救方法。) Here's first aid advice. (這是急救建議。) *Drink water.* 可説成：Drink plenty of water. (要喝很多水。) Drink more water. (多喝點水。) Drink water to stay healthy. (喝水保持身體健康。) *Have coffee.* 可説成：Have some coffee. (喝一些咖啡。) Have a black coffee. (喝杯黑咖啡。) (= *Have a cup of black coffee.*) 當感冒來襲時，最簡單的方法，就是喝大量的溫開水，再喝咖啡，咖啡有利尿的效果，如此可以排毒。

Massage. 可説成：Get a massage. (去按摩。) Try a massage. (試試按摩。) Go for a massage. (去按摩。) 快生病了，沒有運動，用按摩取代，是個好方法。*Coining.* 中的coin 是「硬幣」，刮痧通常用硬幣。可説成：Try coining.

（試試看刮痧。）See a doctor for coining.（找醫生刮痧。）Go get coining therapy.（去接受刮痧治療。）*Cupping.* 中的 cup 是「杯子」，拔罐的罐子有點像杯子。可說成：Chinese cupping.

cupping

（拔罐。）Try cupping.（試試看拔罐。）Cupping might help.（拔罐可能有幫助。）Go for Chinese cupping.（去拔罐。）按摩、刮痧，和拔罐是預防感冒的好方法。

    Take a rest. 可說成：Go take a rest.（去休息。）Take a rest for a day.（休息一天。）*Take medicine.* 可說成：Take some medicine.（吃一些藥。）Try to take some medicine.（吃些藥看看。）「吃藥」不能說 *eat medicine*（誤），要說 take medicine。Take aspirin.（吃阿斯匹靈。）Try some pills.（吃些藥丸試試看。）【這是美國人習慣說的】*See a physician.* 可說成：See a doctor.（去看醫生。）Go see a physician.（去看醫生。）（ = *Go see a doctor*.）Make an appointment and see a physician.（預約去看醫生。）

    藥是三分毒，是指中藥；西藥的毒性更強，吃多了會傷身體。我有一位親戚，連續吃了幾個月的止痛藥，傷了腎臟，不得不去換腎。感冒是萬病之源，當感冒快來時，要做危機處理。我的方法是，立刻喝大量的溫開水，再喝一杯咖啡，上一號就等於排毒。躺在床上不如去按摩，中國人傳統的刮痧和拔罐，效果非常好。總之，一定要想辦法把感冒壓下去才行，吃藥、看醫生，是最後不得已的手段。

10. *He died*.

看英文唸出中文	一 口 氣 説 九 句	看中文唸出英文
die[1] 〔 daɪ 〕 *v.*	He *died*. 他死了。	死亡
dead[1] 〔 dɛd 〕 *adj.*	He's *dead*. 他死了。	死的
depart[4] 〔 dɪ'pɑrt 〕 *v.*	He *departed*. 他離開人世了。	離開
expire[6] 〔 ɪk'spaɪr 〕 *v.*	*Expired*. 他死了。	到期；死亡
perish[5] 〔 'pɛrɪʃ 〕 *v.*	*Perished*. 他死了。	死亡；毀滅
pass away	*Passed away*. 去世了。	去世
funeral[4] 〔 'fjunərəl 〕 *n.*	There's a *funeral*. 有一場葬禮。	葬禮
attend[2] 〔 ə'tɛnd 〕 *v.*	I'll *attend*. 我會參加。	參加
peace[2] 〔 pis 〕 *n.*	May he rest in *peace*. 願他安息。	平靜

Lesson 5

【背景説明 10】

He died. 可加長爲：
He died last year. (他去
年死了。) He died of
cancer. (他死於癌症。)
He's dead. 禮貌的説法
是：He's in heaven. (他
上天堂了。) He's gone to a better place. (他已經到更好的地方去

了。) *He departed.* 可説成：He has departed. (他已經離開人世
了。) He has departed this world. (他已經離開這個世界了。)
He's gone. (他走了。)

Expired. 可説成：He expired. (他死了。) He has expired.
(他已經死了。) *Perished.* 的主要意思是「毀滅」，在此作「死
亡」解。可説成：He perished. (他死了。) He perished in a
house fire. (他在房屋失火時去世了。) *Passed away.* 可説成：
He passed away. (他去世了。) He has passed away. (他已經
去世了。)

There's a funeral. 可説成：There's a funeral tomorrow.
(明天有一場葬禮。) There's a funeral to honor him. (有一場
葬禮要向他致敬。) *I'll attend.* 可説成：I'll attend it. (我會參
加。) I'll attend his funeral. (我會參加他的葬禮。) I'll be
there. (我會去。) *May he rest in peace.* 可説成：May he rest
in eternal peace. (願他永遠安息。)

11. It's true.

看英文唸出中文	一口氣說九句	看中文唸出英文

true[1]
(tru) *adj.*

It's *true*.
是真的。

真的

truth[2]
(truθ) *n.*

It's the *truth*.
是事實。

事實

fact[1]
(fækt) *n.*

It's a *fact*.
是事實。

事實

---

real[1]
('riəl) *adj.*

Real.
是真的。

真的

reality[2]
(rɪ'ælətɪ) *n.*

Reality.
是事實。

事實

happen[1]
('hæpən) *v.*

It really *happened*.
它真的發生了。

發生

---

proof[3]
(pruf) *n.*

There's *proof*.
有證據。

證據

evidence[4]
('ɛvədəns) *n.*

We have *evidence*.
我們有證據。

證據

correct[1]
(kə'rɛkt) *adj.*

It's *correct*.
是正確的。

正確的

【背景説明 11】

It's true. 可説成：It's completely true. (完全眞實。) It's really true. (的確是眞的。) Believe me, it's true. (相信我，它是眞的。) *It's the truth.* 可説成：It's the whole truth. (完全眞實。) It's nothing but the truth. (絕對眞實。) It's the honest truth. (眞的是事實。) *It's a fact.* 可説成：It's a proven fact. (這事實已經被證實。)

Real. 可説成：It's real. (是眞的。) It's a real thing. (是眞的事情。) *Reality.* 可説成：It's a reality. (是事實。) (= *It's reality.*) *It really happened.* 可説成：I know it really happened. (我知道它眞的發生了。) I believe it really happened. (我相信它眞的發生了。)

There's proof. 可説成：There's proof available. (有可獲得的證據。) There's proof you can see. (有你可以看到的證據。) *We have evidence.* 可説成：We have gathered evidence. (我們已經收集了證據。) We have obtained evidence. (我們已經獲得證據。) We have proof. (我們有證據。) *It's correct.* 可説成：It's totally correct. (完全正確。) It's one hundred percent correct. (百分之百正確。) It's true, not false. (是眞的，不是假的。) It's accurate. (它是精確的。)

12. *It's false.*

看英文唸出中文	一口氣說九句	看中文唸出英文
false[1] 〔 fɔls 〕 *adj.*	It's *false*. 是假的。	假的
fiction[4] 〔'fɪkʃən 〕 *n.*	It's *fiction*. 是虛構的事。	虛構的事；小説
fantasy[4] 〔'fæntəsɪ 〕 *n.*	It's *fantasy*. 是幻想。	幻想
make up	*Made up*. 是編造的。	編造
make-believe 〔'mekbɪ,liv 〕 *adj.*	*Make-believe*. 是虛構的。	假裝的；虛構的
pretend[3] 〔 prɪ'tɛnd 〕 *adj.*	Just *pretend*. 只是假想的。	假裝的；假想的
story[1] 〔'storɪ 〕 *n.*	Only a *story*. 只是個故事。	故事
tale[1] 〔 tel 〕 *n.*	Just a *tale*. 只是個故事。	故事
imagine[2] 〔 ɪ'mædʒɪn 〕 *v.*	Totally *imagined*. 完全是想像的。	想像

【背景說明 12】

It's false. 可說成：It's totally false. (完全是假的。)(= *It's completely false.*) *It's fiction.* 可說成：It's all fiction. (全部是虛構的事。) It's not true. (不是眞的。) It's fake. (是假的。) fiction 和 novel 都作「小說」解，但 fiction 是不可數名詞，不加冠詞。*It's fantasy.* 可說成：It's just fantasy. (它只是幻想。) 和 It's fake. 及 It's fiction. 意思相同。

Made up. 可說成：It was made up. (它是編造的。) The story was made up. (這故事是編造的。) It was made up, not real. (是編造的，不是眞的。) *Make-believe.* 是一個複合形容詞，作「假裝的；虛構的」解。可說成：It is make-believe. (是虛構的。) It's not true. It's just a story. (這不是眞的。只是故事。) 不能說成：*It's made-believe.* (誤) 可說成：It's made-up. (它是編造的。)(= *It's made up.*) *Just pretend.* 可說成：It's just pretend. It isn't true. (它是假想的。不是眞的。)

Only a story. 可說成：It is only a story. 或 It was only a story. (只是個故事。) It's only a fake story. (只是假的故事。) *Just a tale.* 可說成：Just a fairy tale. (只是個童話故事。) *Totally imagined.* 可說成：It was totally imagined. (完全是想像的。) I totally imagined it. (完全是我想像的。) It's not true. It was from my imagination. (不是眞的。是我想像的。)

Lesson 5 總複習

1. 激勵；2. 抱怨；3. 協助

1. You *failed*.
   You *dropped* the ball.
   You *let* me *down*.

   You *acquired* nothing.
   You *completed* nothing.
   You *came up short*.

   Start again.
   Try again.
   Make another *attempt*.

2. I'm *frustrated*.
   Disappointed.
   Displeased.

   Depressed.
   Discouraged.
   Dismayed.

   I feel *defeated*.
   Like a *failure*.
   It's a *setback*.

3. Need *help*?
   Can I *assist*?
   Be of *service*?

   Trouble?
   Problem?
   Worried?

   Don't *hesitate*.
   Don't be *polite*.
   I'm *available*.

4.～6. 有話直說

4. Be *direct*.
   Truthful.
   To the *point*.

   Open.
   Frank.
   Specific.

   Explicit.
   Genuine.
   Don't beat around the *bush*.

5. Don't be *shy*.
   Don't be *quiet*.
   You're too *timid*.

   Don't be *scared*.
   Don't be *nervous*.
   Conquer fear.

   Don't be *embarrassed*.
   Don't be *awkward*.
   Be *brave*.

6. *Speak* up!
   Voice your opinion.
   Be *heard*.

   You're *smart*.
   You're *intelligent*.
   Share your ideas.

   You're *bright*.
   You're *on the ball*.
   You have so much to *offer*.

7. 借錢；**8.** 生病；**9.** 急救   **10.** 某人去世；**11.** , **12.** 討論眞假

7. I'm *broke*.
Out of *money*.
No *cash*.

I'*m hard up*.
I'm *penniless*.
I'm *cleaned out*.

May I *borrow* a few bucks?
Could you *lend* me some cash?
How about a *loan*?

8. *Dizzy*.
Tired.
Weak.

Fever.
Headache.
Sore throat.

In *pain*.
Hurting from head to toe.
Symptoms of illness.

9. First *aid*.
Drink *water*.
Have *coffee*.

Massage.
Coining.
Cupping.

Take a *rest*.
Take *medicine*.
See a *physician*.

10. He *died*.
He's *dead*.
He *departed*.

Expired.
Perished.
Passed away.

There's a *funeral*.
I'll *attend*.
May he rest in *peace*.

11. It's *true*.
It's the *truth*.
It's a *fact*.

Real.
Reality.
It really *happened*.

There's *proof*.
We have *evidence*.
It's *correct*.

12. It's *false*.
It's *fiction*.
It's *fantasy*.

Made up.
Make-believe.
Just *pretend*.

Only a *story*.
Just a *tale*.
Totally *imagined*.

Lesson 6　I'm skeptical.

1. What's your job?

看英文唸出中文	一 口 氣 説 九 句	看中文唸出英文
job[1] (dʒɑb) *n.*	What's your *job*? 你做什麼工作？	工作
occupation[4] (ˌɑkjəˈpeʃən) *n.*	*Occupation?* 什麼職業？	職業
line of work	*Line of work?* 什麼行業？	行業
business[2] ('bɪznɪs) *n.*	What's your *business?* 你從事什麼行業？	職業
title[2] ('taɪtḷ) *n.*	*Title?* 是什麼頭銜？	頭銜
position[1] (pəˈzɪʃən) *n.*	*Position?* 是什麼職位？	職位
employ[3] (ɪmˈplɔɪ) *v.*	Are you *employed?* 你現在有工作嗎？	雇用
part-time ('pɑrtˌtaɪm) *adj.*	*Part-time?* 是兼職嗎？	兼職的
full-time ('fʊlˌtaɪm) *adj.*	*Full-time?* 還是全職？	全職的

【背景說明1】

What's your job? 可禮貌地說成：May I ask what your job is?（我可以問你是做什麼工作的嗎？）What do you do?（你做什麼工作？）*Occupation?* 源自 What's your occupation?（你是什麼職業？）*Line of work?* 源自 What's your line of work?（你是什麼行業？）What line of work are you in?（你從事什麼行業？）May I ask your line of work?（我可以問你從事什麼行業嗎？）

What's your business? 可說成：In what area is your business?（你的職業是什麼領域？）（= *What's the area of your business?*）*Title?* 源自 What's your title?（你是什麼頭銜？）What's your job title?（你是什麼職稱？）*Position?* 源自 What's your position?（你是什麼職位？）（= *What position are you in?*）In your company, what's your position?（在你的公司裡，你是什麼職位？）

Are you employed? 字面的意思是「你被雇用嗎？」也就是「你有工作嗎？」（= *Do you have a job?*）可說成：At this time, are you employed?（你現在有工作嗎？）*Part-time?* 源自 Do you work part-time?（你是兼職工作嗎？）Are you part-time?（你是兼職的嗎？）Are you a part-time worker?（你是兼職的員工嗎？）*Full-time?* 源自 Are you full-time?（你是全職的嗎？）可說成：Do you work full-time?（你是不是做全職的工作？）Are you a full-time employee?（你是不是全職的員工？）

2. *How's the pay?*

看英文唸出中文	一口氣說九句	看中文唸出英文
pay[1,3] 〔 pe 〕*n.*	How's the *pay*? 薪水如何？	薪水
salary[4] 〔'sælərɪ 〕*n.*	*Salary* good? 薪水高嗎？	薪水
conditions[3] 〔 kən'dɪʃənz 〕*n. pl.*	Working *conditions*? 工作環境如何？	環境；條件
boss[1] 〔 bɔs 〕*n.*	*Boss* OK? 老闆好嗎？	老闆
colleague[5] 〔'kɑlig 〕*n.*	*Colleagues* friendly? 同事友善嗎？	同事
overtime 〔'ovɚ‚taɪm 〕*n.*	Lots of *overtime*? 要常加班嗎？	加班
benefits[3] 〔'bɛnəfɪts 〕*n. pl.*	*Benefits*? 有什麼福利嗎？	福利
insurance[4] 〔 ɪn'ʃʊrəns 〕*n.*	*Insurance*? 有保險嗎？	保險
bonus[5] 〔'bonəs 〕*n.*	Year-end *bonus*? 有年終獎金嗎？	獎金

【背景説明 2】

How's the pay? 可説成：May I ask how the pay is?（能不能請問你，薪水如何？）How's the pay in your company?（你的公司的薪水如何？）In your opinion, how's the pay?（你覺得薪水如何？）*Salary good?* 源自 Is your salary good?（你的薪水高嗎？）(= *Is your salary high?*）可説成：Is the salary at your company good?（你的公司的薪水高嗎？）*Working conditions?* 可説成：How are the working conditions?（工作環境如何？）Are you happy with the working conditions?（你對你的工作環境滿意嗎？）condition 的主要意思是「情況；條件」，*living conditions* 是「生活環境」，*working conditions* 是「工作環境」。

Boss OK? 源自 Is your boss OK?（你的老闆好嗎？）可説成：Do you like your boss?（你喜歡你的老闆嗎？）*Colleagues friendly?* 源自 Are your colleagues friendly?（你的同事友善嗎？）Do you have good co-workers?（你有沒有好的同事？）*Lots of overtime?* 源自 Do you get lots of overtime?（你有沒有常加班？）Make good money?（賺很多錢嗎？）

Benefits? 源自 How are the benefits?（福利如何？）*Insurance?* 源自 Have good insurance?（有好的保險嗎？）Does your company provide good insurance?（你的公司有沒有提供好的保險？）*Year-end bonus?* 源自 Do you get a year-end bonus?（你有沒有年終獎金？）Does your company provide a year-end bonus?（你們公司有沒有提供年終獎金？）

美國人的文化是，對陌生的人，不講私事，如薪水多少，但是熟的朋友例外，不回答反而有傷友誼。

3. *Make a decision.*

看英文唸出中文	一 口 氣 說 九 句	看中文唸出英文
investigate[3]	*Investigate.*	調查
(ɪn'vɛstə,get) *v.*	要調查。	
research[4]	*Research.*	研究
(rɪ'sɝtʃ , 'risɝtʃ) *v.*	要研究。	
analyze[4]	*Analyze.*	分析
('ænḷ,aɪz) *v.*	要分析。	

compare[2]	*Compare.*	比較
(kəm'pɛr) *v.*	要做比較。	
consider[2]	*Consider.*	考慮
(kən'sɪdə) *v.*	要考慮。	
discuss[2]	*Discuss* it.	討論
(dɪ'skʌs) *v.*	要討論它。	

select[2]	*Select* a couple.	挑選
(sə'lɛkt) *v.*	挑選兩三個。	
choose[2]	*Choose* one.	選擇
(tʃuz) *v.*	選擇一個。	
decision[2]	Make a *decision.*	決定
(dɪ'sɪʒən) *n.*	做出決定。	

【背景說明 3】

　　Investigate. 可説成：Investigate carefully.（小心調查。）
You must investigate well.（你必須好好調查。）Investigate
well before you make a decision.（在你做決定以前，要好好調
查。）*Research.* 可説成：Carefully research.（要小心研究。）
Research well before you make a decision.（在你做決定以前，
要好好研究。）*Analyze.* 可説成：Analyze everything.（每件事
都要分析。）Analyze all factors.（分析所有的因素。）Analyze
well before you make a decision.（在你做決定之前，要好好分
析。）

　　Compare. 可説成：Compare possible outcomes.（比較可能
的結果。）Compare factors before you make a decision.（在你
做決定之前，比較各種因素。）*Consider.* 可説成：Consider
things carefully.（要小心地考慮事情。）Consider everything
before deciding.（在做決定之前，要考慮每件事。）*Discuss it.*
可説成：Discuss it with others.（和別人討論。）Discuss it and
get other opinions.（討論它，並得到其他的意見。）Carefully
discuss it.（要小心地討論它。）

　　Select a couple. 可説成：Select a couple of choices.（選擇
兩三個。）（= *Select a couple of options.*）*Choose one.* 可説成：
Carefully choose one.（要小心地選一個。）Choose the best one.
（選擇最好的。）*Make a decision.* 可説成：After everything,
make a decision.（一切做完後，做個決定。）

4. Traits of a Good Boss

看英文唸出中文	一口氣說九句	看中文唸出英文
firm[2] 〔 fɜm 〕 *adj.*	He's ***firm***. 他很堅定。	堅定的
upright[5] 〔'ʌpˌraɪt 〕 *adj.*	***Upright***. 正直。	直立的;正直的
honorable[4] 〔'ɑnərəbḷ 〕 *adj.*	***Honorable***. 值得尊敬。	值得尊敬的
rational[6] 〔'ræʃənḷ 〕 *adj.*	***Rational***. 理性。	理性的
accessible[6] 〔 æk'sɛsəbḷ 〕 *adj.*	***Accessible***. 容易接近。	容易接近的
opinion[2] 〔 ə'pɪnjən 〕 *n.*	Open to ***opinions***. 願意接受意見。	意見
courteous[4] 〔'kɜtɪəs 〕 *adj.*	***Courteous***. 有禮貌。	有禮貌的
praise[2] 〔 prez 〕 *n. v.*	He gives ***praise***. 他會稱讚。	稱讚
reward[4] 〔 rɪ'wɔrd 〕 *n. v.*	He gives a ***reward***. 他會獎勵。	獎勵

【背景説明 4】

當好老闆的九種特質。

He's firm. (他很堅定。) 可説成：He's firm, not soft. (他很堅定，不軟弱。) He's a firm leader. (他是個堅定的領導者。) *Upright*. 可説成：He's upright. (他很正直。) He's an upright boss. (他是個正直的老闆。) He's honest and upright. (他既誠實又正直。) *Honorable*. 可説成：He's honorable. (他值得尊敬。) (= *He's an honorable man*.) honorable 的意思是「光榮的；高尚的；值得尊敬的」，名詞是 honor (光榮)。當一個人遵守諾言、有誠信，我們就可以用 honorable 來形容他。

Rational. 可説成：He's rational. (他很理性。) He's always rational. (他總是很理性。) He's a rational person. (他是個理性的人。) *Accessible*. 可説成：He's very accessible. (他很容易接近。) He's easy to talk with. (很容易跟他談話。) *Open to opinions*. 可説成：He's open to opinions. (他願意接受意見。) He's open to others' opinions. (他願意接受別人的意見。) He's open to different opinions. (他願意接受不同的意見。)

Courteous. 可説成：He's courteous. (他很有禮貌。) Always courteous. (總是很有禮貌。) He's a courteous boss. (他是個有禮貌的老闆。) *He gives praise*. 可説成：He often gives praise. (他常稱讚。) He's full of praise. (他不停地稱讚。) He likes to praise when it's deserved. (該稱讚他就會稱讚。) *He gives a reward*. 可説成：He often gives a reward. (他常常獎勵。) When it's deserved, he gives a reward. (該獎勵的時候，他就獎勵。) He does rewards. (他會獎勵。)

5. *Traits of a Good Employee*

看英文唸出中文	一口氣說九句	看中文唸出英文
loyal[4] (ˈlɔɪəl) *adj.*	She's *loyal*. 她很忠實。	忠實的
virtuous[4] (ˈvɜtʃuəs) *adj.*	*Virtuous*. 品德高尚。	有品德的
knowledgeable[5] (ˈnɑlɪdʒəbl̩) *adj.*	*Knowledgeable*. 知識豐富。	有知識的
healthy[2] (ˈhɛlθɪ) *adj.*	*Healthy*. 身體健康。	健康的
dependable[4] (dɪˈpɛndəbl̩) *adj.*	*Dependable*. 可靠。	可靠的
dedicated[6] (ˈdɛdəˌketɪd) *adj.*	*Dedicated*. 全心投入。	投入的
punctual[6] (ˈpʌŋktʃuəl) *adj.*	*Punctual*. 守時的。	守時的
productive[4] (prəˈdʌktɪv) *adj.*	*Productive*. 有生產力。	有生產力的
efficient[3] (əˈfɪʃənt) *adj.*	*Efficient*. 有效率。	有效率的

【背景說明 5】

當一個好員工應該要有九種特質。

She's loyal. 可說成：Always loyal.（總是很忠實。）She's a loyal person.（她是個忠實的人。）*Virtuous.* 可說成：She's virtuous.（她有品德。）She's absolutely virtuous.（她絕對有品德。）*Knowledgeable.* 可說成：She's knowledgeable.（她知識豐富。）She's very knowledgeable.（她知識非常豐富。）She's very intelligent.（她很聰明。）She knows a lot.（她懂很多。）

Healthy. 可說成：She's very healthy.（她很健康。）*Dependable.* 可說成：She's dependable.（她很可靠。）（= *She's a dependable person.*）She's always dependable.（她總是很可靠。）*Dedicated.* 可說成：She's very dedicated.（她全心投入。）She's a dedicated employee.（她是個用心的員工。）She's dedicated to her company.（她對公司盡心盡力。）

好的員工要守時，*Punctual.* 可說成：She's punctual.（她很守時。）She's always punctual.（她總是很守時。）（= *She's always on time.*）好的員工要有生產力。*Productive.* 可說成：She's productive.（她有生產力。）She's quite productive.（她相當有生產力。）（= *She's very productive.*）*Efficient.* 可說成：She's efficient.（她很有效率。）She's so efficient.（她非常有效率。）（= *She's quite efficient.* = *She's very efficient.*）

6. *Overcome Challenges*

看英文唸出中文	一口氣説九句	看中文唸出英文
challenge[3] 〔'tʃælɪndʒ〕*n.*	It's a *challenge*. 它是個挑戰。	挑戰
tough[4] 〔 tʌf 〕*adj.*	A *tough* task. 是個艱難的任務。	艱難的
obstacle[4] 〔'ɑbstəkl̩〕*n.*	An *obstacle*. 是個阻礙。	阻礙
trial[2] 〔'traɪəl〕*n.*	A *trial*. 是一項考驗。	考驗
test[2] 〔 tɛst 〕*n.*	A *test*. 是一項測驗。	測驗
difficult[1] 〔'dɪfə‚kʌlt〕*adj.*	A *difficult* situation. 是個困難的情況。	困難的
face[1] 〔 fes 〕*v.*	*Face* it. 要面對它。	面對
accept[2] 〔 ək'sɛpt 〕*v.*	*Accept* it. 接受它。	接受
overcome[4] 〔‚ovɚ'kʌm〕*v.*	*Overcome* it. 克服它。	克服

【背景説明 6】

It's a challenge. 可加長爲：It's a challenge to start a business.
（創業是一項挑戰。）It's usually a challenge to succeed.（要成功
通常是一項挑戰。）*A tough task.* 可説成：It's a tough task.（它是
個艱難的任務。）可加長爲：Getting a Ph.D. is a tough task.（得到
博士學位是個艱難的任務。）Winning a scholarship is a tough task.
（贏得獎學金是個艱難的任務。）*An obstacle.* 可説成：It's an
obstacle.（它是個阻礙。）可加長爲：Poor health is an obstacle.
（不健康是一項阻礙。）Poverty is an obstacle.（貧窮是一項障礙。）
Bad weather is an obstacle.（壞天氣是一項阻礙。）

A trial. 源自 It's a trial.（它是一項考驗。）可説成：Life is a
trial.（人生是一項考驗。）Overcoming illness is a trial.（克服疾病
是一項考驗。）*A test.* 源自 It's a test.（它是一項測驗。）Life is a
test.（人生是一項測驗。）Marriage is a test.（婚姻是一項考驗。）
Learning a new job is a test.（學習新的工作是一項考驗。）*A
difficult situation.* 源自 It's a difficult situation.（它是個困難的情
況。）For children, divorce is a difficult situation.（對孩子來説，
離婚是個困難的情況。）The death of a parent is a difficult
situation.（父親或母親過世是個困難的情況。）

Face it. 可説成：Always face it.（總是要面對它。）When you
have trouble, face it.（如果有困難，就要面對它。）Whatever the
problem, face it.（無論是什麼問題，都要面對它。）*Accept it.* 可説
成：Face reality; accept it.（要面對現實，接受它。）No matter
what, accept it.（無論如何都要接受它。）*Overcome it.* 可説成：
You can overcome it.（你可以克服它。）Try to overcome it.（要
努力克服它。）

7. *Think English*.

看英文唸出中文	一口氣説九句	看中文唸出英文
whatever [2] 〔 hwɑt'ɛvɚ 〕 *pron.*	***Whatever*** you do. 無論你做什麼。	無論什麼
wherever [2] 〔 hwɛr'ɛvɚ 〕 *adv.*	***Wherever*** you go. 無論你去哪裡。	無論何處
whenever [2] 〔 hwɛn'ɛvɚ 〕 *adv.*	***Whenever*** it is. 無論是什麼時候。	無論何時

----

whichever 〔 hwɪtʃ'ɛvɚ 〕 *adj.*	***Whichever*** situation. 無論是哪種情況。	無論哪一個
however [2] 〔 haʊ'ɛvɚ 〕 *adv.*	***However*** tough. 無論有多困難。	無論多麼地
remember [1] 〔 rɪ'mɛmbɚ 〕 *v.*	***Remember*** this. 要記得這一點。	記得

----

think [1] 〔 θɪŋk 〕 *v.*	***Think*** English. 用英文思考。	思考
translate [4] 〔'trænslet 〕 *v.*	***Translate*** into English. 要翻成英文。	翻譯
improve [2] 〔 ɪm'pruv 〕 *v.*	Practice and ***improve***. 要練習和改進。	改善

【背景説明 7】

這一回的主題，是教你要用英文思考。***Whatever you do.*** 在這裡源自：Whatever you do, think English. （無論你做什麼，都要用英文思考。） ***Wherever you go.*** 源自 Wherever you go, think English. （無論你去哪裡，都要用英文思考。） ***Whenever it is.*** 源自 Whenever it is, think English. （無論是什麼時候，都要用英文思考。）

Whichever situation. 源自 Whichever situation you face, think English. （無論你面對哪一種情況，都要用英文思考。） ***However tough.*** 源自 However tough the task, think English. （無論任務有多困難，都要用英文思考。） ***Remember this.*** 可説成：Always remember this advice. （一定要記得這個忠告。） I hope you always remember this. （我希望你永遠記得這個。）

Think English. 可説成：Think in English every day. （每天都用英文思考。） Always think in English. （永遠用英文思考。） ***Translate into English.*** 可説成：Try to translate everything into English. （試著把一切都翻成英文。） Always try to translate into English. （永遠努力翻成英文。） ***Practice and improve.*** 可説成：Every day, practice and improve. （每天都要練習並改進。） You must always practice and improve. （你必須永遠練習並改進。）

Think English.
Translate into English.
Practice and improve.

I will.

8. *Master vocabulary*.

看英文唸出中文	一口氣說九句	看中文唸出英文
vocabulary[2]	Master *vocabulary*.	字彙
〔 və'kæbjə,lɛrɪ 〕 *n.*	要精通字彙。	
memorize[3]	*Memorize* words.	背熟
〔'mɛmə,raɪz 〕 *v.*	要把單字背熟。	
powerful[2]	They are *powerful*.	強有力的
〔'pauɚfəl 〕 *adj.*	它們力量強大。	
expert[2]	Be a word *expert*.	專家
〔'ɛkspɝt 〕 *n.*	做個單字專家。	
respect[2]	Be *respected*.	尊敬
〔 rɪ'spɛkt 〕 *v.*	受人尊敬。	
admire[3]	Be *admired*.	欽佩
〔 əd'maɪr 〕 *v.*	受人欽佩。	
reading[1]	For *reading*.	閱讀
〔'ridɪŋ 〕 *n.*	這是為了閱讀。	
comprehension[5]	For *comprehension*.	理解
〔,kɑmprɪ'hɛnʃən 〕 *n.*	為了理解。	
communication[4]	For better *communication*.	溝通
〔 kə,mjunə'keʃən 〕 *n.*	為了更好的溝通。	

【背景說明 8】

Master vocabulary. 可說成：Try to really master vocabulary.（努力真正地精通字彙。）You must master vocabulary.（你必須精通字彙。）Master vocabulary to be fluent.（為了要把英文說得流利，要精通字彙。）*Memorize words.* 可說成：Memorize words every day.（每天都要背單字。）Memorize important words.（背重要單字。）memorize 是「背熟」，recite 是「背誦；朗誦；背給大家聽」，如 I memorize words so I can recite them.（我把單字背熟，才能背出來。）*Memorize words.* 和 Learn words by heart 及 Commit words to memory. 意思相同。*They are powerful.* 可說成：They are powerful aids to communication.（它們是溝通強有力的輔助工具。）Vocabulary words give you power.（字彙給你力量。）

Be a word expert. 可說成：Try to be a word expert.（努力做個單字專家。）You must be a word expert.（你必須做個單字專家。）*Be respected.* 可說成：Be respected by others.（要受到別人尊敬。）Master vocabulary and you'll be respected.（如果精通字彙，你就會受人尊敬。）*Be admired.* 可說成：Be admired by many.（受很多人欽佩。）You'll be admired.（你將受人欽佩。）Always be admired.（永遠受人欽佩。）

For reading. 可說成：It's useful for reading.（這對閱讀很有用。）It's very helpful for reading.（這對閱讀很有幫助。）*For comprehension.* 可說成：It's necessary for reading comprehension.（這對閱讀理解是必要的。）It's very helpful for understanding.（它非常有助於了解。）*For better communication.* 可說成：For better communication, master vocabulary.（為了更好的溝通，要精通字彙。）It's so important for better communication.（這對更好的溝通很重要。）

9. *Value time*.

看英文唸出中文	一 口 氣 說 九 句	看中文唸出英文
value[2] ('vælju) *v.*	***Value*** time. 要重視時間。	重視
fly[1] (flaɪ) *v.*	It ***flies*** by. 時光飛逝。	飛
short[1] (ʃɔrt) *adj.*	Life is ***short***. 生命很短暫。	短的
decade[3] ('dɛked) *n.*	***Decades*** pass. 幾十年過去了。	十年
week[1] (wik) *n.*	Days to ***weeks***. 好幾天變成好幾個星期。	星期
year[1] (jɪr) *n.*	Months to ***years***. 好幾個月變成好幾年。	年
age[1] (edʒ) *v.*	We ***age*** fast. 我們很快就變老。	變老
seize[3] (siz) *v.*	***Seize*** time. 要把握時間。	抓住
waste[1] (west) *v.*	Don't ***waste*** a minute. 不要浪費任何一分鐘。	浪費

【背景説明 9】

　　Value time. 可説成：Always value time.（一定要重視時間。）You must value time.（你必須重視時間。）To be efficient, value time.（爲了有效率，必須重視時間。）Time is precious.（時間很珍貴。）Don't waste time.（不要浪費時間。）***It flies by.*** 可説成：It flies by quickly.（時間過得很快。）(= *It flies by so fast.*) 也可簡單説：Time flies.（光陰似箭。）***Life is short.*** 可説成：It's so true that life is short.（的確，生命很短暫。）Don't waste time; life is short.（不要浪費時間；生命很短暫。）【慣用句】Old people know that life is short.（年紀比較大的人都知道，生命很短暫。）

　　Decades pass. 可説成：Decades pass quickly.（幾十年很快就過去了。）Decades pass by so fast.（幾十年很快就過去了。）***Days to weeks.*** 可説成：Time flies, as days turn to weeks.（時光飛逝，因爲好幾天會變成好幾星期。）句中 turn to 也可説 turn into（變成）。Days turn to weeks very quickly.（好幾天很快就變成好幾個星期。）***Months to years.*** 可説成：Months become years.（幾個月變成幾年。）Months add up and change to years.（好幾個月加起來，就變成好幾年。）

　　We age fast. 可説成：We are all aging fast.（我們所有的人都很快就變老。）Aging fast is a part of life.（很快變老是生命的一部份。）***Seize time.*** 可説成：Seize time and use it wisely.（把握時間，並聰明地使用它。）***Don't waste a minute.*** 可説成：Please don't waste a single minute.（請不要浪費任何一分鐘。）Take my advice. Don't waste a minute.（聽我的勸告。不要浪費任何一分鐘。）Don't waste time.（不要浪費時間。）Don't waste any time.（不要浪費任何時間。）

10. *Possibly*.

看英文唸出中文	一口氣說九句	看中文唸出英文
maybe[1] (ˈmebɪ) *adv.*	*Maybe*. 也許。	也許
possibly[1] (ˈpasəblɪ) *adv.*	*Possibly*. 有可能。	可能地
slight[4] (slaɪt) *adj.*	There's a *slight* chance. 還是有點機會。	少許的
probably[3] (ˈprabəblɪ) *adv.*	*Probably*. 可能。	可能地
likely[1] (ˈlaɪklɪ) *adv.*	*Likely*. 很有可能。	很可能
hopefully[4] (ˈhopfəlɪ) *adv.*	*Hopefully*. 非常有希望。	有希望地
feasible[6] (ˈfizəbl) *adj.*	It's *feasible*. 這是可實行的。	可實行的
attainable[6] (əˈtenəbl) *adj.*	It's *attainable*. 這是可以達成的。	可達到的
happen[1] (ˈhæpən) *v.*	It can *happen*. 這有可能發生。	發生

【背景說明 10】

Maybe. 可說成：Maybe it will happen. (也許會發生。)
Maybe it could be. (也許可能是。) *Possibly.* 可說成：It could
possibly happen. (它可能會發生。) *There's a slight chance.*
可說成：There's a slight chance it could happen. (還是有點可
能會發生。) There's a small possibility. (可能性很小。) *There's
a slight chance.* 有否定的含意，相當於 There's little chance.
(沒什麼機會。) (= *There's almost no chance.*)

Probably. 可說成：It probably will. (可能會。) (= *It
probably will happen.*) It's probably going to happen. (可能
會發生。) *Likely.* 可說成：It's likely. (有可能。) It's highly
likely. (非常可能。) It's likely to happen. (可能會發生。)
Hopefully. 這個字美國人常說。可說成：Hopefully, it will
happen. (希望它會發生。) Hopefully, it is true. (希望是真
的。) Hopefully, it can come true. (希望它能實現。)

It's feasible. 可說成：I think it's feasible. (我認為它是可
行的。) It's feasible it will happen. (可能會發生。) The plan
is feasible. (這計劃是可行的。) (= *The plan is possible.*)
It's attainable. 可說成：It's very attainable. (非常可能達成。)
I feel it's attainable. (我覺得是可以達成的。) It's an attainable
goal. (這是可以達成的目標。) *It can happen.* 可說成：I think
it can happen. (我認為有可能發生。) Many agree it can
happen. (很多人都同意，這有可能發生。) It can happen soon.
(可能很快就會發生。) It can happen at any time. (這隨時都
可能發生。)

11. *Impossible*.

看英文唸出中文	一口氣說九句	看中文唸出英文
impossible[1] (ɪmˋpɑsəbḷ) *adj.*	*Impossible*. 不可能。	不可能的
never ever	*Never ever*. 永遠都不行。	永不
no way	*No way*. 絕對不行。	絕對不行
zero[1] (ˋzɪro) *adj.*	*Zero* chance. 沒有機會。	零
no can do	*No can do*. 我做不到。	我做不到
absolutely[4] (ˋæbsəˏlutlɪ) *adv.*	*Absolutely* not. 絕對不行。	絕對地
hopeless[1] (ˋhoplɪs) *adj.*	It's *hopeless*. 沒希望。	沒有希望的
question[1] (ˋkwɛstʃən) *n.*	Out of the *question*. 不可能。	問題
million[2] (ˋmɪljən) *n.*	Not in a *million* years. 這輩子休想。	百萬

【背景說明 11】

　　Impossible. 可說成：It's impossible.（不可能。）I believe it's impossible.（我相信不可能。）It's an impossible thing.（這是不可能的事。）*Never ever*. 中的 ever，等於 at any time。這句話字面的意思是「任何時候都不行。」也就是「永遠都不行。」（= *Never at any time*.）It will never ever happen.（它將永遠都不會發生。）I hope it will never ever come true.（我希望它永遠都不會成眞。）*No way*. 可說成：There is no possible way.（沒有什麼可能的方式；不行。）

　　Zero chance. 可說成：There is zero chance.（沒有機會。）There is zero chance it will happen.（發生的機會是零。）*No can do*. 源自 *No*, I *can* not *do* it.（不，我做不到。）也就是 I can't do it.（我做不到。）*Absolutely not*. 可說成：It will absolutely not happen.（絕對不會發生。）

　　It's hopeless. 可說成：It's really hopeless.（眞的沒希望。）It's hopeless to try.（去試是沒有希望的。）*Out of the question*. 源自 It's out of the question.（這是不可能的。）（= *It's impossible*.）

> 【比較】*Out of the question*. 字面的意思是「在這個問題之外。」引申為「不可能。」此時 question 是普通名詞。
>
> 　　　　Out of question.（沒問題。）【誤】現在美語已經不用，現在多用 Without question. 或 Beyond question. 此時 question 是抽象名詞，所以不加冠詞。

　　Not in a million years. 可說成：It could not happen in a million years. 字面的意思是「一百萬年之內都不會發生。」引申為「永遠都不可能。」（= *I believe it's impossible*.）

12. *I doubt it*.

看英文唸出中文	一 口 氣 說 九 句	看中文唸出英文
doubt[2] 〔 daʊt 〕 *v.*	I *doubt* it. 我懷疑。	懷疑
believe[1] 〔 bə'liv 〕 *v.*	Don't *believe* it. 不相信。	相信
sure[1] 〔 ʃʊr 〕 *adj.*	You *sure*? 你確定嗎？	確定的
skeptical[6] 〔 'skɛptɪkḷ 〕 *adj.*	I'm *skeptical*. 我懷疑。	懷疑的
doubtful[3] 〔 'daʊtfəl 〕 *adj.*	*Doubtful*. 我懷疑。	懷疑的
questionable[1] 〔 'kwɛstʃənəbḷ 〕 *adj.*	It's *questionable*. 有問題。	有問題的
joke[1] 〔 dʒok 〕 *v.*	Are you *joking?* 你在說笑嗎？	開玩笑
kid[1] 〔 kɪd 〕 *v.*	*Kidding?* 開玩笑嗎？	開玩笑
buy[1] 〔 baɪ 〕 *v.*	I don't *buy* it. 我不相信。	買；相信

【背景説明 12】

I doubt it. 可説成：I really doubt it.（我真的懷疑。）I seriously doubt it.（我真的懷疑。）這個句子表示「我不相信。」（＝*I don't think it's true.*）*Don't believe it.* 可説成：I don't believe it.（我不相信。）I don't believe it's true.（我不相信它是真的。）I don't believe it will happen.（我不相信會發生。）*You sure?* 源自 Are you sure?（你確定嗎？）可説成：Are you really sure?（你真的確定嗎？）How can you be so sure?（你怎麼能如此確定？）

I'm skeptical. 可説成： I'm very skeptical.（我非常懷疑。）I'm skeptical about it.（我懷疑它。）*Doubtful.* 可説成：I'm doubtful.（我懷疑。）或 It's doubtful.（這令人懷疑。）doubtful 可以形容「人」和「非人」，作「懷疑的」或「令人懷疑的」解。I feel it's doubtful.（我覺得它令人懷疑。）*It's questionable.* 可説成：It's questionable that it could happen.（會發生這件事是有問題的。）

Are you joking? 可説成：Are they joking?（他們在説笑嗎？）Is someone joking?（有人在説笑嗎？）*Kidding?* 可説成：Are you kidding?（你在開玩笑嗎？）*I don't buy it.* 可説成：I honestly don't buy it.（老實説我不相信。）buy 的主要意思是「買」，在這裡作「相信」（＝*believe*）解。*I don't buy it.* 等於 I don't believe it.（我不相信。）I don't think it's true.（我不相信這是真的。）

Lesson 6　總複習

1. , 2. 工作；3. 如何做決定

1. What's your *job*?
   Occupation?
   Line of work?

   What's your *business*?
   Title?
   Position?

   Are you *employed*?
   Part-time?
   Full-time?

2. How's the *pay*?
   Salary good?
   Working *conditions*?

   Boss OK?
   Colleagues friendly?
   Lots of *overtime*?

   Benefits?
   Insurance?
   Year-end *bonus*?

3. *Investigate*.
   Research.
   Analyze.

   Compare.
   Consider.
   Discuss it.

   Select a couple.
   Choose one.
   Make a *decision*.

4.～6. 好老闆、好員工、接受挑戰

4. He's *firm*.
   Upright.
   Honorable.

   Rational.
   Accessible.
   Open to *opinions*.

   Courteous.
   He gives *praise*.
   He gives a *reward*.

5. She's *loyal*.
   Virtuous.
   Knowledgeable.

   Healthy.
   Dependable.
   Dedicated.

   Punctual.
   Productive.
   Efficient.

6. It's a *challenge*.
   A *tough* task.
   An *obstacle*.

   A *trial*.
   A *test*.
   A *difficult* situation.

   Face it.
   Accept it.
   Overcome it.

7. , 8. 學英文；9. 把握時間　　　　**10.～12. 有可能、不可能、懷疑**

7. *Whatever* you do.
   Wherever you go.
   Whenever it is.

   Whichever situation.
   However tough.
   Remember this.

   Think English.
   Translate into English.
   Practice and *improve*.

8. Master *vocabulary*.
   Memorize words.
   They are *powerful*.

   Be a word *expert*.
   Be *respected*.
   Be *admired*.

   For *reading*.
   For *comprehension*.
   For better *communication*.

9. *Value* time.
   It *flies* by.
   Life is *short*.

   Decades pass.
   Days to *weeks*.
   Months to *years*.

   We *age* fast.
   Seize time.
   Don't *waste* a minute.

10. *Maybe*.
    Possibly.
    There's a *slight* chance.

    Probably.
    Likely.
    Hopefully.

    It's *feasible*.
    It's *attainable*.
    It can *happen*.

11. *Impossible*.
    Never ever.
    No way.

    Zero chance.
    No can do.
    Absolutely not.

    It's *hopeless*.
    Out of the *question*.
    Not in a *million* years.

12. I *doubt* it.
    Don't *believe* it.
    You *sure*?

    I'm *skeptical*.
    Doubtful.
    It's *questionable*.

    Are you *joking*?
    Kidding?
    I don't *buy* it.

Lesson 7　Traveling is fascinating.

1. Been abroad?

看英文唸出中文	一口氣說九句	看中文唸出英文
abroad[2] 〔 ə'brɔd 〕 *adv.*	Been **abroad**? 出過國嗎？	到國外
overseas[2] 〔'ovɚ'siz 〕 *adv.*	Been **overseas**? 出過國嗎？	在海外
foreign[1] 〔'fɔrɪn〕 *adj.*	Been to any **foreign** countries? 去過任何外國嗎？	外國的
travel[2] 〔'trævl̩ 〕 *v.*	***Travel!*** 去旅行！	旅行
tour[2] 〔 tʊr 〕 *v. n.*	***Tour!*** 去旅遊！	旅遊
sightsee[4] 〔'saɪt,si 〕 *v.*	Go ***sightseeing***! 去觀光！	觀光
exciting[2] 〔 ɪk'saɪtɪŋ〕 *adj.*	It's **exciting**. 它很刺激。	刺激的
adventure[3] 〔 əd'vɛntʃɚ 〕 *n.*	It's an **adventure**. 它是種冒險。	冒險
lifetime[3] 〔'laɪf,taɪm 〕 *adj.*	Create **lifetime** memories. 要創造終生的回憶。	終生的

Lesson 7

【背景説明1】

Been abroad? 源自 Have you been abroad?（你出過國嗎？）可加強語氣説成：Been abroad before?（以前出過國嗎？）*Been overseas?* 源自 Have you been overseas?（你出過國嗎？）可加強語氣説成：Been overseas before?（以前出過國嗎？）或 Ever been overseas?（曾經出過國嗎？）語言就是這麼奇怪，美國人不説 *Ever been abroad?*（誤）*Been to any foreign countries?* 源自 Have you been to any foreign countries?（你去過任何外國嗎？）可説成：Been to any foreign countries before?（以前去過任何外國嗎？）

Travel! 源自 You should travel!（你應該去旅行！）可加長爲：Travel as much as you can!（儘量去旅行！）Travel a lot to learn a lot.（越常旅遊學得越多。）*Tour!* 源自 Take a tour!（去旅遊！）可説成：Join a travel tour!（參加旅行團！）Try to tour many countries.（儘量到許多國家去旅遊。）*Go sightseeing!* 可説成：You should go sightseeing.（你應該去觀光。）I suggest you go sightseeing.（我建議你去觀光。）

It's exciting. 可加強語氣説成：It's very exciting.（它非常刺激。）It's exciting to travel.（旅行很刺激。）It's always exciting to go abroad.（出國總是很刺激。）*It's an adventure.* 可説成：It's always an adventure to travel.（去旅行一定是種冒險。）It's an adventure to travel overseas.（出國旅遊是種冒險。）*Create lifetime memories.* 源自 You create lifetime memories.（你創造了終生的回憶。）可説成：Traveling helps create lifetime memories.（旅遊有助於創造終生的回憶。）Going overseas creates lifetime memories.（出國能創造終生的回憶。）

2. *Traveling is fascinating*.

看英文唸出中文	一 口 氣 説 九 句	看中文唸出英文
fascinating[5]	Traveling is *fascinating*.	迷人的
(ˈfæsn̩ˌetɪŋ) *adj.*	旅行很迷人。	
fan[3,1]	I'm a big *fan*.	迷；粉絲
(fæn) *n.*	我是超級粉絲。	
support[2]	I *support* it.	支持；贊成
(səˈport) *v.*	我贊成它。	
cherish[4]	*Cherish* it.	珍惜
(ˈtʃɛrɪʃ) *v.*	我珍惜它。	
relish[6]	*Relish* it.	享受
(ˈrɛlɪʃ) *v.*	我享受它。	
savor	I *savor* every minute.	慢慢品嚐
(ˈsevɚ) *v.*	我會細細體會每一分鐘。	
fancy[3]	*Fancy* it.	幻想；喜歡
(ˈfænsɪ) *v.*	我喜歡它。	
fond[3]	Be *fond* of it.	喜歡的
(fɑnd) *adj.*	我喜歡它。	
nuts[2]	I'm *nuts* about it.	發瘋的；狂熱的
(nʌts) *adj.*	我為它瘋狂。	

【背景説明 2】

Traveling is fascinating. 可加長爲：I think traveling is fascinating. (我認爲旅行很迷人。) To me, traveling abroad is fascinating. (對我而言，出國旅行很迷人。) *I'm a big fan.* 可説成：I'm a big fan of traveling. (我很喜歡旅行。) I'm a big fan of independent travel. (我非常喜歡自助旅行。) *I support it.* 可説成：I support it wholeheartedly. (我全心全意贊成它。) I encourage travel. (我鼓勵旅遊。)

Cherish it. 源自 I cherish it. (我珍惜它。) 可加強語氣説成：I always cherish it. (我總是很珍惜它。) *Relish it.* 源自 I relish it. (我享受它。) 可加強語氣説成：Relish every day of it. (享受旅行的每一天。) Relish it while you can. (在你能享受時，儘量享受。) *I savor every minute.* 可説成：While traveling, I savor every minute. (當旅行的時候，我會細細體會每一分鐘。)

Fancy it. 源自 I fancy it. (我喜歡它。) 可加強語氣説成：I fancy it so much. (我非常喜歡它。) 也可説成：I really love it. (我眞的很喜歡它。) fancy 的主要意思是「幻想」，幻想的東西，都是你最喜歡的，所以才會引申出「喜歡」的意思。 *Be fond of it.* 源自 I'm fond of it. (我喜歡它。) 可加強語氣説成：I'm very fond of traveling. (我非常喜歡旅行。) *I'm nuts about it.* 可説成：I'm crazy about it. (我爲它瘋狂。) I'm totally nuts about it. (我完全爲它瘋狂。)

3. *Join me*.

看英文唸出中文	一口氣說九句	看中文唸出英文
join[1] 〔 dʒɔɪn 〕 *v.*	*Join* me. 和我一起參加。	加入
register[4] 〔'rɛdʒɪstɚ〕 *v.*	*Register*. 去登記。	登記
sign up	*Sign up*. 去報名。	報名
ask[1] 〔 æsk 〕 *v.*	I *ask* you. 我請求你。	請求
invite[2] 〔 ɪn'vaɪt 〕 *v.*	I *invite* you. 我邀請你。	邀請
accompany[4] 〔 ə'kʌmpənɪ 〕 *v.*	*Accompany* me. 陪伴我。	陪伴
beg[2] 〔 bɛg 〕 *v.*	I *beg* you. 我拜託你。	乞求
urge[4] 〔 ɝdʒ 〕 *v.*	I *urge* you. 我懇求你。	催促;懇求
insist[2] 〔 ɪn'sɪst 〕 *v.*	I *insist*. 我堅持。	堅持

Lesson 7

【背景説明3】

Join me. 可説成：You should join me.（你應該和我一起參加。）Please join me.（請和我一起參加。）Why don't you join me?（你為什麼不和我一起參加？）*Register.* 可説成：You should register.（你應該去登記。）You have to register for it.（你必須去登記。）*Sign up.* 可説成：You must sign up.（你必須去報名。）源自參加學校活動時，會有一張 sign-up sheet，要參加者簽名。

I ask you. 可説成：I ask you now.（我現在請求你。）I want to ask you.（我要請求你。）I ask you to join me.（我請求你和我一起去。）*I invite you.* 可説成：I invite you to attend.（我邀請你參加。）I want to invite you.（我要邀請你。）I invite you to join me.（我邀請你和我一起去。）*Accompany me.* 可説成：Please accompany me.（請陪伴我。）（= *Please join me.*）I'd like you to accompany me.（我要你陪伴我。）（= *Let's go together.*）

I beg you. 可説成：I beg you to join me.（我拜託你和我一起去。）Please, I beg you.（求求你，我拜託你。）I beg you to consider it.（我拜託你考慮一下。）*I urge you.* 可説成：I urge you to join me.（我懇求你加入我的行列。）*I insist.* 可説成：Please, I insist.（拜託，我堅持。）I insist that you join us.（我堅持你加入我們的行列。）可連續説三句：You must! You can't say no. You have to.（你必須！你不能説不。你一定要。）

4. Airport Advice

看英文唸出中文	一口氣說九句	看中文唸出英文
airport[1] (ˈɛrˌport) *n.*	Get to the *airport* early. 早點去機場。	機場
airline[2] (ˈɛrˌlaɪn) *n.*	Know which *airline*. 要知道是哪家航空公司。	航空公司
terminal[5] (ˈtɝmənḷ) *n.*	Which *terminal*. 哪個航廈。	航空站
international[2] (ˌɪntɚˈnæʃənḷ) *adj.*	*International*. 是國際線。	國際的
domestic[3] (dəˈmɛstɪk) *adj.*	Not *domestic*. 不是國內線。	國內的
check[1] (tʃɛk) *v.*	*Check* in on time. 要準時辦理登機手續。	檢查
departure[4] (dɪˈpartʃɚ) *n.*	*Departure*. 是出境。	離開
arrival[3] (əˈraɪvḷ) *n.*	Not *arrival*. 不是入境。	到達
leave[1] (liv) *v.*	*Leave* yourself time. 要給自己留點時間。	離開；留

Lesson 7

【背景説明 4】

Get to the airport early. 可説成：Always get to the airport two hours early. (一定要提早兩個小時到機場。) Go to the airport several hours early. (要提早幾個小時到機場。) Get to 可以用 Go to 來代替。*Know which airline*. 可説成：Know which airline you're on. (要知道你搭乘哪一家航空公司。) airline 指「航空公司」時，可用單、複數形式，但航空公司名稱，一定用複數，因爲不只一條航線，如 China Airlines (中華航空)。*Which terminal*. 源自 Know which terminal. (要知道哪個航廈。) 可説成：Which terminal to go to. (要去哪個航廈。) Know which terminal your airline is at. (要知道你的航空公司在哪個航廈。)

International. 可説成：Go to the international terminal. (去國際航廈。) Your flight is at the international terminal. (你的班機在國際航廈。) *Not domestic*. 可説成：Do not go to the domestic terminal. (不要去國內航廈。) It's not at the domestic terminal. (不是在國內航廈。) *Check in on time*. 可説成：You must check in on time. (你必須準時辦理登機手續。) Always check in on time. (一定要準時辦理登機手續。) Make sure you check in on time. (你一定要準時辦理登機手續。)

Departure. 的主要意思是「離開；出發。」在機場，是指「出境區。」(*the departure area*) *Not arrival*. 源自 You want departure, not arrival. (你是要出境，不是入境。) 可説成：Departure is not the same as arrival. (出境區和入境區不一樣。) *Leave yourself time*. 可説成：Leave yourself enough time. (要給自己留足夠的時間。) Always leave yourself time. (一定要留給自己時間。) You must leave yourself enough time. (你必須留給自己足夠的時間。)

5. *I enjoy scenery*.

看英文唸出中文	一口氣說九句	看中文唸出英文
scenery[4] (´sinərɪ) *n.*	I enjoy *scenery*. 我喜歡風景。	風景
sight[1] (saɪt) *n.*	Natural *sights*. 自然的風景。	風景
view[1] (vju) *n.*	Outdoor *views*. 戶外的景色。	景色
sunny[2] (´sʌnɪ) *adj.*	*Sunny* skies. 晴朗的天空。	晴朗的
starry[1] (´starɪ) *adj.*	*Starry* nights. 佈滿星星的夜晚。	佈滿星星的
beach[1] (bitʃ) *n.*	Beautiful *beaches*. 美麗的海灘。	海灘
tranquil[6] (´træŋkwɪl) *adj.*	*Tranquil*. 很寧靜。	寧靜的
pleasant[2] (´plɛzn̩t) *adj.*	*Pleasant*. 令人愉快。	令人愉快的
peaceful[2] (´pisfəl) *adj.*	So calm and *peaceful*. 非常寧靜。	寧靜的

Lesson 7

【背景説明 5】

到了户外，你可以説：*I enjoy scenery*. 可加強語氣説成：
I enjoy watching scenery best. (我最喜歡看風景。) I really
enjoy mountain scenery. (我眞的很喜歡山景。) *Natural
sights*. 在這裡源自 I enjoy natural sights.(我喜歡自然的風景。)
可説成：I prefer natural sights. (我比較喜歡自然的風景。)
Natural sights relax me. (自然的風景能使我放鬆。)

Sunny skies. 在此源自 I love sunny skies. (我喜歡晴朗
的天空。) 可説成：Blue sunny skies are best. (藍色的晴朗
天空最棒。)*Starry nights*. 可説成：Starry nights are beautiful.
(佈滿星星的夜晚很漂亮。) Starry nights are romantic. (佈
滿星星的夜晚很浪漫。) *Beautiful beaches*. 可説成：I love
beautiful beaches. (我喜歡美麗的海灘。) Beautiful beaches
are my favorite places. (美麗的海灘是我最喜愛的地方。)

Tranquil. 源自 It's tranquil. (很寧靜。) tranquil 的意思
是「平靜的；寧靜的；安靜的」(= *calm, still and quiet*)。可説
成：It's tranquil here. (這裡很寧靜。) It's a tranquil place.
(這個地方很寧靜。) *Pleasant*. 可説成：It's so pleasant. (眞
令人愉快。) Being out in nature is pleasant. (在外面的大自
然裡很愉快。) Traveling is pleasant. (旅遊很愉快。) *So
calm and peaceful*. 可説成：It's so calm and peaceful. (非
常寧靜。) At night, it's so calm and peaceful. (在晚上非常
寧靜。) and 連接兩個同義的形容詞 calm 和 peaceful，有加
強語氣的作用。

6. Movies!

看英文唸出中文	一 口 氣 說 九 句	看中文唸出英文
movie [1] (ˈmuvɪ) *n.*	*Movies!* 電影！	電影
screen [2] (skrin) *n.*	The silver *screen*! 銀幕！	螢幕
fan [3,1] (fæn) *n.*	I'm a movie *fan*. 我是個電影迷。	(影、歌、球)迷
frequently [3] (ˈfrikwəntlɪ) *adv.*	I go *frequently*. 我常去看。	經常
weekly [4] (ˈwiklɪ) *adv.*	I watch *weekly*. 我每週都會看。	每週地
weekend [1] (ˈwikˈɛnd) *n.*	Especially on *weekends*. 尤其是在週末。	週末
reading [1] (ˈridɪŋ) *n.*	Watching is like *reading*. 看電影就像在閱讀。	閱讀
novel [2] (ˈnɑvḷ) *n.*	A movie is a *novel*. 電影就像小說。	小說
gain [2] (gen) *v.*	You *gain* information. 你會得到一些資訊。	獲得

* *the silver screen* 「銀幕」是「電影」的暱稱。

Lesson 7

【背景説明 6】

Movies! 源自 I love movies!（我喜歡電影！）可説成：I really like watching movies!（我真的很喜歡看電影！）I'm crazy about movies.（我很喜歡電影。）*The silver screen!* 源自 I enjoy the silver screen!（我喜歡看電影！）I'm a big fan of the silver screen.（我很喜歡電影。）

I go frequently. 可説成：I go watch movies frequently.（我常常去看電影。）I go all the time（我一直去。）I go a lot.（我常常去。）*I watch weekly.* 可説成：I watch movies weekly.（我每週都去看電影。）I see movies every week.（我每個禮拜都看電影。）*Especially on weekends.* 可説成：I go often, especially on weekends.（我常去，尤其是在週末。）I watch movies a lot, especially on weekends.（我常看電影，尤其是在週末。）

Watching is like reading. 可説成：To me, watching a movie is like reading a book.（對我而言，看一部電影就像讀一本書。）Movie watching is like reading a book.（看電影就像讀一本書。）*A movie is a novel.* 可説成：Watching a movie is like reading a novel.（看一部電影就像讀一本小說。）In my opinion, a movie is like a novel.（我認爲一部電影就像一本小說。）*You gain information.* 可説成：When viewing a movie, you gain information.（當你看電影的時候，你會得到資訊。）By watching movies, you can gain information.（藉由看電影，你可以獲得資訊。）Movies can teach you.（電影會教導你。）You can learn from watching movies.（你可以從看電影學到東西。）

7. *I enjoy action.*

看英文唸出中文	一口氣說九句	看中文唸出英文

action[1]
('ækʃən) *n.*

I enjoy action.
我喜歡動作片。

動作

thriller[1]
('θrɪlɚ) *n.*

Thrillers are exciting.
驚悚片很刺激。

驚悚片

comedy[4]
('kɑmədɪ) *n.*

Comedy is funny.
喜劇很好笑。

喜劇

---

serious[2]
('sɪrɪəs) *adj.*

I prefer *serious.*
我比較喜歡嚴肅的。

嚴肅的

deep[1]
(dip) *adj.*

I like *deep.*
我喜歡有深度的。

深的

shallow[3]
('ʃælo) *adj.*

Don't like *shallow.*
不喜歡膚淺的。

淺的;膚淺的

---

fiction[4]
('fɪkʃən) *n.*

No science *fiction.*
不喜歡科幻片。

小說

cartoon[2]
(kɑr'tun) *n.*

No *cartoons.*
不喜歡卡通片。

卡通

reality[2]
(rɪ'ælətɪ) *n.*

Reality is best.
寫實是最好的。

真實

【背景説明 7】

I enjoy action. 源自 I enjoy action movies. (我喜歡動作片。) 可説成：I enjoy action movies most. (我最喜歡動作片。) I enjoy movies with lots of action. (我喜歡有很多動作的電影。) *Thrillers are exciting.* 可説成：Thrillers are most exciting. (驚悚片最刺激。) Thriller movies are exciting. (驚悚片很刺激。) *Comedy is funny.* 可説成：Most comedy is funny. (大部份的喜劇都很好笑。) To me, comedy is so funny. (對我而言，喜劇很好笑。)

I prefer serious. 源自 I prefer serious movies. (我比較喜歡嚴肅的電影。) 可説成：I like realistic movies. (我喜歡寫實的電影。) *I like deep.* 源自 I like deep movies. (我喜歡有深度的電影。) 可説成：I prefer deep movies. (我比較喜歡有深度的電影。) I like movies with deep meaning. (我喜歡意義深遠的電影。) *Don't like shallow.* 源自 I don't like shallow movies. (我不喜歡膚淺的電影。) 可説成：I don't like shallow stories. (我不喜歡膚淺的故事。) I prefer stories with deeper meaning. (我比較喜歡意義較深遠的故事。) I don't like simple movies. (我不喜歡簡單的電影。)

No science fiction. 可説成：No science fiction for me. (我不喜歡科幻片。) I don't care for science fiction movies. (我不喜歡科幻片。) *No cartoons.* 可説成：No cartoon movies for me. (我不喜歡卡通片。) I'm not a cartoon movie fan. (我不是卡通片的影迷。) *Reality is best.* 可説成：A realistic movie is what I like best. (寫實電影是我最喜歡的。) A realistic movie is the best kind of movie for me. (寫實電影是我最喜歡的類型。) I like real, truthful movies. (我喜歡眞實的電影。) I like movies based on true stories. (我喜歡由眞實故事改編的電影。)

8. *Ordering Coffee*

看英文唸出中文	一口氣說九句	看中文唸出英文
ready[1] 〔'rɛdɪ〕 *adj.*	*Ready.* 準備好了。	準備好的
coffee[1] 〔'kɔfɪ〕 *n.*	*Coffee.* 要咖啡。	咖啡
Americano 〔ə͵mɛrɪ'kano〕 *n.*	*Americano.* 美式咖啡。	美式咖啡
hot[1] 〔hɑt〕 *adj.*	*Hot.* 熱的。	熱的
medium[3] 〔'midɪəm〕 *adj.*	*Medium.* 中杯。	中等的
vanilla[6] 〔və'nɪlə〕 *n.*	Add *vanilla.* 要加香草。	香草
cream[2] 〔krim〕 *n.*	Two *creams.* 兩個奶精。	奶油
sugar[1] 〔'ʃugɚ〕 *n.*	Two *sugars.* 兩小包糖。	糖
to go	*To go.* 外帶。	外帶

【背景説明 8】

Ready. 源自 I'm ready. (我準備好了。) 可説成：Hi, I'm ready. (嗨，我準備好了。) Ready to order. (準備好要點了。) I'm ready to order. (我準備好要點了。) 美國人常説：I know what I want. (我知道我要點什麼了。) *Coffee*. 可説成：Coffee, please. (麻煩給我咖啡。) (= *A coffee, please*.) I want a coffee. (我要咖啡。) (= *I'd like a coffee*.) I want to order a coffee. (我想點咖啡。) *Americano*. 可説成：Give me an Americano. (給我美式咖啡。) I'd like an Americano. (我要美式咖啡。) I'd like to order an Americano. (我想點美式咖啡。)

Hot. 源自 I want it hot. (我要熱的。) (= *I'd like it hot*.) *Medium*. 源自 Medium size cup. (中杯。) 可説成：Please give me a medium. (請給我中杯。) I want a medium. (我要中杯。) *Add vanilla*. 可説成：Please add vanilla. (請加香草。) Add vanilla to it. (上面加香草。)

Two creams. 可説成：Also two creams. (還要兩個奶精。) I'd like two creams. (我要兩個奶精。) Put two creams in it. (放兩個奶精進去。) *Two sugars*. 可説成：Please give me two sugars. (請給我兩小包糖。) Add two sugars, please. (請加兩小包糖。) I'd like two sugars in it. (我要在裡面放兩小包糖。) *To go*. 可説成：Make it to go. (要外帶。) To go, please. (外帶，麻煩你。) I'd like that coffee to go. (那杯咖啡我要外帶。) 「內用」是 For here.

9. *What a day!*

看英文唸出中文	一 口 氣 說 九 句	看中文唸出英文
what[1] 〔 hwɑt 〕*adj.*	***What** a day!* 多麼美好的一天！	多麼的
sensational[5] 〔 sɛnˈseʃənḷ 〕*adj.*	***Sensational!*** 好極了！	極好的；很棒的
exceptional[5] 〔 ɪkˈsɛpʃənḷ 〕*adj.*	***Exceptional!*** 不同凡響！	例外的；卓越的
amusing[4] 〔 əˈmjuzɪŋ 〕*adj.*	***Amusing!*** 很好玩！	有趣的
entertaining[4] 〔ˌɛntɚˈtenɪŋ 〕*adj.*	***Entertaining!*** 令人愉快！	令人愉快的
thrilling[5] 〔ˈθrɪlɪŋ 〕*adj.*	***Thrilling!*** 令人興奮！	令人興奮的
perfect[2] 〔ˈpɝfɪkt 〕*adj.*	***Perfect!*** 很完美！	完美的
satisfied[2] 〔ˈsætɪsˌfaɪd 〕*adj.*	***Satisfied!*** 很滿意！	滿意的
unforgettable[1] 〔ˌʌnfɚˈgɛtəbḷ 〕*adj.*	***Unforgettable!*** 眞是令人難忘！	令人難忘的

【背景説明 9】

當你玩了一天,要結束時,你可以説這九句話,表達你的滿意和快樂。

What a day! 可説成:What a fantastic day!(多麼美好的一天!)What a wonderful day!(多麼棒的一天!)What a beautiful day!(多麼美好的一天!)*Sensational!* 可説成:It was sensational!(好極了!)It was truly sensational!(眞的好極了!)(= *I had a sensational day!*)*Exceptional!* 可説成:It was exceptional!(眞是不同凡響!)(= *It was an exceptional day!*)

Amusing! 可説成:It was amusing!(眞有趣!)How amusing!(眞有趣!)*Entertaining!* 可説成:It was entertaining!(眞令人愉快!)How entertaining!(多麼令人愉快!)*Thrilling!* 可説成:It was thrilling!(很令人興奮!)How thrilling!(眞令人興奮!)Absolutely thrilling!(非常令人興奮!)

Perfect! 可説成:It was perfect!(很完美!)It was a perfect day!(眞是完美的一天!)Everything was perfect!(一切都很完美!)*Satisfied!* 可説成:I was satisfied!(我很滿意!)I was very satisfied today.(我今天非常滿意。)*Unforgettable!* 可説成:It's unforgettable!(眞令人難忘!)不可説成:*I'm unforgettable.*(誤)也可説成:I'll never forget.(我永遠都不會忘記。)I won't forget it.(我不會忘記。)It was a day I won't forget.(這是我不會忘記的一天。)I won't ever forget this day.(我永遠都不會忘記這一天。)

10. *Strange!*

看英文唸出中文	一 口 氣 説 九 句	看中文唸出英文

strange[1]　　　　　*Strange!*　　　　　奇怪的
〔 strendʒ 〕 *adj.*　　　奇怪！

weird[5]　　　　　*Weird!*　　　　　怪異的
〔 wɪrd 〕 *adj.*　　　　奇怪！

odd[3]　　　　　How *odd*!　　　　　古怪的
〔 ɑd 〕 *adj.*　　　　眞奇怪！

---

unusual[2]　　　　*Unusual!*　　　　不尋常的
〔 ʌnˈjuʒʊəl 〕 *adj.*　　不尋常！

normal[3]　　　　Not *normal*!　　　正常的
〔ˈnɔrml̩ 〕 *adj.*　　　不正常！

ordinary[4]　　　That's not *ordinary*!　一般的
〔ˈɔrdn̩ˌɛrɪ 〕 *adj.*　　那不尋常！

---

puzzle[2]　　　　It's a *puzzle*.　　　謎
〔ˈpʌzl̩ 〕 *n.*　　　　它是個謎。

mystery[3]　　　　It's a *mystery*.　　奧祕；謎
〔ˈmɪstrɪ 〕 *n.*　　　它是個謎。

figure out　　　No one can *figure* it *out*.　了解
　　　　　　　　沒有人能理解。

Lesson 7

【背景説明 10】

　　Strange! 可説成：It's strange!（奇怪！）So strange!（好奇怪！）It's strange to me.（我覺得很奇怪。）I feel it's very strange.（我覺得非常奇怪。）*Weird!* 可説成：It's weird!.（奇怪！）Very weird!（非常奇怪！）*How odd!* 可説成：How odd it is!（真奇怪！）So very odd!（很奇怪！）這是美國人常用的慣用句。

　　Unusual! 可説成：It's unusual!（不尋常！）It's very unusual!（非常不尋常！）(= *It's so unusual!*) *Not normal!* 也可説成：It's not normal!（不正常！）It's not a normal thing!（不是一件正常的事！）It's not something normal!（不是正常的事！）*That's not ordinary!* 可説成：That's not an ordinary thing!（這不是一件尋常的事！）It's very unordinary!（這非常不尋常！）

　　It's a puzzle. 可説成：It's such a puzzle.（它真是個謎。）It's puzzling to me.（我覺得很困惑。）(= *I'm confused.*) *It's a mystery.* 可説成：It's a real mystery.（它真是個謎。）It's a mystery to me.（我覺得它是個謎。）It's such a mystery.（它真是個謎。）There is no explanation.（無法解釋。）No one knows how or why.（沒有人知道怎麼回事。）(= *No one knows how or why it happens.*) *No one can figure it out.* 中的 figure 的意思有：① *n.* 數字；人物 ② *v.* 認為；估計；揣測。figure out 是「理解；明白；想出」(= *be able to understand*)。這句話可説成：No one can explain it.（沒有人能解釋。）No one knows.（沒有人知道。）

11. *It beats me*.

看英文唸出中文	一 口 氣 說 九 句	看中文唸出英文
beat 〔 bit 〕 *v.*	It *beats* me. 我不知道。	打敗
understand¹ 〔ˌʌndɚˈstænd 〕 *v.*	I don't *understand*. 我不了解。	了解
confused³ 〔 kənˈfjuzd 〕 *adj.*	I'm *confused*. 我很困惑。	困惑的

meaning² 〔ˈminɪŋ 〕 *n.*	What's the *meaning*? 是什麼意思？	意思
mean¹ 〔 min 〕 *v.*	What do you *mean*? 你是什麼意思？	意思是
have no idea	I *have no idea*. 我不知道。	不知道

beyond² 〔 bɪˈjɑnd 〕 *prep.*	It's *beyond* me. 我不懂。	超過
make sense	It doesn't *make sense*. 那不合理。	合理
more¹ 〔 mor 〕 *pron.*	Tell me *more*. 多告訴我一些。	更多的人或物

Lesson 7

Lesson 7

【背景説明 11】

It beats me. 中的 beat，主要意思是「打敗」，這句話字面的意思是「它打敗了我。」引申為「我不知道。」(= *I don't know.*)
I don't understand. 可説成：I don't understand it. (我不了解。)
I don't really understand. (我真的不了解。) *I'm confused.* 可説成：I'm confused about it. (對這件事我很困惑。) I'm totally confused. (我非常困惑。) It's confusing to me. (我覺得很困惑。)

What's the meaning? 可説成：What's the meaning of this? (這是什麼意思？) I don't know what the meaning is. (我不知道是什麼意思。)*What do you mean?* 可説成：What's your meaning? (你是什麼意思？) Please explain what you mean. (請解釋你是什麼意思。) *I have no idea.* 可説成：I really have no idea. (我真的不知道。) I don't understand. (我不了解。) I'm in the dark. (我不知道。)

It's beyond me. 字面的意思是「它超過我。」引申為「我不懂。」可説成：It's totally beyond me. (我全然不懂。) I can't understand it. (我無法了解。) *It doesn't make sense.* 可説成：It doesn't make any sense to me. (我覺得不合理。) make sense 的意思「合理；有道理」(= *be reasonable*)。*Tell me more.* 可説成：Tell me more about it. (多告訴我一些。) Please tell me more. (請多告訴我一些。) Could you please tell me more? (能不能請你多告訴我一些？) Explain it to me. (解釋給我聽。) Explain it more to me. (跟我多解釋一點。)

12. *I don't follow.*

看英文唸出中文	一口氣說九句	看中文唸出英文

follow [1]
(ˈfɑlo) *v.*

I don't *follow*.
我沒聽懂。

跟隨

get it

I don't *get it*.
我不了解。

了解

grasp [3]
(græsp) *v.*

I can't *grasp* it.
我無法理解。

抓住;理解

---

explain [2]
(ɪkˈsplen) *v.*

Explain it.
解釋一下。

解釋

define [3]
(dɪˈfaɪn) *v.*

Define it.
解釋一下。

下定義;解釋

point [1]
(pɔɪnt) *n.*

What's the *point*?
重點是什麼?

重點

---

clarify [4]
(ˈklærəˌfaɪ) *v.*

Clarify.
要清楚地說明。

清楚地說明

clear [1]
(klɪr) *adj.*

Make it *clear*.
要明確一點。

清楚的

information [4]
(ˌɪnfɚˈmeʃən) *n.*

I need more *information*.
我需要更多的資訊。

資訊

【背景説明 12】

I don't follow. 可説成：I don't follow what you're saying.
（我沒聽懂你說的話。）I don't follow what you mean.（我沒聽懂你的意思。）follow 的主要意思是「跟隨」，在這裡作「聽懂」（= *understand*）解。*I don't get it.* 可説成：I don't get the meaning of it.（我不了解它的意思。）I don't comprehend.（我不了解。）*I can't grasp it.* 字面的意思是「我無法抓住它。」引申為「我無法理解。」(= *I don't understand it.*) 也就是 I don't comprehend it.（我無法理解。）understand 和 comprehend 為及物和不及物兩用動詞，可加或不加 it。

Explain it. 可説成：Explain it more.（多解釋一下。）*Define it.* 可説成：Define it for me.（為我解釋一下。）define 的主要意思是「下定義」，在這裡作「解釋」解。Define it more.（多解釋一下。）*What's the point?* 可説成：What's the main point?（主要的重點是什麼？）What's the main idea?（主要的想法是什麼？）

Clarify. 可説成：Clarify it.（要清楚地說明它。）Clarify it more.（要更清楚地說明它。）Please clarify it more.（請更清楚地說明它。）*Make it clear.* 可説成：Make it clear to me.（對我說得明確一點。）(= *Make it clear for me.*) Explain it clearly.（要清楚地解釋它。）Explain it to me.（要向我解釋它。）*I need more information.* 可説成：I need you to give me more information.（我需要你給我更多的資訊。）(= *I need more information from you.*) I need more information, please.（我需要更多的資訊，拜託。）Tell me more.（多告訴我一些。）Give me more information.（給我更多的資訊。）

Lesson 7 總複習

1.～3. 邀約出國旅遊

4. 搭飛機指南；**5., 6.** 風景、電影

1. Been *abroad*?
   Been *overseas*?
   Been to any *foreign* countries?

   Travel!
   Tour!
   Go *sightseeing*!

   It's *exciting*.
   It's an *adventure*.
   Create *lifetime* memories.

2. Traveling is *fascinating*.
   I'm a big *fan*.
   I *support* it.

   Cherish it.
   Relish it.
   I *savor* every minute.

   Fancy it.
   Be *fond* of it.
   I'm *nuts* about it.

3. *Join* me.
   Register.
   Sign up.

   I *ask* you.
   I *invite* you.
   Accompany me.

   I *beg* you.
   I *urge* you.
   I *insist*.

4. Get to the *airport* early.
   Know which *airline*.
   Which *terminal*.

   International.
   Not *domestic*.
   Check in on time.

   Departure.
   Not *arrival*.
   Leave yourself time.

5. I enjoy *scenery*.
   Natural *sights*.
   Outdoor *views*.

   Sunny skies.
   Starry nights.
   Beautiful *beaches*.

   Tranquil.
   Pleasant.
   So calm and *peaceful*.

6. *Movies!*
   The silver *screen*!
   I'm a movie *fan*.

   I go *frequently*.
   I watch *weekly*.
   Especially on *weekends*.

   Watching is like *reading*.
   A movie is a *novel*.
   You *gain* information.

Lesson 7

7. 電影；**8.** 點咖啡；**9.** 快樂的一天

7. I enjoy *action*.
   Thrillers are exciting.
   Comedy is funny.

   I prefer *serious*.
   I like *deep*.
   Don't like *shallow*.

   No science *fiction*.
   No *cartoons*.
   Reality is best.

8. *Ready*.
   Coffee.
   Americano.

   Hot.
   Medium.
   Add *vanilla*.

   Two *creams*.
   Two *sugars*.
   To go.

9. *What* a day!
   Sensational!
   Exceptional!

   Amusing!
   Entertaining!
   Thrilling!

   Perfect!
   Satisfied!
   Unforgettable!

10.~12. 看到奇怪的事，請求解釋

10. *Strange*!
    Weird!
    How *odd*!

    Unusual!
    Not *normal*!
    That's not *ordinary*!

    It's a *puzzle*.
    It's a *mystery*.
    No one can *figure* it *out*.

11. It *beats* me.
    I don't *understand*.
    I'm *confused*.

    What's the *meaning*?
    What do you *mean*?
    I *have no idea*.

    It's *beyond* me.
    It doesn't *make sense*.
    Tell me *more*.

12. I don't *follow*.
    I don't *get it*.
    I can't *grasp* it.

    Explain it.
    Define it.
    What's the *point*?

    Clarify.
    Make it *clear*.
    I need more *information*.

Lesson 8 I'm touched.

1. She's cute.

看英文唸出中文	一口氣說九句	看中文唸出英文
cute[1] (kjut) *adj.*	She's *cute.* 她很可愛。	可愛的
clever[2] ('klɛvɚ) *adj.*	*Clever.* 很聰明。	聰明的
curious[2] ('kjurɪəs) *adj.*	*Curious.* 很好奇。	好奇的
appealing[3] (ə'pilɪŋ) *adj.*	*Appealing.* 很吸引人。	吸引人的
adorable[5] (ə'dorəbḷ) *adj.*	*Adorable.* 很可愛。	可愛的
affectionate[6] (ə'fɛkʃənɪt) *adj.*	*Affectionate.* 充滿了愛。	摯愛的
sweet[1] (swit) *adj.*	*Sweet.* 很可愛。	甜的
innocent[3] ('ɪnəsṇt) *adj.*	*Innocent.* 很天眞。	天眞的
charming[3] ('tʃɑrmɪŋ) *adj.*	*Charming.* 很迷人。	迷人的

Lesson 8

【背景說明 1】

稱讚不花一毛錢,卻是給人最好的禮物。利用各種的稱讚方式,可增加自己的字彙。看到了兩三歲的小女孩,你可以說: *She's cute.* She's a cute girl. (她是可愛的女孩。) She's such a cute girl. (她是個非常可愛的女孩。) *Clever.* 可說成:She's a clever kid. (她是個聰明的小孩。) *Curious.* 可說成:She's so curious. (她很好奇。)

Appealing. 可說成:She's appealing. (她很吸引人。) She's quite appealing. (她相當吸引人。) (= *She's very appealing.* = *She's very attractive.*) *Adorable.* 可說成:She's an adorable child. (她是個可愛的小孩。)

Affectionate. 可說成:She's very affectionate. (她非常愛大家。) 名詞是 affection (愛)。在字典上,affectionate 翻成:「表示愛的;摯愛的;充滿深情的;溫柔親切的」(= *showing that you love or care about someone or something*)。例如:They are affectionate parents. (他們是充滿了愛的父母。) The couple are affectionate with each other. (這對夫妻很愛彼此。)

Sweet. 可說成:She's a sweet girl. (她是個可愛的女孩。) *Innocent.* 可說成:She's an innocent child. (她是個天真的小孩。) *Charming.* 可說成:She's charming. (她很迷人。) (= *She's a charming girl.*) She has a charming personality. (她的個性很迷人。)

2. Beautiful!

看英文唸出中文	一口氣說九句	看中文唸出英文
beautiful[1] 〔'bjutəfəl 〕*adj.*	***Beautiful!*** 漂亮！	漂亮的
gorgeous[5] 〔'gɔrdʒəs 〕*adj.*	***Gorgeous!*** 非常漂亮！	非常漂亮的
stunning[5] 〔'stʌnɪŋ 〕*adj.*	***Stunning!*** 非常迷人！	迷人的
striking[2] 〔'straɪkɪŋ 〕*adj.*	***Striking!*** 令人印象深刻！	顯著的
dazzling[5] 〔'dæzl̩ɪŋ 〕*adj.*	***Dazzling!*** 令人目眩！	耀眼的
breathtaking 〔'brɛθ,tekɪŋ 〕*adj.*	***Breathtaking!*** 令人驚嘆！	令人驚嘆的
attractive[3] 〔 ə'træktɪv 〕*adj.*	***Attractive!*** 很吸引人！	吸引人的
irresistible[3] 〔,ɪrɪ'zɪstəbl̩ 〕*adj.*	***Irresistible!*** 令人無法抗拒！	令人無法抗拒的
knock-out 〔'nɑk,aʊt 〕*n.*	She's a ***knock-out***. 她是個大美女。	大美女

Lesson 8

Lesson 8

【背景説明 2】

Beautiful! 可説成：She's beautiful!（她很漂亮！）
Gorgeous! 可説成：She's gorgeous!（她非常漂亮！）*Stunning!*
可説成：She's stunning!（她很迷人！）She looks stunning.（她
看起來很迷人。）She has a stunning smile.（她笑起來很迷人。）
She's a stunning lady.（她是個有魅力的女士。）

Striking! 可説成：She's striking!（她令人印象深刻！）
strike 的主要意思是「打」(= *hit against*)，引申出 striking 這個
形容詞，作「顯著的；醒目的；令人印象深刻的」解。She has a
striking appearance.（她的外型令人難忘。）*Dazzling!* 可説成：
She's dazzling!（她很耀眼！）Her appearance is dazzling.（她
的外表很耀眼。）Her beauty is dazzling.（她的美麗令人目眩。）
Breathtaking! 可説成：She's breathtaking!（她令人驚嘆！）
She's so beautiful. She takes my breath away.（她非常漂亮。
她令我目瞪口呆。）

Attractive! 可説成：She's very attractive!（她很吸引人！）
I am attracted to her.（我被她吸引。）*Irresistible!* 可説成：
She's irresistible!（她令人無法抗拒！）Her beauty makes her
irresistible.（她的美麗令人無法抗拒。）*She's a knock-out.* 可説
成：With so much beauty, she's a knock-out.（她非常漂亮，是個
大美女。）knock 的意思是「敲；擊；打」，knock out 源自拳擊，
作「把…擊昏」解。knock-out 這個複合名詞，字面的意思是「擊
昏；打出去」，引申為「大美女；非常迷人的人」。美國人常説：She's
so gorgeous. She's a knock-out.（她很漂亮。她是個大美女。）

3. Who's that?

看英文唸出中文	一 口 氣 說 九 句	看中文唸出英文
who [1] 〔 hu 〕*pron.*	***Who***'s that? 那是誰？	誰
recognize [3] 〔'rɛkəɡ,naɪz 〕*v.*	***Recognize*** them? 認得他們嗎？	認得
familiar [3] 〔 fə'mɪljə˙ 〕*adj.*	***Familiar*** with them? 和他們熟嗎？	熟悉的
information [4] 〔,ɪnfə'meʃən 〕*n.*	Any ***information***? 有任何資訊嗎？	資訊
detail [3] 〔'ditel 〕*n.*	***Details***? 詳細情況如何？	細節
status [4] 〔'stetəs 〕*n.*	Marital ***status***? 婚姻狀況如何？	地位；狀況
single [2] 〔'sɪŋɡl̩ 〕*adj.*	***Single***? 單身嗎？	單身的
married [1] 〔'mærɪd 〕*adj.*	***Married***? 結婚了嗎？	已婚的
available [3] 〔 ə'veləbl̩ 〕*adj.*	***Available***? 可以追嗎？	可獲得的

Lesson 8

4. Be careful.

看英文唸出中文	一口氣說九句	看中文唸出英文
careful[1] 〔'kɛrfəl〕 adj.	Be *careful*. 要小心。	小心的
cautious[5] 〔'kɔʃəs〕 adj.	Be *cautious*. 要謹慎。	謹慎的
take care	You *take care*. 你要注意。	注意
alert[4] 〔ə'lɜt〕 adj.	Be *alert*. 要機警。	機警的
aware[3] 〔ə'wɛr〕 adj.	Be *aware*. 要有危機意識。	知道的；察覺到的
watch out	*Watch out*. 要小心。	小心
listen to	*Listen to* me. 聽我的話。	聽
heed[5] 〔hid〕 v.	*Heed* my words. 注意我說的話。	注意
advice[3] 〔əd'vaɪs〕 n.	Follow my *advice*. 聽從我的勸告。	勸告

【背景説明 3】

> *Who's that?* 可説成：Who's that man over there?（在那裡的那個人是誰？）*Recognize them?* 可説成：Do you recognize them?（你認得他們嗎？）依據美國人説話的習慣，即使一個人，也用 them。只有在強調那一個特別的人時，才會説 Recognize him?（認得他嗎？）
>
> 　【比較】A：*Who's that? Recognize them?*【一般語氣】
> 　　　　　B：Who's that? Recognize him?【強調某一個人】
> 　　　　　在美國口語中，常用 them 來代替 him 或 her，特別在不確定性別時，如：If *anyone* calls while I'm out, tell *them* I'll be back at noon.（如果我出去時有人打電話來，告訴他們我中午會回來。）

Familiar with them? 源自 Are you familiar with them?（你和他們熟嗎？）可説成：Know them?（認識他們嗎？）Friends with them?（和他們是朋友嗎？）（= *Are you friends with them?* ）Seen them before?（以前見過他們嗎？）（= *Have you seen them before?* ）美國人書寫英語和口説英語不同，書寫英語規規矩矩，説起來，美國人聽起來不舒服；口説英語簡短、輕鬆。這三句一説出來，就會讓聽的人有親切感。*Who's that? Recognize them? Familiar with them?*

　　Any information? 可説成：Do you have any information?（你有任何資訊嗎？）Have any news?（有任何消息嗎？）*Details?* 可説成：Do you have any details?（你有任何詳細情況嗎？）*Marital status?* 美國人常問：What's your marital status?（你的婚姻狀況如何？）

Single? 可說成：Are you single?（你是單身嗎？）Are you still single?（你還是單身嗎？）*Married?* 可說成：Are you single or married?（你是單身，還是已婚？）Have you been married before?（你以前結過婚嗎？）*Available?* 男人和男人之間喜歡談論女生，看到了美女，常問：Is she available? 表示她是否單身，沒有男朋友，可以追嗎？女人之間，如果看到男生，可問身旁的人：Is he available?（他沒有對象嗎？；他能交往嗎？）Is he still available?（他還沒有對象嗎？）Is he available for a date?（能不能和他約會？）

【背景說明 4】

Be careful. 可說成：Please be careful.（請小心。）Remember to be careful.（記得要小心。）*Be cautious.* 可說成：Use caution.（要謹慎。）Always be cautious.（一定要謹慎。）Be a cautious person.（要謹慎。）*You take care.* 可說成：I want you to take care of yourself.（我要你好好照顧自己。）

Be alert. 可說成：Be on alert.（要機警。）可加長為：Be alert tonight. The weather is bad.（今天晚上要機警。天氣不好。）*Be aware.* 可加長為：Always be aware of strangers.（一定要注意陌生人。）Always be aware of safety while traveling.（旅行時，一定要注意安全。）*Watch out.* 可加長為：Watch out on slippery surfaces.（小心地面很滑。）

Listen to me. 可說成：Please listen to me.（請聽我的話。）I want you to listen.（我要你注意聽。）*Heed my words.* 可說成：I advise you to heed my words.（我勸你要注意聽我說的話。）*Follow my advice.* 可說成：You had better follow my advice.（你最好聽從我的勸告。）Please follow my advice.（請聽從我的勸告。）Do what I say.（照我說的去做。）

5. *She was rude*.

看英文唸出中文	一口氣說九句	看中文唸出英文
rude[2] 〔 rud 〕*adj.*	She was ***rude***. 她很粗魯。	粗魯的
arrogant[6] 〔'ærəgənt 〕*adj.*	So ***arrogant***. 非常自大。	自大的
impolite[2] 〔͵ɪmpə'laɪt 〕*adj.*	So ***impolite***. 很沒禮貌。	沒禮貌的
insulting[4] 〔 ɪn'sʌltɪŋ 〕*adj.*	***Insulting***. 很侮辱人。	侮辱人的
ignorant[4] 〔'ɪgnərənt 〕*adj.*	***Ignorant***. 很無知。	無知的
sharp-tongued[4] 〔͵ʃɑrp'tʌŋd 〕*adj.*	Very ***sharp-tongued***. 說話非常尖酸刻薄。	說話尖酸刻薄的
ill-bred[4] 〔'ɪl'brɛd 〕*adj.*	***Ill-bred***. 很沒教養。	無教養的
etiquette 〔'ɛtɪ͵kɛt 〕*n.*	Poor ***etiquette***. 禮節很差。	禮節
manners[2] 〔'mænɚz 〕*n. pl.*	No ***manners*** at all. 沒有半點禮貌。	禮貌

Lesson 8

【背景説明5】

She was rude. 可説成：What she said was rude. （她說的話很粗魯。）美國人常説：She was rude to her parents. （她對她的父母很粗魯。）She was rude to me. （她對我很粗魯。）She's often rude. （她常常很粗魯。）*So arrogant.* 源自 She's so arrogant. （她非常自大。）可説成：What she did was so arrogant. （她的行為非常自大。）Her manner was so arrogant. （她的態度非常自大。）*So impolite.* 源自 She's so impolite. （她很沒禮貌。）She's often so impolite. （她常常很沒禮貌。）

Insulting. 源自 It was insulting to me. （這對我是種侮辱。）可説成：How insulting. （真是侮辱人。）*Ignorant.* 源自 She was ignorant. （她很無知。）可加強語氣説成：She was so ignorant. （她很無知。）（= *She was very ignorant.* ）*Very sharp-tongued.* 可説成：She was very sharp-tongued. （她說話非常尖酸刻薄。）She is often very sharp-tongued. （她說話時常很尖酸刻薄。）

Ill-bred. 可説成：She's ill-bred. （她沒教養。）She has an ill-bred style. （她的作風很沒教養。）*Poor etiquette.* 可説成：It was poor etiquette. （很沒禮貌。）What she did was poor etiquette. （她的行為很沒禮貌。）*No manners at all.* 可説成：She has no manners at all. （她一點禮貌也沒有。）She was not polite at all. （她非常沒禮貌。）

6. So disturbing.

看英文唸出中文	一口氣說九句	看中文唸出英文
disturbing[6] 〔 dɪ'stɝbɪŋ 〕 *adj.*	So *disturbing*. 眞令人不安。	令人不安的
annoying[4] 〔 ə'nɔɪɪŋ 〕 *adj.*	So *annoying*. 眞令人心煩。	令人心煩的
upsetting[3] 〔 ʌp'sɛtɪŋ 〕 *adj.*	Very *upsetting*. 讓人非常不高興。	令人不高興的
scare[1] 〔 skɛr 〕 *v.*	It *scared* me. 它使我害怕。	使害怕
frighten[2] 〔'fraɪtn̩ 〕 *v.*	It *frightened* me. 它使我受到驚嚇。	使驚嚇
hurt[1] 〔 hɝt 〕 *v.*	It *hurt* me a lot. 它對我傷害很大。	傷害
blow[1] 〔 blo 〕 *n.*	Like a *blow*. 像打了一拳。	一拳
punch[3] 〔 pʌntʃ 〕 *n. v.*	A *punch* to the gut. 一拳打在肚子上。	一拳
slap[5] 〔 slæp 〕 *n. v.*	A *slap* in the face. 在臉上打了一個耳光。	打耳光

Lesson 8

【背景説明 6】

So disturbing. 可説成：It's so disturbing. (眞令人不安。)
The situation is so disturbing. (情況眞令人不安。) It makes me
feel awful. (這讓我覺得很糟。) *So annoying.* 可説成：It's so
annoying. (眞令人心煩。) It's so annoying to me. (眞令我心煩。)
His behavior was so annoying. (他的行爲眞令人心煩。) *Very
upsetting.* 可説成：It's very upsetting. (眞讓人不高興。) It's
very upsetting to me. (眞令我不高興。)

It scared me. 可説成：It scared me a lot. (它使我非常害怕。)
It scared me half to death. (它把我嚇得半死。) What happened
scared me. (發生的事使我害怕。) *It frightened me.* 可説成：It
really frightened me. (它眞的嚇死我了。) It frightened me
terribly. (它使我受到很大的驚嚇。) *It hurt me a lot.* 可説成：It
caused me great pain. (它使我受到極大的痛苦。) It was painful.
(很痛苦。) 不能説成：*I was painful.* (誤) 可説：I was in pain.
(我很痛苦。)

Like a blow. 可説成：It felt like a blow. (像是打了一拳。)
It hurt like a blow to my head. (像是一拳打到我頭上那麼痛。)
A punch to the gut. 可説成：It hurt me like a punch to the gut.
(這對我的傷害就像是一拳打在肚子上。) punch 可當動詞，如：He
punched the wall. (他用拳頭打在牆上。) 也可當名詞，如：He can
take a punch. (他能忍受一拳。) gut〔gʌt〕*n.* 腸子，在這裡是作「肚
子；腹部」解。*A slap in the face.* 可説成：It felt like a slap in the
face. (感覺像是在臉上打了一耳光。) It shocked me like a slap in
the face. (像是在臉上打了一耳光使我震驚。) It hurt like a slap in
the face. (就像在臉上打了一耳光那麼痛。)

7. *I was cheated.*

看英文唸出中文	一口氣說九句	看中文唸出英文
cheat[2] (tʃit) *v.*	I was *cheated*. 我被騙了。	欺騙
fool[2] (ful) *v.*	*Fooled*. 被騙了。	欺騙
trick[2] (trɪk) *v.*	*Tricked*. 被欺騙了。	欺騙
set up	I was *set up*. 我被陷害了。	陷害
deceive[5] (dɪ'siv) *v.*	*Deceived*. 被欺騙了。	欺騙
mislead[4] (mɪs'lid) *v.*	*Misled*. 被誤導了。	誤導
unfair[2] (ʌn'fɛr) *adj.*	It was *unfair*. 很不公平。	不公平的
dishonest[2] (dɪs'ɑnɪst) *adj.*	So *dishonest*. 非常不誠實。	不誠實的
exploit[6] (ɪk'splɔɪt) *v.*	I was *exploited*. 我被利用了。	利用

Lesson 8

【背景説明 7】

I was cheated. 可説成：I feel like I was cheated.（我覺得我被騙了。）I was cheated and it hurt a lot.（我被騙了，而且傷害很大。）*Fooled.* 可説成：I was fooled by her.（我被她騙了。）She really fooled me.（她真的騙了我。）*Tricked.* 可説成：She tricked me.（她騙了我。）I was tricked by her.（我被她騙了。）

I was set up. 可説成：I felt like I was set up.（我覺得我被陷害了。）I was set up by her.（我被她陷害了。）*Deceived.* 可説成：I was deceived.（我被騙了。）I was deceived by her.（我被她騙了。）Her actions deceived me.（她的行為欺騙了我。）*Misled.* 可説成：I was misled.（我被誤導了。）She misled me.（她誤導了我。）

It was unfair. 可説成：For me, it was very unfair.（對我來說，這非常不公平。）It was a very unfair thing to happen.（發生這樣的事很不公平。）*So dishonest.* 可説成：It was so dishonest.（非常不誠實。）What she did was so dishonest.（她的行為很不誠實。）Her actions were so dishonest.（她的行為很不誠實。）*I was exploited.* 可説成：I was exploited by her group.（我被她們那一群人利用了。）They used me.（他們利用了我。）（= *They took advantage of me.*）

8. *I was shocked*.

看英文唸出中文	一口氣說九句	看中文唸出英文
shock² 〔ʃɑk〕*v.*	I was *shocked*. 我很震驚。	使震驚
stun⁵ 〔stʌn〕*v.*	I was *stunned*. 我目瞪口呆。	使目瞪口呆
shake¹ 〔ʃek〕*v.*	I was *shaken* up. 我很震驚。	搖動
sudden² 〔'sʌdn̩〕*adj.*	So *sudden*. 非常突然。	突然的
happen¹ 〔'hæpən〕*v.*	It *happened* so fast. 它發生得很快。	發生
quick¹ 〔kwɪk〕*adj.*	Just too *quick*. 真的太快了。	快的
unprepared¹ 〔͵ʌnprɪ'pɛrd〕*adj.*	I was *unprepared*. 我沒有準備。	無準備的
unexpected² 〔͵ʌnɪk'spɛktɪd〕*adj.*	It was *unexpected*. 它真的出乎意料。	出乎意料的
bombshell 〔'bɑm͵ʃɛl〕*n.*	Hit me like a *bombshell*. 突然襲擊我。	炸彈

【背景説明 8】

I was shocked. 可加強語氣説成：I was totally shocked.
（我非常震驚。）（= *I was completely shocked.*）*I was stunned.*
可説成：I was stunned by his words.（他說的話讓我目瞪口呆。）
I was stunned by her hatred.（她的怨恨讓我目瞪口呆。）*I was*
shaken up. 可説成：I was shaken up by the bad news.（那個壞
消息使我震驚。）Because of the tragedy, I was shaken up.（因
爲那場悲劇，我很震驚。）

So sudden. 可説成：It was all so sudden.（這一切都非常突
然。）The action was so sudden.（這個行動非常突然。）*It*
happened so fast. 可説成：To me, it all happened so fast.（對
我而言，這一切都發生得很快。）*Just too quick.* 可説成：It was
just too quick for me.（對我來說這眞的太快了。）美國人常説：
His departure was just too quick.（他離開得太快了。）

I was unprepared. 可説成：I wasn't ready.（我沒準備好。）
I was not prepared.（我沒有準備。）美國人常説：I was unprepared
for the exam.（我考試還沒準備好。）*It was unexpected.* 美國人
常説：It was an unexpected quiz.（這是出乎意料的小考。）*Hit*
me like a bombshell. 可説成：It hit me like a bombshell.（突然襲
擊我。）The awful news hit me like a bombshell.（這可怕的消息
突然襲擊我。）shell 的意思有：①（海洋動物的）殼 ②（蛋或堅果
的）殼 ③（汽車或飛機等的）外殼 ④ 砲彈。bombshell 是「炸彈」
（= *bomb* = *shell*），「炸彈殼」是 bomb casing，不是 *bombshell*；
「子彈殼」是 bullet casing。

9. *I was depressed*.

看英文唸出中文	一口氣說九句	看中文唸出英文
depressed [4] (dɪ'prɛst) *adj.*	I was *depressed*. 我很沮喪。	沮喪的
dejected (dɪ'dʒɛktɪd) *adj.*	*Dejected*. 很沮喪。	沮喪的
miserable [4] ('mɪzərəbḷ) *adj.*	*Miserable*. 很悲慘。	悲慘的
discontented [4] (ˌdɪskən'tɛntɪd) *adj.*	*Discontented*. 不滿意。	不滿意的
distressed [5] (dɪ'strɛst) *adj.*	*Distressed*. 很苦惱。	苦惱的
pessimistic [4] (ˌpɛsə'mɪstɪk) *adj.*	*Pessimistic*. 很悲觀。	悲觀的
downcast ('daʊnˌkæst) *adj.*	*Downcast*. 心情沮喪。	沮喪的
downhearted (ˌdaʊn'hɑrtɪd) *adj.*	*Downhearted*. 很灰心。	灰心的
low-spirited (ˌlo'spɪrɪtɪd) *adj.*	So *low-spirited*. 情緒很低落。	情緒低落的

Lesson 8

【背景說明 9】

I was depressed. 可説成：It depressed me. (這件事令我沮喪。) *Dejected.* 可説成：I felt dejected. (我覺得沮喪。) *Miserable.* 可説成：I was miserable. (我很悲慘。) It was miserable. (很悲慘。) It was a miserable day. (很悲慘的一天。) It was a miserable thing to do. (做這件事很悲慘。)

Discontented. 可説成：I was discontented. (我不滿意。) (= *I was not satisfied.*) I felt so discontented. (我覺得非常不滿意。) (= *I felt so unhappy.*) discontent (不滿意) 是名詞，不能當形容詞用，和 discontented (不滿意的) 不相同。
Distressed. 可説成：I was distressed. (我很苦惱。) I was somewhat distressed. (我有點苦惱。) I was so distressed. (我非常苦惱。) *Pessimistic.* 可説成：I was pessimistic. (我很悲觀。) 看到悲觀的人，可以説：What a pessimistic person! (多麼悲觀的人！)

Downcast. 可説成：I was downcast. (我很沮喪。) I felt so downcast. (我覺得很沮喪。) *Downhearted.* 可説成：I felt so downhearted. (我覺得非常灰心。) It made me feel so downhearted. (它使我覺得很灰心。) *So low-spirited.* 可説成：I felt so low-spirited. (我情緒非常低落。) It left me so low-spirited. (它使我情緒非常低落。)

10. Be tough.

看英文唸出中文	一口氣說九句	看中文唸出英文
tough[4] 〔 tʌf 〕 *adj.*	Be *tough*. 要堅強。	堅強的
firm[2] 〔 fɝm 〕 *adj.*	*Firm*. 要堅定。	堅定的
powerful[2] 〔'paʊəfəl 〕 *adj.*	*Powerful*. 要強而有力。	強有力的
durable[4] 〔'djʊrəbḷ 〕 *adj.*	*Durable*. 要耐操。	耐用的
rugged[5] 〔'rʌgɪd 〕 *adj.*	*Rugged*. 要能吃苦耐勞。	崎嶇的
resolute[6] 〔'rɛzə,lut 〕 *adj.*	*Resolute*. 要堅決。	堅決的
strong[1] 〔 strɔŋ 〕 *adj.*	*Strong*. 要強壯。	強壯的
sturdy[5] 〔'stɝdɪ 〕 *adj.*	*Sturdy*. 要強健。	強健的
solid[3] 〔'sɑlɪd 〕 *adj.*	Be as *solid* as a rock. 要穩固如磐石；要非常 可靠。	堅固的

Lesson 8

Lesson 8

【背景説明 10】

天天都可以勸朋友，説：*Be tough.* 可加長爲：Always try
to be tough. （一定要儘量堅強。） When you meet difficulty, be
tough. （碰到困難時，要堅強。） Be a tough person. （做一個堅強
的人。） *Firm.* 可説成：Stand firm. （要堅定。） Stand firm on
important issues. （關於重要的問題要堅定。） Stand firm for
what you believe in. （對你信仰的事要堅定。） *Powerful.* 可説
成：Be powerful. （要強而有力。） Be a powerful person. （做一
個有力量的人。） Have a powerful personality. （要有強大的個
性。）

Durable. 可説成：Be a durable person. （做一個耐操的人。）
Be durable during difficult times. （在困難的時候要耐操。）
Rugged. 可説成：Be rugged. （要能吃苦耐勞。） Be a rugged
person. （做個能吃苦耐勞的人。） rugged 的主要意思是「崎嶇
的」，在此作「能吃苦耐勞的」解。*Resolute.* 可説成：Be
resolute. （要堅決。） Be resolute in your actions. （你的行動要堅
決。） Be resolute in everything you do. （做什麼事都要堅決。）

Strong. 可説成：Be strong. （要強壯。） Always be honest
and strong. （一定要誠實和強壯。） *Sturdy.* 這個字背不下來時，
和 study （讀書）比較，就背下來了。可説成：Be sturdy and
reliable. （既要強健，也要可靠。） *Be as solid as a rock.* 可説成：
Be reliable and as solid as a rock. （要做一個非常可靠的人。）
Be the type of person who is as solid as a rock. （要做一個穩固
如磐石的人。） solid 的主要意思是「固體的」，在此作「堅固的；
可靠的」解。

11. I'm touched. (I)

看英文唸出中文	一口氣說九句	看中文唸出英文
touch[1] (tʌtʃ) *v.*	I'm ***touched***. 我很感動。	使感動
move[1] (muv) *v.*	I'm ***moved***. 我很感動。	使感動
honor[3] ('ɑnɚ) *n.*	It's an ***honor***. 這是種榮耀。	光榮;榮耀
value[2] ('væljʊ) *v.*	I ***value*** this. 我很重視這個。	重視
mean[1] (min) *v.*	It ***means*** a lot. 這意義重大。	意思是
cherish[4] ('tʃɛrɪʃ) *v.*	I'll ***cherish*** it. 我會珍惜它。	珍惜
inspire[4] (ɪn'spaɪr) *v.*	This ***inspires*** me. 這激勵了我。	激勵
motivate[4] ('motə,vet) *v.*	It ***motivates*** me. 它激勵了我。	激勵
encouraging[2] (ɪn'kɝdʒɪŋ) *adj.*	It's ***encouraging***. 它鼓勵了我。	鼓勵的

Lesson 8

Lesson 8

【背景説明 11】

I'm touched. 可説成：I'm touched by your words.（你的話讓我感動。）It touches my heart.（這使我感動。）It makes me feel so great.（這讓我感覺非常好。）*I'm moved.* 可説成：I'm almost moved to tears of joy.（我幾乎感動得流下高興的眼淚。）It's very moving.（這很令人感動。）*It's an honor.* 可説成：It's such an honor to me.（對我而言非常光榮。）

I value this. 可説成：I really value this.（我真的很重視這個。）美國人常説：I really value this award.（我真的很重視這個獎。）I value this gift so much.（我非常重視這個禮物。）I value this moment.（我重視這個時刻。）*It means a lot.* 可説成：It means a lot to me at this time.（在這一刻，它對我意義重大。）It's important to me.（這對我很重要。）*I'll cherish it.* 可説成：I'll cherish it forever.（我將永遠珍惜它。）（= *I'll always cherish it.*）

This inspires me. 可説成：This honor inspires me to do better.（這項榮譽激勵我要做得更好。）This praise inspires me to try harder.（這個稱讚激勵我要更努力。）*It motivates me.* 可説成：It motivates me to keep trying hard.（它激勵我不斷努力。）It motivates me not to quit.（它激勵我不要放棄。）*It's encouraging.* 可説成：It's so encouraging to receive this.（得到這個，使我得到極大的鼓勵。）It's encouraging to me.（它鼓勵了我。）It's really encouraging for me to receive praise.（受到稱讚真的鼓勵了我。）

12. *I'm touched*. (II)

看英文唸出中文	一口氣說九句	看中文唸出英文
wonderful[2] ﹝'wʌndəˌfəl﹞*adj.*	How ***wonderful!*** 眞棒！	很棒的
fantastic[4] ﹝fæn'tæstɪk﹞*adj.*	Truly ***fantastic!*** 眞的很棒！	極好的
uplifting ﹝ʌp'lɪftɪŋ﹞*adj.*	It's ***uplifting!*** 眞的很振奮人心！	振奮人心的
remember[1] ﹝rɪ'mɛmbɚ﹞*v.*	I'll always ***remember***. 我會一直記得。	記得
forget[1] ﹝fɚ'gɛt﹞*v.*	I'll never ***forget***. 我絕不會忘記。	忘記
forever[3] ﹝for'ɛvɚ﹞*adv.*	I'll keep it ***forever***. 我會永遠記住。	永遠
impress[3] ﹝ɪm'prɛs﹞*v.*	I'm ***impressed***. 我很感動。	使印象深刻
joy[1] ﹝dʒɔɪ﹞*n.*	I'm filled with ***joy***. 我充滿了喜悅。	喜悅
thanks[1] ﹝θæŋks﹞*n. pl.*	A big ***thanks*** to you. 非常感謝你。	感謝

Lesson 8

【背景説明 12】

How wonderful! 可説成：How wonderful I feel!（我覺得眞棒！）How wonderful you are!（你眞棒！）*Truly fantastic!* 可説成：This is truly fantastic!（這眞的很棒！）*It's uplifting!* 可説成：It's so uplifting to me!（這非常令我振奮！）I feel it's uplifting!（我覺得這令人精神爲之一振！）It really lifts my spirits!（它眞的使我精神爲之一振！）

I'll always remember. 可説成：I'll always remember it.（我會一直記得。）This is something I'll always remember.（這是我會一直記得的事。）*I'll never forget.* 可説成：For as long as I live, I'll never forget.（只要我還活著，就絕對不會忘記。）*I'll keep it forever.* 可説成：I'll keep it as long as I live.（只要我活著，我就會記住。）*I'll keep it forever.* 字面的意思是「我會永遠保存它。」引申爲「我會永遠記住。」

I'm impressed. 可説成：I'm impressed by this.（這使我很感動。）*I'm impressed.* 有很多意思，可以作「我很佩服；我很感動；我很心動；我很難忘；令我回味無窮」解。【詳見「一口氣背會話」p.199】*I'm filled with joy.* 可説成：Honestly speaking, I'm filled with joy.（老實說，我充滿了喜悅。）*A big thanks to you.* 這句話是慣用語，不合乎文法規則，因爲 thanks 是複數。可説成：Big thanks to you.（非常感謝你。）A big thanks to you from the bottom of my heart.（我由衷地感謝你。）

Lesson 8 總複習

1., 2. 稱讚；3. 詢問

1. She's *cute*.
   Clever.
   Curious.

   Appealing.
   Adorable.
   Affectionate.

   Sweet.
   Innocent.
   Charming.

2. *Beautiful*!
   Gorgeous!
   Stunning!

   Striking!
   Dazzling!
   Breathtaking!

   Attractive!
   Irresistible!
   She's a *knock-out*.

3. *Who*'s that?
   Recognize them?
   Familiar with them?

   Any *information*?
   Details?
   Marital *status*?

   Single?
   Married?
   Available?

4.～6. 勸朋友小心

4. Be *careful*.
   Be *cautious*.
   You *take care*.

   Be *alert*.
   Be *aware*.
   Watch out.

   Listen to me.
   Heed my words.
   Follow my *advice*.

5. She was *rude*.
   So *arrogant*.
   So *impolite*.

   Insulting.
   Ignorant.
   Very *sharp-tongued*.

   Ill-bred.
   Poor *etiquette*.
   No *manners* at all.

6. So *disturbing*.
   So *annoying*.
   Very *upsetting*.

   It *scared* me.
   It *frightened* me.
   It *hurt* me a lot.

   Like a *blow*.
   A *punch* to the gut.
   A *slap* in the face.

Lesson 8

Lesson 8

7.～9. 受騙、沮喪

7. I was *cheated*.
Fooled.
Tricked.

I was *set up*.
Deceived.
Misled.

It was *unfair*.
So *dishonest*.
I was *exploited*.

8. I was *shocked*.
I was *stunned*.
I was *shaken* up.

So *sudden*.
It *happened* so fast.
Just too *quick*.

I was *unprepared*.
It was *unexpected*.
Hit me like a *bombshell*.

9. I was *depressed*.
Dejected.
Miserable.

Discontented.
Distressed.
Pessimistic.

Downcast.
Downhearted.
So *low-spirited*.

10. 激勵；11. , 12. 回答激勵

10. Be *tough*.
Firm.
Powerful.

Durable.
Rugged.
Resolute.

Strong.
Sturdy.
Be as *solid* as a rock.

11. I'm *touched*.
I'm *moved*.
It's an *honor*.

I *value* this.
It *means* a lot.
I'll *cherish* it.

This *inspires* me.
It *motivates* me.
It's *encouraging*.

12. How *wonderful!*
Truly *fantastic!*
It's *uplifting!*

I'll always *remember*.
I'll never *forget*.
I'll keep it *forever*.

I'm *impressed*.
I'm filled with *joy*.
A big *thanks* to you.

Lesson 9 — **Let's kill time.**

1. *Chinese Breakfast*

看英文唸出中文	一口氣說九句	看中文唸出英文
bake[2]	*Baked* bread.	烘烤
(bek) *v.*	燒餅。	
fry[3]	*Fried* breadstick.	油炸
(fraɪ) *v.*	油條。	
soybean[2]	*Soybean* milk.	黃豆
('sɔɪ,bin) *n.*	豆漿。	
stuff[3]	*Stuffed* steamed bun.	填塞
(stʌf) *v.*	包子。	
steam[2]	*Steamed* bun.	蒸
(stim) *v.*	饅頭。	
rice[1]	*Rice* ball.	米飯
(raɪs) *n.*	飯糰。	
congee	*Congee.*	稀飯
('kɑndʒi) *n.*	稀飯。	
pancake[3]	*Pancakes.*	薄煎餅
('pæn,kek) *n.*	蛋餅。	
dumpling[2]	*Dumplings.*	肉餡湯圓
('dʌmplɪŋ) *n.*	小籠包。	

Lesson 9

2. *Chinese Dishes*

看英文唸出中文	一 口 氣 説 九 句	看中文唸出英文
pot² 〔 pɑt 〕 *n.*	Hot *pot*. 火鍋。	鍋子
noodle² 〔'nud!〕 *n.*	Beef *noodles*. 牛肉麵。	麵
duck¹ 〔 dʌk 〕 *n.*	Peking *duck*. 北京烤鴨。	鴨子
pork² 〔 pɔrk 〕 *n.*	Red-cooked *pork*. 紅燒肉。	豬肉
twice¹ 〔 twaɪs 〕 *adv.*	*Twice*-cooked pork. 回鍋肉。	兩次
chicken¹ 〔'tʃɪkən 〕 *n.*	Three-cup *chicken*. 三杯雞。	雞
soup¹ 〔 sup 〕 *n.*	Egg drop *soup*. 蛋花湯。	湯
sour¹ 〔 saʊr 〕 *adj.*	Hot and *sour* soup. 酸辣湯。	酸的
sticky-rice 〔'stɪkɪ͵raɪs 〕 *adj.*	*Sticky-rice* dumpling. 粽子。	糯米的

Lesson 9

【背景說明 1】

中國人所謂的「燒餅」，美國人看起來就像烤的麵包，所以翻成 *baked bread*，最能被他們接受。你也可以用漢語拼音，說成：shaobing，或 baked flatbread。「油條」除了 *fried breadstick* 以外，還可說成：youtiao，或 deep-fried dough stick。「豆漿」可說成：*soybean milk*，soy milk，或 bean milk。

「包子」*stuffed steamed bun*，字面的意思是「有塞東西，蒸過的小圓麵包」，講這個外國人聽得懂，也可說成：baozi 或 bao。「饅頭」是 *steamed bun*，也可說成：mantou。

stuffed steamed bun

「稀飯」是 *congee*，也可說成：rice porridge，也有人說成 rice soup。「蛋餅」除了 *pancakes* 以外，也可說成 omelet crepe。「小籠包」是 *dumplings*，也可說成：xialongbao，或 soup dumplings。凡是放入水中煮的或蒸的，都稱作 dumpling，如「粽子」是 sticky-rice dumpling，「餃子」是 Chinese dumpling。

sticky-rice dumpling

【背景說明 2】

Peking duck（北京烤鴨）有名到已經是固定說法了，一般的烤鴨，則說成：roast duck。

「蛋花湯」是 *egg drop soup*，源自把雞蛋（egg）攪拌後，放（drop）進湯裡。如果你說 *egg flower soup*（誤），美國人聽不懂。

3. *Too noisy*.

看英文唸出中文	一口氣說九句	看中文唸出英文
noisy[1] 〔'nɔɪzɪ〕 *adj.*	Too *noisy*. 太吵了。	吵鬧的
loud[1] 〔laʊd〕 *adj.*	Too *loud*. 太大聲了。	大聲的
hurt[1] 〔hɜt〕 *v.*	*Hurts* my ears. 傷害我的耳朵。	傷害
bother[2] 〔'baðɚ〕 *v.*	It *bothers* me. 它打擾了我。	打擾
annoying[4] 〔ə'nɔɪɪŋ〕 *adj.*	It's *annoying*. 很令人心煩。	令人心煩的
irritating[6] 〔'ɪrə,tetɪŋ〕 *adj.*	*Irritating*. 令人生氣。	令人生氣的
disturbing[6] 〔dɪ'stɜbɪŋ〕 *adj.*	*Disturbing*. 令人困擾。	令人困擾的
distracting[6] 〔dɪ'stræktɪŋ〕 *adj.*	*Distracting*. 使人分心。	使人分心的
disrupt 〔dɪs'rʌpt〕 *v.*	It's *disrupting* us. 它會打斷我們。	使中斷

Lesson 9

【背景説明 3】

Too noisy. 可説成：It's too noisy here.（這裡太吵了。）
Let's move. It's too noisy.（我們走吧。太吵了。）*Too loud*.
可説成：It's too loud here.（這裡太大聲了。）覺得別人聲音
太大時，可説：Your voice is too loud.（你的聲音太大了。）
説這句話要小心，免得別人揍你。*Hurts my ears*. 可説成：It
hurts my ears.（傷害我的耳朵。）The loud noise hurts my
ears.（大的吵雜聲傷害我的耳朵。）

It bothers me. 可加強語氣説成：It really bothers me.
（真的打擾了我。）It bothers me quite a bit.（它使我很困擾。）
（= *It bothers me a lot.*）*It's annoying*. 可説成：It's so
annoying.（它真令人心煩。）（= *It's very annoying.* = *It's quite
annoying.*）*Irritating*. 可説成：It's irritating.（它令人生氣。）
It's quite irritating.（非常令人生氣。）（= *It's so irritating.*
= *It's very irritating.*）irritating 的動詞是 irritate（激怒），
irritating 這個形容詞是「令人生氣的；令人不耐煩的」。

Disturbing. 可説成：It's disturbing.（令人困擾。）It's
so disturbing.（真令人困擾。）（= *It's very disturbing.*）
Distracting. 可説成：It's distracting.（令人分心。）It's so
distracting.（真令人分心。）（= *It's very distracting.*）*It's
disrupting us*. 中的 disrupt 是動詞，disrupting 是進行式的
動詞，如 It's disrupting my work.（它打斷了我的工作。）
It's disrupting the speech.（它打斷了談話。）

4. I rent.

看英文唸出中文	一 口 氣 說 九 句	看中文唸出英文
rent[3] 〔 rɛnt 〕 *v.*	**I *rent*.** 我租房子。	租用
tenant[5] 〔'tɛnənt 〕 *n.*	**I'm a *tenant*.** 我是房客。	房客
landlord[5] 〔'lænd,lɔrd 〕 *n.*	**Have a *landlord*.** 我有房東。	房東
apartment[2] 〔 ə'pɑrtmənt 〕 *n.*	**Got an *apartment*.** 我有公寓。	公寓
building[1] 〔'bɪldɪŋ 〕 *n.*	**In a *building*.** 在大樓裡。	大樓
resident[5] 〔'rɛzədənt 〕 *n.*	**I'm a *resident*.** 我是居民。	居民
contract[3] 〔'kɑntrækt 〕 *n.*	**Have a *contract*.** 我有合約。	合約
fee[2] 〔 fi 〕 *n.*	**I pay *fees*.** 我付費用。	費用
deposit[3] 〔 dɪ'pɑzɪt 〕 *n.*	**Paid a *deposit*.** 我付了押金。	押金

Lesson 9

【背景説明 4】

I rent. 可説成：I rent an apartment.（我租了一間公寓。）
I'm a tenant. 中，tenant 這個字，要先背 ten（十），再加上 ant
（人），如 servant「傭人」、merchant「商人」，都是 ant 結尾。
可説成：I pay rent.（我付房租。）*Have a landlord.* 可説成：
I have a landlord.（我有房東。）

Got an apartment. 可説成：I've got an apartment.（我有
公寓。）I live in an apartment.（我住在公寓裡。）*In a building.*
可説成：It's in a residential building.（它是在住宅大樓裡。）
（= *It's in an apartment building.*）*I'm a resident.* 可説成：
I'm a resident in that building.（我是那棟大樓的居民。）

Have a contract. 可説成：I have a rental contract.（我有
租約。）My landlord and I have a contract.（房東和我有合約。）
I pay fees. 可説成：I pay fees monthly.（我每個月付費用。）
I pay the rental fee the first week of every month.（我每個月
的第一週付房租。）*Paid a deposit.* 可説成：I paid a deposit.
（我付了押金。）（= *I paid a security deposit.*）不可説成：*I paid
a deposit fee.*（誤）「押金」是 deposit 或 security deposit，而
且不能用現在式：*I pay a deposit.*（誤）因爲押金已經付了。
I pay fees. 用現在式，因爲是每個月都要付的錢。

在美國租房子，通常付一個月的押金（pay one month's
deposit），並預付一個月的房租（pay one month's rent in
advance）。

5. *Daily chores.*

看英文唸出中文	一 口 氣 説 九 句	看中文唸出英文
chore[4] 〔 tʃor 〕*n.*	Daily *chores*. 每天的雜事。	雜事
task[2] 〔 tæsk 〕*n.*	Simple *tasks*. 簡單的任務。	任務
duty[2] 〔 'djutɪ 〕*n.*	It's a *duty*. 這是一種責任。	責任
bed[1] 〔 bɛd 〕*n.*	Make your *bed*. 要整理你的床舖。	床
hang[2] 〔 hæŋ 〕*v.*	*Hang* up clothes. 要把衣服掛起來。	懸掛
dish[1] 〔 dɪʃ 〕*n.*	Do the *dishes*. 要洗碗盤。	盤子
floor[1] 〔 flor 〕*n.*	Keep the *floor* clean. 地板要保持乾淨。	地板
tidy[3] 〔 'taɪdɪ 〕*adj.*	Keep your desk *tidy*. 你的書桌要保持整齊。	整齊的
trash[3] 〔 træʃ 〕*n.*	Throw away the *trash*. 要把垃圾丟掉。	垃圾

Lesson 9

【背景説明 5】

Daily chores. 可説成：Daily chores are important. (每天的雜事很重要。) One chore for me is taking out the trash. (我的雜事之一就是倒垃圾。) *Simple tasks.* 可説成：I help my parents by doing simple tasks. (我幫助我的父母做簡單的任務。) I do simple tasks like sweeping and cleaning. (我做簡單的任務，像是掃地和清潔。) *It's a duty.* 源自 Doing daily chores is a duty. (做家事是一種責任。) 可説成：It's a family duty. (這是一種家庭責任。)

Make your bed. 可説成：Make your bed every day. (每天都要整理你的床舖。) Always make your bed in the morning. (早上一定要整理你的床舖。) *Hang up clothes.* 可説成：Take off and hang up your clothes. (把衣服脫掉，然後掛起來。) Hang up your clothes in the closet. (把你的衣服掛在櫥櫃裡。) *Do the dishes.* 可説成：Wash the dishes. (要洗碗盤。) I often do the dishes for my mom. (我常替媽媽洗碗盤。)

Keep the floor clean. 可説成：Wash the floor. (要洗地板。) Sweep the floor. (要掃地。) *Keep your desk tidy.* 可説成：Always try to keep your desk tidy. (你的書桌一定要儘量保持整齊。) Keep your desk neat. (你的書桌要保持整潔。) *Throw away the trash.* 可説成：Remember to throw away the trash. (記得要丟垃圾。) Throw away the garbage. (要把垃圾丟掉。)

6. *Keep the household clean.*

看英文唸出中文	一口氣說九句	看中文唸出英文
household[4] (ˈhaʊsˌhold) *n.*	Keep the *household* clean. 家裡要保持乾淨。	家；家庭
sanitary[6] (ˈsænəˌtɛrɪ) *adj.*	Be *sanitary*. 要衛生。	衛生的
hygiene[6] (ˈhaɪdʒin) *n.*	Have good *hygiene*. 要有良好的衛生。	衛生
flush[4] (flʌʃ) *v.*	*Flush* the toilet. 要沖馬桶。	沖洗（馬桶）
sink[2] (sɪŋk) *n.*	Keep the *sink* dry. 洗臉台要保持乾燥。	洗臉台；水槽
cockroach[2] (ˈkɑkˌrotʃ) *n.*	Keep *cockroaches* away. 使蟑螂遠離。	蟑螂
germ[4] (dʒɝm) *n.*	Fight *germs*. 要對抗病菌。	病菌
mice[1] (maɪs) *n. pl.*	Fight *mice*. 要對抗老鼠。	老鼠
rat[1] (ræt) *n.*	Fight *rats*. 要對抗老鼠。	老鼠

Lesson 9

【背景説明 6】

Keep the household clean. 中的 household，可作「一家人；家庭」解，也可作「家」(= *home*)、「房子」(= *house*) 解。*Keep the household clean.* 可説成：Keep your home clean.（家裡要保持乾淨。）(= *Keep your house clean.*)

Be sanitary. 可説成：Be a clean person.（做個愛乾淨的人。）Be sanitary to live a healthy life.（要注重衛生，才能過健康的生活。）*Have good hygiene.* 可説成：Keep your body and home clean.（你的身體和家都要保持清潔。）You must have good hygiene.（你必須要有良好的衛生。）

Flush the toilet. 可説成：Always flush the toilet.（一定要沖馬桶。）Maintain a clean toilet.（馬桶要保持清潔。）*Keep the sink dry.* 可説成：Try to keep household sinks dry.（家裡的洗臉台要保持乾燥。）*Keep cockroaches away.* 可説成：Keep roaches away.（使蟑螂遠離。）It's vital to keep cockroaches away.（使蟑螂遠離是很重要的。）

Fight germs. 可説成：Always try to fight against germs.（一定要努力對抗病菌。）Prevent germs.（阻止病菌。）Try to destroy germs.（努力摧毀病菌。）*Fight mice.* 可説成：Take action against mice.（採取行動對抗老鼠。）Fight to prevent mice from getting into your house.（努力防止老鼠進入家裡。）*Fight rats.* 可説成：Work hard to prevent rats.（努力阻止老鼠入侵。）Keep your house clean to prevent rats.（房子保持乾淨，以防止老鼠入侵。）

mouse

rat

7. Let's kill time.

看英文唸出中文	一 口 氣 說 九 句	看中文唸出英文
kill time	Let's *kill time*. 我們來打發時間吧。	打發時間
stroll[5] 〔 strol 〕v.	*Stroll*. 去散步。	散步
people-watch 〔'pipḷˌwɑtʃ 〕v.	*People-watch*. 去看人群。	觀看人群
explore[4] 〔 ɪk'splor 〕v.	*Explore*. 去探險。	探險
exercise[2] 〔'ɛksəˌsaɪz 〕v.	*Exercise*. 做運動。	運動
interact[4] 〔ˌɪntə'ækt 〕v.	*Interact*. 和人互動。	互動
wander[3] 〔'wɑndə 〕v.	*Wander*. 隨便走走。	徘徊
around[1] 〔 ə'raʊnd 〕adv.	Walk *around*. 四處走走。	到處
browse[5] 〔 braʊz 〕v.	*Browse* around. 四處看看。	瀏覽

Lesson 9

【背景説明 7】

Let's kill time. 可説成：Let's kill some time together, OK? (我們一起打發一些時間吧，好嗎？) *Stroll.* 可説成：Let's stroll around. (我們去四處散步吧。) Let's take a stroll. (我們去散步吧。) Let's stroll around for a while. (我們到處散步一會兒吧。) Let's take a walk. (我們去散步吧。) (= *Let's walk around.*) *People-watch.* 可説成：Let's people-watch. (我們看看人群吧。) Let's watch people. (我們看看人群吧。) (= *Let's watch the crowd.*) I like to people-watch. (我喜歡看人群。)

Explore. 可説成：Let's explore. (我們去探險吧。) (= *Let's go explore.* = *Let's look around.* = *Let's check things out.* = *Let's see what we can find.*) explore 這個字，除了是「探險」，還可作「考察」解 (= *travel around an area in order to learn about it*)。即使只是四處走走，都稱作 explore。 *Exercise.* 可説成：Let's exercise. (我們去運動吧。) (= *Let's get some exercise.*) *Interact.* 可説成：Let's interact. (我們去和人互動吧。) (= *Let's try to meet some people.* = *Let's talk to people.*)

Wander. 可説成：Let's wander. (我們隨便走走吧。) (= *Let's wander around.*) wander 的主要意思是「徘徊；流浪」，在此作「(漫無目的地) 到處走」解。 *Walk around.* 可説成：Let's walk around. (我們四處走走吧。) (= *Let's take a walk around.*) *Browse around.* 可説成：Let's browse around. (我們到處看看吧。) Let's browse around for a while. (我們去到處看一下吧。) browse 的意思是「瀏覽」，也就是「隨便看看」。

8. *It's raining hard.*

看英文唸出中文	一口氣說九句	看中文唸出英文
hard[1] 〔 hɑrd 〕*adv.*	**It's raining *hard*.** 雨下得很大。	猛烈地
pour[3] 〔 por 〕*v.*	***Pouring*.** 下傾盆大雨。	下傾盆大雨
come down	***Coming down*.** 下大雨。	下大雨
shower[2] 〔'ʃaʊɚ 〕*n.*	**A *shower*.** 陣雨。	陣雨
downpour[4] 〔'daʊn͵por 〕*n.*	**A *downpour*.** 傾盆大雨。	傾盆大雨
heavy[1] 〔'hɛvɪ 〕*adj.*	***Heavy* rain.** 大雨。	激烈的
storm[2] 〔 stɔrm 〕*v.*	***Storming*.** 有暴風雨。	有暴風雨
bucket[3] 〔'bʌkɪt 〕*n.*	**Raining *buckets*.** 雨傾盆而下。	水桶
rain cats and dogs	***Raining cats and dogs*.** 下傾盆大雨。	下傾盆大雨

【背景説明 8】

It's raining hard. 可説成：It's raining very hard.（雨下得非常大。）It's really raining hard outside.（外面雨眞的下得很大。）*Pouring.* 可説成：It's pouring.（正在下傾盆大雨。）It's pouring outside.（外面在下傾盆大雨。）(= *It's pouring out.*) *Coming down.* 可説成：It's coming down.（正在下大雨。）The rain is coming down hard.（雨下得很大。）It's really coming down.（雨眞的下得很大。）

A shower. 可説成：It's a shower.（是陣雨。）There's a shower outside.（外面下陣雨。）shower 多用於天氣預報，如：You can expect afternoon showers.（你可以預期午後會有陣雨。）*A downpour.* 可説成：It's a downpour.（是傾盆大雨。）It's really a downpour outside.（外面眞的下起傾盆大雨。）*Heavy rain.* 可説成：It's a heavy rain.（雨下得很大。）(= *It's raining heavily.*)

Storming. 可説成：It's storming out today.（今天外面有暴風雨。）*Raining buckets.* 可説成：It's raining buckets.（雨正在傾盆而下。）bucket 的主要意思是「水桶」，複數形 buckets 可作「大量」解，所以 rain buckets 是慣用語，作「下大雨」解。*Raining cats and dogs.* 可説成：It's raining cats and dogs.（正在下傾盆大雨。）不能説成：*It's raining dogs and cats.*【誤】只要記住：<u>c</u>ats and <u>d</u>ogs，c 在 d 前面即可。rain cats and dogs 是慣用語，固定用法，不可改變。

9. It's slippery.

看英文唸出中文	一 口 氣 説 九 句	看中文唸出英文
slippery[3] (ˈslɪpərɪ) *adj.*	It's *slippery*. 很滑。	滑的
slick (slɪk) *adj.*	*Slick*. 很光滑。	光滑的
smooth[3] (smuð) *adj.*	*Smooth*. 很平滑。	平滑的
unsteady[3] (ʌnˈstɛdɪ) *adj.*	*Unsteady*. 不穩定。	不穩定的
unstable[3] (ʌnˈstebḷ) *adj.*	*Unstable*. 不穩定。	不穩定的
perilous[5] (ˈpɛrələs) *adj.*	*Perilous*. 很危險。	危險的
trip[1] (trɪp) *v.*	Don't *trip*. 不要絆倒。	絆倒
slip[2] (slɪp) *v.*	Don't *slip*. 不要滑倒。	滑倒
fall down	Don't *fall down*. 不要摔倒。	摔倒

Lesson 9

【背景説明 9】

It's slippery. 可説成：Be careful. It's slippery.（小心。地很滑。）*Slick.* 可説成：It's slick.（很光滑。）(= *The ground is slick.*) Walk slowly. The ground is slick.（走慢一點。地面很滑。）slick 這個字雖然超出 7000 字範圍，但是常用，還是把它收錄進來。*Smooth.* 可説成：It's smooth.（很平滑。）slippery-slick-smooth 三個字都是 s 開頭，前兩個是 sli 開頭，都是同義字，唸一遍就記得。

Unsteady. 可説成：It's very unsteady.（非常不穩定。）It's kind of unsteady.（有點不穩定。）*Unstable.* 可説成：It's unstable.（不穩定。）It's quite unstable.（相當不穩定。）(= *It's very unstable.*) *Perilous.* 它的名詞是 peril（危險）(= *danger*)。可説成：It's perilous.（很危險。）It's quite perilous.（相當危險。）(= *It's very perilous.*) It's exceptionally perilous.（超級危險。）一個字難背，unsteady-unstable-perilous 三個字一起背就容易了，因爲前兩個都是 unst 開頭，而且意思相同。

Don't trip. 可説成：Don't trip on the slippery surface.（在滑溜的地面上，不要被絆倒。）trip 主要的意思是「旅行」，在此作「絆倒」解。*Don't slip.* 可説成：Don't slip in the shower room.（在淋浴間不要滑倒。）*Don't fall down.* 可説成：Don't fall.（不要跌倒。）Don't slip and fall down.（不要滑倒。）(= *Don't trip and fall down.*)

10. *Don't speed*.

看英文唸出中文	一 口 氣 説 九 句	看中文唸出英文
speed[2] 〔 spid 〕 *v.*	Don't *speed*. 不要超速。	超速
alone[1] 〔 ə'lon 〕 *adv.*	Don't swim *alone*. 不要單獨游泳。	單獨地
text[3] 〔 tɛkst 〕 *v.*	Don't *text* while walking. 走路時不要傳簡訊。	傳簡訊
smoke[1] 〔 smok 〕 *v.*	Don't *smoke*. 不要抽煙。	抽煙
drink[1] 〔 drɪŋk 〕 *v.*	Don't *drink*. 不要喝酒。	喝酒
drug[2] 〔 drʌg 〕 *n.*	Don't use *drugs*. 不要吸毒。	毒品
harmful[3] 〔'hɑrmfəl 〕 *adj.*	Could be *harmful*. 可能會有害。	有害的
hurtful[1] 〔'hɝtfəl 〕 *adj.*	*Hurtful*. 是有害的。	有害的
hazardous[6] 〔'hæzədəs 〕 *adj.*	*Hazardous*. 是危險的。	危險的

Lesson 9

【背景説明 10】

Don't speed. 可說成：Don't speed while driving.（開車時不要超速。）(= *Don't go over the speed limit.*) *Don't text while walking.* 中的 text，主要意思是「內文」，在此作「傳簡訊」解。可說成：Don't text on your phone while walking.（走路時不要用你的手機傳簡訊。）Don't text and drive.（不要一邊開車，一邊傳簡訊。）

Don't smoke. 可說成：Don't smoke cigarettes.（不要抽煙。）Don't smoke too much.（不要抽太多煙。）*Don't drink.* 的意思是「不要喝酒。」不能說成：*Don't drink alcohol.*【誤】但可說成：Don't abuse alcohol.（不要酗酒。）除了酒之外，其他飲料都要說清楚，如：Don't drink too much water.（不要喝太多水。）Don't drink too much soda.（不要喝太多汽水。）*Don't use drugs.* 可說成：Don't do drugs.（不要吸毒。）Stay away from drugs.（遠離毒品。）在這裡的 drugs 就是指「毒品」。drug 也可以指「藥」，如 drugstore（藥房）。

Could be harmful. 可說成：It could be harmful.（可能會有害。）That could be harmful to you.（那可能對你有害。）*Hurtful.* 可說成：It could be hurtful.（可能會有害。）Could be hurtful and dangerous.（可能既有害又危險。）*Hazardous.* 可說成：It could be hazardous.（可能很危險。）(= *It could be dangerous.*)

11. I was scared.

看英文唸出中文	一口氣說九句	看中文唸出英文
scared[1] 〔 skɛrd 〕 adj.	I was **scared**. 我很害怕。	害怕的
nervous[3] 〔'nɝvəs 〕 adj.	**Nervous**. 很緊張。	緊張的
concerned[3] 〔 kən'sɝnd 〕 adj.	**Concerned**. 很擔心。	擔心的
startle[5] 〔'startl̩ 〕 v.	I was **startled**. 我嚇了一跳。	使嚇一跳
tense[4] 〔 tɛns 〕 adj.	**Tense**. 很緊張。	緊張的
uptight 〔 ʌp'taɪt 〕 adj.	**Uptight**. 很緊張。	緊張的
chilling[3] 〔'tʃɪlɪŋ 〕 adj.	It was **chilling**. 它令人恐懼。	令人恐懼的
nightmare[4] 〔'naɪt,mɛr 〕 n.	A **nightmare**. 是一場惡夢。	惡夢
dream[1] 〔 drim 〕 n.	A bad **dream**. 是一場惡夢。	夢

Lesson 9

12. *I'm spent.*

看英文唸出中文	一口氣説九句	看中文唸出英文
spent[1] 〔 spɛnt 〕 *adj.*	*I'm spent.* 我筋疲力盡。	筋疲力盡的
drained[3] 〔 drend 〕 *adj.*	*Drained.* 筋疲力盡。	筋疲力盡的
dead[1] 〔 dɛd 〕 *adv.*	*Dead* tired. 非常疲倦。	非常
worn out	*Worn out.* 筋疲力盡。	筋疲力盡的
wiped out	*Wiped out.* 筋疲力盡。	筋疲力盡的
weak[1] 〔 wik 〕 *adj.*	Feeling *weak.* 覺得很虛弱。	虛弱的
gas[1] 〔 gæs 〕 *n.*	Out of *gas.* 體力耗盡。	汽油 (= *gasoline*)
juice[1] 〔 dʒus 〕 *n.*	Out of *juice.* 沒有活力了。	果汁;活力
left[1] 〔 lɛft 〕 *adj.*	Nothing *left.* 沒有精力了。	剩下的

Lesson 9

Lesson 9

【背景説明 11】

I was scared. 可説成：I was scared about it.（我很怕它。）I was scared for my safety.（我害怕不安全。）I was afraid.（我很害怕。）*Nervous.* 可説成：I was nervous.（我很緊張。）（= *It made me nervous.*）*Concerned.* 源自 I was concerned.（我很擔心。）動詞 concern 是「使擔心」，concerned 已經變成純粹的形容詞，作「擔心的；關心的」解。可説成：I was so concerned.（我很擔心。）（= *I was very concerned.*）I was concerned about you.（我非常擔心你；我非常關心你。）

I was startled. 可説成：I was startled by it.（它使我嚇一跳。）*Tense.* 可説成：I was tense.（我很緊張。）（= *It made me tense.*）*Uptight.* 可説成：I was uptight.（我很緊張。）可加強語氣説成：I felt nervous and uptight.（我感到非常緊張。）*It was chilling.* 可説成：It was so scary.（它很可怕。）*A nightmare.* 可説成：It was a nightmare.（它是一場惡夢。）（= *It was an awful dream.*）*A bad dream.* 可説成：It was a bad dream.（它是一場惡夢。）

【背景説明 12】

I'm spent. 可説成：I'm exhausted.（我筋疲力盡。）I've used up all my energy.（我已經用完我所有的精力。）spent 的主要意思是 spend（花費）的過去式和過去分詞，spent 已經變成純粹的形容詞了，表示「筋疲力盡的」。*Drained.* 可説成：I'm drained.（我體力耗盡了。）drain 的主要意思是「排水」，drained 的字面意思是「水流乾了」，引申爲「筋疲力盡的」。I'm drained of all my energy.（我體力耗盡了。）（= *I feel out of energy.* = *I feel empty.*）*Dead tired.* 可説成：I'm dead tired.（我非常疲倦。）dead 的主要意思是「死的」，在這裡作「非常」解。I feel dead tired.（我覺得非常累。）I feel like I am dead.（我覺得好像死了一樣。）

Worn out. 可説成：I'm worn out.（我筋疲力盡。）(= *I feel worn out.*) wear out 字面的意思是「穿破；穿壞」，I wore out the shoes.（我把鞋子穿壞了。）worn out 原來是過去分詞，現在已經變成純粹的形容詞，表示「穿壞的；筋疲力盡的」。These shoes are worn out.（這雙鞋子已經穿壞了。）*Wiped out.* 可説成：I feel wiped out.（我覺得筋疲力盡。）wipe out 字面的意思是「（用布）把…裡面擦乾淨」，如：Wipe out the empty container.（把空的容器裡面擦乾淨。）wiped out 已經變成純粹形容詞，字面的意思是「被擦乾淨了」，表示「筋疲力盡的」。可加強語氣説成：I feel totally wiped out.（我覺得完全筋疲力盡。）這是美國人的幽默用語。當你説 I'm wiped out. 別人會笑。*Feeling weak.* 可説成：I'm feeling very weak.（我覺得非常虛弱。）I'm tired and feeling weak.（我很疲倦，覺得很虛弱。）Right now I'm feeling weak.（現在我覺得很虛弱。）

Out of gas. 字面的意思是「沒有汽油了。」如：The car is out of gas.（汽車沒油了。）I'm out of gas.「我沒油了。」表示「我體力耗盡了。」(= *I have no energy left.*) *Out of juice.* 可説成：I'm out of juice. 字面的意思是「我沒有果汁了。」引申爲「我體力耗盡了。」(= *I feel out of juice.*) *Nothing left.* 可説成：I have nothing left. 字面的意思是「我沒有東西剩下來了。」引申爲「我沒有精力了。」

這一回九句話，意思接近，你會感覺到美國人的幽默，以後你累了，不要只説 I'm tired. 你可以説：I'm out of gas. I'm out of juice. 説幽默的話，自己高興，也讓身旁的人高興。

Lesson 9 總複習

1. 中式早餐；**2.** 中國菜；**3.** 餐廳太吵　　**4.~6.** 租房子做家事

1. *Baked* bread.
   Fried breadstick.
   Soybean milk.

   Stuffed steamed bun.
   Steamed bun.
   Rice ball.

   Congee.
   Pancakes.
   Dumplings.

2. Hot *pot*.
   Beef *noodles*.
   Peking *duck*.

   Red-cooked *pork*.
   Twice-cooked pork.
   Three-cup *chicken*.

   Egg drop *soup*.
   Hot and *sour* soup.
   Sticky-rice dumpling.

3. Too *noisy*.
   Too *loud*.
   Hurts my ears.

   It *bothers* me.
   It's *annoying*.
   Irritating.

   Disturbing.
   Distracting.
   It's *disrupting* us.

4. I *rent*.
   I'm a *tenant*.
   Have a *landlord*.

   Got an *apartment*.
   In a *building*.
   I'm a *resident*.

   Have a *contract*.
   I pay *fees*.
   Paid a *deposit*.

5. Daily *chores*.
   Simple *tasks*.
   It's a *duty*.

   Make your *bed*.
   Hang up clothes.
   Do the *dishes*.

   Keep the *floor* clean.
   Keep your desk *tidy*.
   Throw away the *trash*.

6. Keep the *household* clean.
   Be *sanitary*.
   Have good *hygiene*.

   Flush the toilet.
   Keep the *sink* dry.
   Keep *cockroaches* away.

   Fight *germs*.
   Fight *mice*.
   Fight *rats*.

7. 打發時間；**8.** 下雨；**9.** 地滑

7. Let's *kill time*.
Stroll.
People-watch.

Explore.
Exercise.
Interact.

Wander.
Walk *around*.
Browse around.

8. It's raining *hard*.
Pouring.
Coming down.

A *shower*.
A *downpour*.
Heavy rain.

Storming.
Raining *buckets*.
Raining cats and dogs.

9. It's *slippery*.
Slick.
Smooth.

Unsteady.
Unstable.
Perilous.

Don't *trip*.
Don't *slip*.
Don't *fall down*.

10.~12. 告誡、害怕、勞累

10. Don't *speed*.
Don't swim *alone*.
Don't *text* while walking.

Don't *smoke*.
Don't *drink*.
Don't use *drugs*.

Could be *harmful*.
Hurtful.
Hazardous.

11. I was *scared*.
Nervous.
Concerned.

I was *startled*.
Tense.
Uptight.

It was *chilling*.
A *nightmare*.
A bad *dream*.

12. I'm *spent*.
Drained.
Dead tired.

Worn out.
Wiped out.
Feeling *weak*.

Out of *gas*.
Out of *juice*.
Nothing *left*.

Lesson 9

Lesson 10　Get well soon.

1. Get better quickly. (I)

看英文唸出中文	一口氣説九句	看中文唸出英文
sick[1] 〔 sɪk 〕*adj.*	Heard you were ***sick***. 聽說你生病了。	生病的
hold up	***Holding up*** OK? 撐得下去嗎？	撐住
survive[2] 〔 sɚ'vaɪv 〕*v.*	Gonna ***survive***? 會活下去吧？	生還
quickly[1] 〔'kwɪklɪ 〕*adv.*	Get better ***quickly***. 要快點好起來。	很快地
ASAP (= *as soon as* 　*possible*)	Get stronger ***ASAP***. 要儘快變得更強壯。	儘快
strength[3] 〔 strɛŋθ 〕*n.*	Regain your ***strength***. 要恢復你的體力。	力量
help[1] 〔 hɛlp 〕*v.*	Can I ***help***? 我能幫忙嗎？	幫忙
thought[1] 〔 θɔt 〕*n.*	You're in my ***thoughts***. 我一直想到你。	想法
prayer[3] 〔 prɛr 〕*n.*	You're in my ***prayers***. 我在為你祈禱。	祈禱；祈禱文

【背景説明 1】

Heard you were sick. 可説成：I heard you were sick.（我聽說你生病了。）*Holding up OK?* 可説成：Are you holding up OK?（你撐得下去嗎？）(= *Are you doing OK?*) Are you hanging in there?（你撐得下去嗎？）暗示：Do you need help?（你需要幫助嗎？）*Gonna survive?* 可説成：Are you going to survive?（你會活下去吧？）(= *Are you going to be OK?*) gonna 等於 going to（將要），例如：I think I'm gonna need some help.（我想我需要一些幫助。）

Get better quickly. 可説成：I hope you get better quickly.（我希望你快點好起來。）*Get stronger ASAP.* 可説成：Get stronger as soon as possible.（要儘快變得更強壯。）ASAP 可唸成四個字母 A-S-A-P 或〔'esæp〕，前者較常用。可説成：Get well fast.（要快點好起來。）*Regain your strength.* 可説成：We want you to regain your strength.（我們希望你能恢復你的體力。）

Can I help? 可説成：Can I help you?（我能幫助你嗎？）(= *May I help you?*) What can I do to help?（有什麼我能幫忙的嗎？）*You're in my thoughts.* 可加強語氣説成：Please know that you're in my thoughts.（請你一定要知道，我一直想到你。）*You're in my prayers.* 可説成：Please know that you're in my prayers.（請你一定要知道，我在為你祈禱。）(= *I'm praying for you.*) Please know that you're in my thoughts and prayers.（請你一定要知道，我一直想到你，並為你祈禱。）pray（祈禱）是動詞，prayer 是名詞，作「祈禱；祈禱文」解，「祈禱的人」是 devotee〔,dɛvə'ti〕(= *a person who prays*)。

2. *Get better quickly*. (*II*)

看英文唸出中文	一口氣說九句	看中文唸出英文
well[1] 〔 wɛl 〕 *adj.*	Get *well* soon. 要快點痊癒。	健康的
recover[3] 〔 rɪˈkʌvɚ 〕 *v.*	*Recover* fast. 要快點康復。	康復
normal[3] 〔ˈnɔrml̩ 〕 *n.*	Return to *normal*. 要恢復正常狀態。	常態
healthy[2] 〔ˈhɛlθɪ 〕 *adj.*	Eat *healthy*. 要吃得健康。	健康的
rest[1] 〔 rɛst 〕 *v.*	*Rest* and sleep. 要休息和睡覺。	休息
cure[2] 〔 kjʊr 〕 *n.*	That's the best *cure*. 那是最佳療法。	治療法
medicine[2] 〔ˈmɛdəsn̩ 〕 *n.*	Take any *medicine*? 有吃任何藥嗎？	藥
doctor[1] 〔ˈdɑktɚ 〕 *n.*	See a *doctor*? 看醫生了嗎？	醫生
Western[2] 〔ˈwɛstɚn 〕 *adj.*	Chinese or *Western*? 中醫還是西醫？	西方的

Lesson 10

【背景説明 2】

Get well soon. 可説成：Get better soon.（要快點好轉。）Get well quickly.（要快點康復。）*Recover fast.* 可説成：I want you to recover fast.（我希望你趕快康復。）Recover ASAP.（儘快康復。）*Return to normal.* 可説成：

I want you to return to normal.（我希望你恢復正常。）Get back to your normal self.（要恢復正常。）

Eat healthy. 可説成：Eat healthy food.（吃健康的食物。）（= *Eat healthy foods.*）Eat a healthy diet.（飲食要健康。）Eat better.（要吃好一點。）Start to eat healthy meals.（要開始吃健康的餐點。）Eat more nutritious foods.（多吃點有營養的食物。）*Rest and sleep.* 可説成：Get lots of rest and sleep.（要多休息和睡覺。）Get enough rest and sleep.（要有充足的休息和睡眠。）*That's the best cure.* 可説成：That's the best way to cure yourself.（那是痊癒最好的方法。）

Take any medicine? 可説成：Did you take any medicine?（你有吃任何藥嗎？）*See a doctor?* 可説成：Did you see a doctor?（你有沒有看醫生？）Have you gone to see a doctor?（你有沒有去看醫生？）See a physician?（看醫生了嗎？）*Chinese or Western?* 可説成：Did you see a Chinese or a Western doctor?（你有沒有看中醫或西醫？）（= *Did you go to a Chinese or Western doctor?*）

3. Experience is valuable.

看英文唸出中文	一口氣説九句	看中文唸出英文
valuable[3] 〔'væljʊəbḷ 〕*adj.*	Experience is *valuable*. 經驗很珍貴。	珍貴的
invaluable[6] 〔 ɪn'væljʊəbḷ 〕*adj.*	*Invaluable*. 是無價的。	無價的
valued[2] 〔'væljʊd 〕*adj.*	It's *valued*. 很寶貴。	寶貴的
precious[3] 〔'prɛʃəs 〕*adj.*	*Precious*. 是珍貴的。	珍貴的
priceless[5] 〔'praɪslɪs 〕*adj.*	*Priceless*. 是無價的。	無價的
prized[2] 〔 praɪzd 〕*adj.*	*Prized*. 很珍貴。	珍貴的
beneficial[5] 〔ˌbɛnə'fɪʃəl 〕*adj.*	*Beneficial*. 是有益的。	有益的
profitable[4] 〔'prɑfɪtəbḷ 〕*adj.*	*Profitable*. 是有利可圖的。	有利可圖的
worth[2] 〔 wɝθ 〕*adj.*	*Worth* a lot. 是很有價值的。	值得…

【背景説明 3】

　　Experience is valuable. 可説成：Every experience in life is valuable. (人生中的每個經驗都很珍貴。) *Invaluable.* 可説成：Experience is invaluable. (經驗是無價的。) *It's valued.* 可説成：It's highly valued. (它非常寶貴。)

　　Precious. 可説成：It's precious. (它很珍貴。) (= *It's very valuable.*) *Priceless.* 可説成：It's priceless. (它是無價的。) It's considered priceless. (它被認爲是無價的。) *Prized.* 可説成：It's a prized thing in life. (它是人生中珍貴的事物。)

下面都是常考的單字，意思相同，程度略有差異：

$$\begin{cases} \text{It's } \underline{\textbf{\textit{valuable}}}. \text{ (它很珍貴。)} \\ = \text{It's } \underline{\textbf{\textit{in}}_|\textbf{\textit{valuable}}}. \text{ (它是無價的。)} \end{cases}$$
　　　　　not¦　　　　　　【無法估價，即是「無價的」】

$$\begin{cases} = \text{It's } \underline{\textbf{\textit{precious}}}. \text{ (它是珍貴的。)} \\ = \text{It's } \underline{\textbf{\textit{priceless}}}. \text{ (它是無價的。)} \end{cases}$$

$$\begin{cases} = \text{It's } \underline{\textbf{\textit{valued}}}. \text{ (它是寶貴的。)} \\ = \text{It's } \underline{\textbf{\textit{prized}}}. \text{ (它是珍貴的。)} \end{cases}$$

$$\begin{cases} \text{It's } \underline{\textbf{\textit{value}}_|\textbf{\textit{less}}}. \text{ (它是沒價值的。)} \\ \quad\quad ¦ \text{ not } \quad 【價值變少，就是「沒價值的」】 \\ = \text{It's } \underline{\textbf{\textit{worthless}}}. \text{ (它是沒價值的。)} \end{cases}$$

　　Beneficial. 可説成：It's beneficial. (它是有益的。) (= *It's very helpful.*) *Profitable.* 可説成：It's profitable. (它是有利的。) It can be profitable. (它可能是有利可圖的。) (= *It can be worth money to you.* = *It can help you make money.*) *Worth a lot.* 可説成：It's worth a lot. (它很有價值。) It's worth a lot of money. (它值很多錢。) Experience is worth a lot. (經驗很有價值。)

4. Eat together! (I)

看英文唸出中文	一口氣說九句	看中文唸出英文
together[1] 〔 tə'gɛðɚ 〕adv.	Eat *together!* 一起吃飯！	一起
break bread	Break *bread!* 一起吃飯！	一起吃飯
meal[2] 〔 mil 〕n.	Share a *meal!* 一起吃飯！	一餐
feast[4] 〔 fist 〕n. v.	*Feast?* 要吃大餐？	大餐；吃大餐
snack[2] 〔 snæk 〕n.	*Snack?* 還是小吃？	小吃
dine[3] 〔 daɪn 〕v.	*Dine?* 要用餐嗎？	用餐
invite[2] 〔 ɪn'vaɪt 〕v.	I'm *inviting* you. 我邀請你。	邀請
chat[3] 〔 tʃæt 〕v.	Let's eat and *chat*. 我們邊吃邊聊吧。	聊天
catch up	Let's *catch up*. 我們聊聊近況吧。	聊近況

【背景説明 4】

Eat together! 可説成：Let's eat together!（我們一起吃飯吧！）
Let's you and I eat together!（我們兩個一起吃飯吧！）I want to
eat together.（我想要一起吃飯。）*Break bread!* 可説成：Let's
break bread!（我們一起吃飯吧！）(*= Let's break bread together!*)
break bread 字面的意思是「把麵包折成兩半」，兩個人一起吃，引申
爲「一起吃飯」，源自聖經。*Share a meal!* 可説成：Let's share a
meal!（我們一起吃飯吧！）

Feast? 可説成：Shall we feast?（我們要不要大吃大喝？）
Want to feast?（要不要大吃一頓？）(*= Want to eat a lot? = Want
a big meal?*) feast 也可當名詞，作「大餐」解，如 Let's have a
feast.（我們去大吃大喝吧。）Would you like to join our feast?
（你願不願意和我們一起吃大餐？）但是現在 feast 多當動詞用，表
示「吃大餐；大吃大喝」。

【比較】 Shall we feast? 【正，常用】
Shall we have a feast? 【正，現在少用】

Snack? 可説成：Shall we grab a snack?（我們要不要吃點東西？）
(*= Shall we grab a bite?*)「小吃店」叫 snack bar。*Dine?* 可説
成：Shall we dine together?（我們一起用餐如何？）Shall we
dine tonight?（我們今晚用餐如何？）

I'm inviting you. 可説成：I'm inviting you to eat.（我邀請你
去吃東西。）Allow me to invite you to eat.（讓我來邀請你去吃
飯。）*Let's eat and chat.* 可説成：Let's talk over a meal.（讓我
們邊用餐邊聊。）Let's discuss things over a meal.（我們邊吃飯邊
討論事情。）*Let's catch up.* 可説成：Let's catch up on all the
news.（讓我們聊聊所有發生的事。）(*= Let's update our news.*)

5. *Eat together!* (*II*)

看英文唸出中文	一口氣說九句	看中文唸出英文
available[3] 〔ə'veləbḷ〕*adj.*	**You *available*?** 你有空嗎？	有空的
free[1] 〔fri〕*adj.*	**You *free*?** 你有空嗎？	有空的
busy[1] 〔'bɪzɪ〕*adj.*	***Busy?*** 忙嗎？	忙碌的
starve[3] 〔stɑrv〕*v.*	**I'm *starving*.** 我快餓死了。	飢餓
famish[6] 〔'fæmɪʃ〕*v.*	**I'm *famished*.** 我肚子餓。	使挨餓
stuff[3] 〔stʌf〕*v.*	**Let's *stuff* ourselves.** 我們要吃得很飽。	填飽（某人肚子）
indulge[5] 〔ɪn'dʌldʒ〕*v.*	**Let's *indulge*!** 我們放縱一下吧！	放縱
pig out	***Pig out!*** 要大吃一頓！	大吃一頓
chow down	***Chow down!*** 要大快朵頤！	大快朵頤

【背景説明 5】

You available? 可説成：
Are you available?（你有空
嗎？）Are you available to
eat?（你有沒有空吃飯？）Are
you available now?（你現在
有空嗎？）*You free?* 可説成：

Are you free now?（你現在有空嗎？）Are you free to eat with
me?（你有沒有空和我一起吃飯？）Do you have free time?（你有
沒有空？）*Busy?* 可説成：Are you busy?（你忙嗎？）Are you
too busy?（你會不會太忙？）Are you busy now?（你現在忙嗎？）

I'm starving. 可説成：I'm starving, are you?（我很餓，你
呢？）*I'm famished.* 可説成：I'm so famished.（我很餓。）
（= *I'm very hungry.*）*Let's stuff ourselves.* 可説成：Let's really
stuff ourselves while eating.（我們吃飯時一定要吃得很飽。）

Let's indulge! 可説成：Let's indulge ourselves!（我們放縱
一下吧！）*Pig out!* 可説成：Let's really pig out!（我們真的要大
吃一頓！）pig 是「豬」，out 是「出去」，豬放出去吃東西時，會
拼命吃個不停，所以 pig out 就引申為「狼吞虎嚥地大吃」。*Chow
down!* 可説成：Let's really chow down!（讓我們真的大吃一頓！）
（= *Let's pig out!*）chow 當名詞是「食物」，當動詞是「吃」。這句
話還可説成：Let's eat as much as we can!（我們大吃一頓吧！）

6. Fantastic restaurant!

看英文唸出中文	一 口 氣 說 九 句	看中文唸出英文
fantastic [4] 〔 fæn'tæstɪk 〕 *adj.*	*Fantastic* restaurant! 很棒的餐廳！	極好的
delicious [2] 〔 dɪ'lɪʃəs 〕 *adj.*	*Delicious* food. 好吃的食物。	美味的
cuisine [5] 〔 kwɪ'zin 〕 *n.*	Healthy *cuisine*. 健康的菜餚。	菜餚
relaxing [3] 〔 rɪ'læksɪŋ 〕 *adj.*	*Relaxing*. 很讓人放鬆。	令人放鬆的
cozy [5] 〔 'kozɪ 〕 *adj.*	*Cozy*. 溫暖而舒適。	溫暖而舒適的
enjoyable [3] 〔 ɪn'dʒɔɪəbḷ 〕 *adj.*	*Enjoyable*. 令人愉快。	令人愉快的
quality [2] 〔 'kwɑlətɪ 〕 *adj.*	*Quality* service. 高品質的服務。	高品質的
courteous [4] 〔 'kɝtɪəs 〕 *adj.*	*Courteous* staff. 有禮貌的員工。	有禮貌的
recommend [5] 〔 ͵rɛkə'mɛnd 〕 *v.*	Highly *recommended*. 非常推薦。	推薦

Lesson 10

【背景説明 6】

Fantastic restaurant! 可説成：It's a fantastic restaurant! （這是很棒的餐廳！）(= *It's a great restaurant! = It's an excellent restaurant!*) *Delicious food.*
可説成：This is delicious food. （這是好吃的食物。）This restaurant has delicious food. （這間餐廳有美食。）Excellent food. （很棒的食物。）*Healthy cuisine.*

可説成：This restaurant has healthy cuisine. （這間餐廳有健康的菜餚。）Nutritious food. （營養的食物。）Good quality food. （品質很好的食物。）

Relaxing. 可説成：It's a relaxing place. （它是個令人放鬆的地方。）(= *It feels very relaxing.*) *Cozy.* 可説成：It feels cozy. （它使人感覺溫暖而舒適。）(= *It's small and comfortable.*) *Enjoyable.* 可説成：It's an enjoyable place. （它是個令人愉快的地方。）(= *I like it a lot.*)

Quality service. 可説成：They have quality service. （他們有高品質的服務。）*Courteous staff.* 可説成：They have courteous staff. （他們的員工很有禮貌。）*Highly recommended.* 可説成：It's highly recommended. （非常推薦。）(= *Many say it's excellent.*)

7. *Controversial subjects*.

看英文唸出中文	一 口 氣 說 九 句	看中文唸出英文
controversial[6] (ˌkɑntrəˈvɝʃəl) *adj.*	***Controversial*** subjects. 有爭議的主題。	有爭議的
politics[3] (ˈpɑləˌtɪks) *n.*	***Politics***. 政治。	政治
religion[3] (rɪˈlɪdʒən) *n.*	***Religion***. 宗教。	宗教
abortion[5] (əˈbɔrʃən) *n.*	***Abortion***. 墮胎。	墮胎
animal[1] (ˈænəml̩) *n.*	***Animal*** testing. 動物測試。	動物
population[2] (ˌpɑpjəˈleʃən) *n.*	***Population*** control. 人口控制。	人口
divorce[4] (dəˈvɔrs) *n.*	***Divorce***. 離婚。	離婚
penalty[4] (ˈpɛnl̩tɪ) *n.*	The death ***penalty***. 死刑。	刑罰
uniform[2] (ˈjunəˌfɔrm) *n.*	School ***uniforms***. 學校制服。	制服

【背景説明 7】

Controversial subjects. 可説成：Avoid controversial subjects.（避免有爭議的主題。）(= *Avoid sensitive subjects.*)
Politics. 可説成：Avoid politics.（避免談論政治。）(= *Try not to talk about politics.*) *Religion.* 可説成：Avoid religion.（避免談論宗教。）

Abortion. 可説成：Avoid abortion.（避免談論墮胎。）(= *Don't discuss abortion.*) *Animal testing.* 可説成：Avoid talking about animal testing.（避免談論動物測試。）*Population control.* 可説成：Avoid discussing population control.（避免討論人口控制。）

Divorce. 可説成：Don't discuss divorce.（不要討論離婚。）Divorce is a sensitive topic.（離婚是個敏感的主題。）*The death penalty.* 可説成：Avoid discussing the death penalty.（避免討論死刑。）*School uniforms.* 可説成：Talking about school uniforms is controversial.（談論學校制服是有爭議的。）

Lesson 10

8. *Controversy everywhere*.

看英文唸出中文	一 口 氣 說 九 句	看中文唸出英文
false¹ 〔 fɔls 〕 *adj.*	True or *false*. 對或錯。	錯誤的
wrong¹ 〔 rɔŋ 〕 *adj.*	Right or *wrong*. 正確還是錯誤。	錯誤的
against¹ 〔 ə'gɛnst 〕 *prep.*	For or *against*. 贊成或反對。	反對
argue² 〔 'ɑrgjʊ 〕 *v.*	We *argue*. 我們會爭執。	爭論
dispute⁴ 〔 dɪ'spjut 〕 *v.*	*Dispute*. 爭論。	爭論
quarrel³ 〔 'kwɔrəl 〕 *v.*	*Quarrel*. 爭吵。	爭吵
debate² 〔 dɪ'bet 〕 *n.*	We have *debates*. 我們進行辯論。	辯論
difference² 〔 'dɪfərəns 〕 *n.*	*Differences*. 我們意見不合。	不同
controversy⁶ 〔 'kɑntrə,vɝsɪ 〕 *n.*	*Controversy* everywhere. 到處都有爭論。	爭論

Lesson 10

【背景説明 8】

True or false. 可説成：It could be true or could be false.
（可能是對，也可能是錯。）Who knows if it's true or false.
（誰知道是對還是錯。）*True or false.* 可翻成：「對的或錯
的。」或「真的或是假的。」*Right or wrong.* 可説成：Maybe
it's right or maybe it's wrong.（也許它是對的，也許它是錯
的。）They disagree on whether it's right or wrong.（關於
對或錯，他們意見不一致。）*For or against.* 可説成：You can
be for or against it.（你可以贊成或反對。）Are you for or
against it?（你贊成還是反對？）(= *Are you for or against?*)

We argue. 可説成：We sometimes argue.（我們有時會爭
執。）We have disagreements.（我們意見不合。）*Dispute.*
可説成：We often dispute.（我們常常爭論。）*Quarrel.* 可説
成：We quarrel once in a while.（我們偶爾會爭吵。）(= *We
argue once in a while.*)

We have debates. 可説成：We often have debates.（我們
常會辯論。）*Differences.* 可説成：We have our differences.
（我們意見不合。）difference 的主要意思是「不同」，在此指
「意見不同；意思不合」。*Controversy everywhere.* 可説成：
There is controversy everywhere.（到處都有爭論。）Many
things are controversial today.（現在很多事情是有爭議的。）
(= *Many topics are controversial everywhere.*)

9. *Don't say toilet*.

看英文唸出中文	一 口 氣 說 九 句	看中文唸出英文
toilet [2] (ˈtɔɪlɪt) *n.*	Don't say ***toilet***. 不要說馬桶。	馬桶；廁所
dirty [1] (ˈdɜtɪ) *adj.*	It sounds ***dirty***. 聽起來很髒。	髒的
image [3] (ˈɪmɪdʒ) *n.*	The ***image*** is ugly. 會有醜陋的印象。	印象
floor [1] (flor) *n.*	Wet ***floor***. 潮濕的地板。	地板
smelly [1] (ˈsmɛlɪ) *adj.*	***Smelly*** room. 發臭的房間。	臭的
bacteria [3] (bækˈtɪrɪə) *n. pl.*	***Bacteria*** on sinks. 洗手台上有細菌。	細菌
restroom [2] (ˈrɛstˌrum) *n.*	Saying ***restroom*** is good. 說洗手間比較好。	洗手間
bathroom [1] (ˈbæθˌrum) *n.*	***Bathroom*** is better. 說化妝室更好。	化妝室
washroom (ˈwɑʃˌrum) *n.*	***Washroom*** is best. 說盥洗室最好。	盥洗室

【背景說明 9】

Don't say toilet. 源自 Don't say the word toilet. (不要說 toilet 這個字。) toilet 這個字,在英國、歐洲是指「廁所」,美國卻指「馬桶」。【詳見「一口氣背會話」p.331】在美國,問人家: *Where's the toilet?* (誤) 他們聽得懂,但因為 toilet 也作「馬桶」解,較不合適。

toilet

It sounds dirty. 可說成: It sounds unclean. (聽起來不乾淨。) It's not nice. (這樣不太好。) *The image is ugly.* 可說成: It's an ugly image. (這是醜陋的印象。) The image is impolite. (給人的印象不禮貌。)

Wet floor. 可說成: You think of a wet floor. (你會想到潮濕的地板。) *Smelly room.* 可說成: You imagine a smelly room. (你會想像一個發臭的房間。) *Bacteria on sinks.* 可說成: You picture bacteria on sinks. (你會想像在洗手台上的細菌。)

sink

Saying restroom is good. 可說成: I recommend saying restroom. (我建議說洗手間。) It's OK to say restroom. (可以說洗手間。) *Bathroom is better.* 可說成: Saying bathroom is better. (說化粧室更好。) It's also polite to say bathroom. (說化粧室也比較禮貌。) *Washroom is best.* 可說成: Saying washroom is best. (說盥洗室最好。)

10. Responses to Thank You (I)

看英文唸出中文	一口氣説九句	看中文唸出英文
welcome[1] (ˈwɛlkəm) *adj.*	You're **welcome**. 不客氣。	受歡迎的
pleasure[2] (ˈplɛʒɚ) *n.*	My **pleasure**. 是我的榮幸。	榮幸
mention[3] (ˈmɛnʃən) *v.*	Don't **mention** it. 不要客氣。	提到
certainly[1] (ˈsɝtn̩lɪ) *adv.*	*Certainly.* 當然沒問題。	當然
of course	*Of course.* 當然沒問題。	當然
sure thing	*Sure thing.* 當然沒問題。	當然
problem[1] (ˈprɑbləm) *n.*	No **problem**. 沒問題。	問題
trouble[1] (ˈtrʌbl̩) *n.*	No **trouble**. 沒什麼。	麻煩
sweat[3] (swɛt) *n.*	No **sweat**. 沒問題。	流汗

* 爲什麼回答説：Certainly. Of course. Sure thing. 詳見「背景説明」。

【背景説明 10】

對別人的道謝，最常用的回答是：*You're welcome.* 字面的意思是「你是受歡迎的。」引申爲「不客氣。」常加強語氣説成：You're very welcome.（你太客氣了。）You're most welcome.（你太客氣了。）You're quite welcome.（你十分客氣。）*My pleasure.* 可説成：It's my pleasure.（這是我的榮幸。）It's been my pleasure.（這是我的榮幸。）用現在式或現在完成式都可以，用完成式語氣較強。*Don't mention it.* 字面意思是「不要提了。」引申爲「不客氣。」可説成：Don't worry about it. 字面意思是「不要擔心。」引申爲「不客氣。」

Certainly. Of course. Sure thing. 這三句話，跟中國文化不合，中國人不太會用。因爲別人跟你道謝，你怎麼能説「當然」呢？可看成源自：No problem, certainly.（當然沒問題。）No problem, of course.（當然沒問題。）No problem, sure thing.（當然沒問題。）

No problem. 可説成：It's no problem.（沒問題。）*No trouble.* 可説成：It's no trouble.（沒什麼。）It's no trouble at all.（一點麻煩都沒有。）*No sweat.* 可説成：It's no sweat.（沒問題。）sweat 的主要意思是「流汗」，*No sweat.*「不流汗」，表示「小事一椿」，即是「沒問題；沒關係。」別人跟你説：Thanks for your help.（謝謝你的幫助。）你可回答：*No sweat.*（小事一椿。）別人説：I'm sorry.（很抱歉。）你也可以回答：*No sweat.*（沒關係。）

Lesson 10

11. *Responses to Thank You* (*II*)

看英文唸出中文	一口氣說九句	看中文唸出英文
worry[1] (ˈwɝɪ) *n.*	No *worries*. 不用擔心。	擔心
deal[1] (dil) *n.*	No big *deal*. 小事一樁。	了不起的事
bother[2] (ˈbɑðɚ) *n.*	No *bother* at all. 一點都不麻煩。	麻煩
any[1] (ˈɛnɪ) *adj.*	*Any* time. 隨時爲你效勞。	任何的
nothing[1] (ˈnʌθɪŋ) *pron.*	It was *nothing*. 沒什麼。	什麼也沒有
service[1] (ˈsɝvɪs) *n.*	At your *service*. 隨時爲你效勞。	服務
say[1] (se) *v.*	Don't *say* that. 別那麼說。	說
least[1] (list) *adj.*	It's the *least* I could do. 這是我最起碼能做的。	最少；最小
polite[2] (pəˈlaɪt) *adj.*	You're too *polite*. 你太客氣了。	客氣的

12. Responses to an Apology

看英文唸出中文	一口氣說九句	看中文唸出英文
OK[1] (ˈoˈke) *adj.*	It's **OK**. 沒關係。	好的；沒問題的
all right	It's **all right**. 沒關係。	沒有什麼； 不要緊
mind[1] (maɪnd) *v.*	I don't **mind**. 我不介意。	介意
thanks[1] (θæŋks) *n. pl.*	**Thanks**. 謝謝。	謝謝
appreciate[3] (əˈpriʃɪˌet) *v.*	I **appreciate** that. 我很感激你那麼說。	感激
apology[4] (əˈpɑlədʒɪ) *n.*	**Apology** accepted. 我接受道歉。	道歉
more[1] (mor) *pron.*	Say no **more**. 不要再說了。	額外的人或物
forgive[2] (fɚˈgɪv) *v.*	All is **forgiven**. 我全都原諒。	原諒
forget[1] (fɚˈgɛt) *v.*	Forgive and **forget**. 既往不咎。	忘記

【背景説明 11】

No worries. 可説成：Hey, no worries.（嘿，不用擔心。）
這句話和中國人的思想不太一樣，有背才會説出來。

> 【比較】 A：Thank you.（謝謝。）
> B：*No worry.*【误】
> **No worries.**（不用擔心。）【正】
> 英文就是這麼難，差一點點就錯，即使天天和美國人
> 在一起，也不見得學得好。背短句是最簡單的方法。

No big deal. 可説成：It's no big deal.（小事一椿。）（= *It's
nothing.*）deal 的主要意思是「交易」，不是大的交易，即是小
事。*No bother at all.* 可説成：It's no bother at all.（一點都不
麻煩。）（= *It was no bother at all.*）

　　Any time. 的字面意思是「任何時候。」表示「任何時候都
可以幫助你。」即「隨時爲你效勞。」可説成：No problem,
any time.（沒問題，隨時爲你效勞。）*It was nothing.* 可加強
語氣説成：It was really nothing at all.（眞的沒什麼。）*At
your service.* 可説成：I'm at your service anytime.（我隨時
爲你效勞。）

　　Don't say that. 可説成：You don't need to say that.（你
不需要那麼說。）Please don't say that.（請不要那麼說。）*It's
the least I could do.* 可説成：It was the least I could do.（這是
我最起碼能做的。）*You're too polite.* 可説成：You're just too
polite.（你眞的太客氣了。）

　　一般中國人遇到別人説 "Thank you."，只會回答 "You're welcome." 背了第 10 及 11 兩回，你的口才就和別人不一樣了。

國人最不會回答的有：

A：Thank you.（謝謝。）

B：Certainly.（當然沒問題。）

　　Of course.（當然沒問題。）

　　Sure thing.（當然沒問題。）

　　Any time.（隨時為你效勞。）

　　It was nothing.（沒什麼。）

　　At your service.（隨時為你效勞。）

中外文化不同，如果照字典上，把 Any time. 翻成「不客氣」，就不好背了。如果把 Certainly. 翻成「當然」，別人跟你道謝，你不能説「當然」，要説「當然沒問題」才對。

【背景説明 12】

　　It's OK. 可説成：Forget it.（算了。）Never mind.（沒關係。）
It's all right. 可説成：No big deal.（沒什麼。）(= *Not a big deal.*)
I don't mind. 可説成：I don't mind at all.（我一點都不介意。）

　　Apology accepted. 可説成：The apology is accepted.（你的道歉已經被接受。）I accept your apology.（我接受你的道歉。）

　　Say no more. 可説成：Please say no more.（請不要再説了。）
All is forgiven. 可説成：You're forgiven.（你已經被原諒了。）
I forgive you.（我原諒你。）*Forgive and forget.* 這是諺語，可説成：I'm ready to forgive and forget.（我準備好要既往不咎。）
It's over.（都過去了。）Let's let it go.（我們讓這件事過去吧。）

Lesson 10　總複習

1., 2. 探病；3. 經驗的重要

1. Heard you were *sick*.
   Holding up OK?
   Gonna *survive*?

   Get better *quickly*.
   Get stronger *ASAP*.
   Regain your *strength*.

   Can I *help*?
   You're in my *thoughts*.
   You're in my *prayers*.

2. Get *well* soon.
   Recover fast.
   Return to *normal*.

   Eat *healthy*.
   Rest and sleep.
   That's the best *cure*.

   Take any *medicine*?
   See a *doctor*?
   Chinese or *Western*?

3. Experience is *valuable*.
   Invaluable.
   It's *valued*.

   Precious.
   Priceless.
   Prized.

   Beneficial.
   Profitable.
   Worth a lot.

4., 5. 邀約用餐；6. 討論餐廳

4. Eat *together!*
   Break *bread!*
   Share a *meal!*

   Feast?
   Snack?
   Dine?

   I'm *inviting* you.
   Let's eat and *chat*.
   Let's *catch up*.

5. You *available*?
   You *free*?
   Busy?

   I'm *starving*.
   I'm *famished*.
   Let's *stuff* ourselves.

   Let's *indulge!*
   Pig out!
   Chow down!

6. *Fantastic* restaurant!
   Delicious food.
   Healthy *cuisine*.

   Relaxing.
   Cozy.
   Enjoyable.

   Quality service.
   Courteous staff.
   Highly *recommended*.

7. , 8. 閒聊；9. 勸告

7. *Controversial* subjects.
   Politics.
   Religion.

   Abortion.
   Animal testing.
   Population control.

   Divorce.
   The death *penalty*.
   School *uniforms*.

8. True or *false*.
   Right or *wrong*.
   For or *against*.

   We *argue*.
   Dispute.
   Quarrel.

   We have *debates*.
   Differences.
   Controversy everywhere.

9. Don't say *toilet*.
   It sounds *dirty*.
   The *image* is ugly.

   Wet *floor*.
   Smelly room.
   Bacteria on sinks.

   Saying *restroom* is good.
   Bathroom is better.
   Washroom is best.

10. , 11. 回答感謝；12. 回答道歉

10. You're *welcome*.
    My *pleasure*.
    Don't *mention* it.

    Certainly.
    Of course.
    Sure thing.

    No *problem*.
    No *trouble*.
    No *sweat*.

11. No *worries*.
    No big *deal*.
    No *bother* at all.

    Any time.
    It was *nothing*.
    At your *service*.

    Don't *say* that.
    It's the *least* I could do.
    You're too *polite*.

12. It's *OK*.
    It's *all right*.
    I don't *mind*.

    Thanks.
    I *appreciate* that.
    Apology accepted.

    Say no *more*.
    All is *forgiven*.
    Forgive and *forget*.

Lesson 10

INDEX・索引

INDEX

本書所有人

姓 名 ＿＿＿＿＿＿＿＿＿＿＿＿　電 話 ＿＿＿＿＿＿＿＿＿

地 址 ＿＿＿＿＿＿＿＿＿＿＿＿＿＿＿＿＿＿＿＿＿＿＿＿＿

（如拾獲本書，請通知本人領取，感激不盡。）

「一口氣必考字彙極短句」背誦記錄表

篇　　名	口試通過日期			口試老師簽名
Lesson 1	年	月	日	
Lesson 2	年	月	日	
Lesson 3	年	月	日	
Lesson 4	年	月	日	
Lesson 5	年	月	日	
Lesson 6	年	月	日	
Lesson 7	年	月	日	
Lesson 8	年	月	日	
Lesson 9	年	月	日	
Lesson 10	年	月	日	

「財團法人臺北市一口氣英語教育基金會」
提供 *100* 萬元獎金，領完為止！

1. 凡在 2 分鐘內背完一個 Lesson，108 句，
　 即可領獎金 *500* 元。

2. 在 15 分鐘之內，背完 10 回，1,080 句，可再領獎金 *5,000* 元。

3. 背完整本「**一口氣必考字彙極短句**」，共可領 *1* 萬元。

4. 每天只能口試 2 次，限背一個 Lesson。

5. 背誦地點：台北市許昌街 17 號 6F–6【一口氣英語教育基金會】
　　 TEL: (02) 2389-5212

劉毅老師千人公開課、全國校長師訓
上海站成功舉辦

—— 菁尚教育沈韜校長

　　2017年10月14日晚上，由菁尚教育主辦的「劉毅一口氣英語千人講座」在上海交大菁菁堂舉行，齊聚各路大咖、彙集了千人學子，共同見證大師風采，領略「一口氣英語」的獨特魅力。

劉毅老師熱情地與學員分享「一口氣英語」

由菁尚教育在上海主辦的「劉毅一口氣英語千人講座」座無虛席

「一口氣英語」是根據最科學的分析和實際檢測的背誦經驗，以特殊的組合，三句為一組，九句為一段。它要求學習者大聲朗讀，反覆練習，然後背誦，自然加快速度，最終能夠在5秒鐘之內背出這九句話，達到英文脫口而出的水準。此時，所有的內容，就會變成自己大腦裡存儲記憶的一部分，一輩子也不會忘記，需要用時隨時取用，依照此法日積月累，自然就能出口成章，能夠說最道地的英語了。此方法的發明，震撼兩岸教育界，數以萬計的學子因此而受益。

　　緊接著，10月17日、18日全國校長師訓拉開帷幕。此次師訓彙集了全國英語教培機構的精英校長們，全國一口氣英語明星講師，更有瘋狂英語李陽校長知名大咖到場出席本場英語盛宴。

劉毅老師與李陽校長、沈韜校長

　　劉毅老師、李陽校長現場即興互飆一口氣英語演講，帶領全場校長們高呼"Follow our passion. Follow our hearts. Anything is possible."令來自海峽兩岸的知名校長們激情澎湃。兩岸教培天王齊聚上海，同堂飆課的精彩師訓場面，成為此次活動中，激動人心而又令人難忘的一幕。

劉毅老師師訓金句：

1. 教材要能讓老師能夠教學相長，越教越喜歡教。只有全身心投入，才能真正感受到教書的魅力。

2. 每一位學生都是老師的恩人，要不斷鼓勵孩子。英文不好，要誇國文好；功課不好，要誇身體好；身體不好，要誇品格好。

3. 課堂上的每一分鐘，都要讓學生驚喜和感動，讓孩子下課後回家很振奮，要想盡辦法不斷提高學生成績。

4. 只有用心編寫、震撼靈魂的書，才不會隨著時間流逝被大家遺忘。你無我有，是勝過別人的關鍵。

　　為期兩天的精彩師訓課程，令全國校長們意猶未盡。劉毅老師獨創的英語教學法，以及研發的教材，經過長年的努力，令大陸老師們大受啟發，決心在傳承教學理念和技巧的同時，努力將學習英語的獨特方法發揚光大。

　　授課過程中，由劉毅老師精心編製的適合不同人群、不同程度學生的教材，不斷免費贈予與會老師，無不體現著一名教育者的大愛情懷。《一分鐘背九個單字》、《用會話背7000字》、《英語自我介紹》等演講、《臺灣、大陸高考全真試題》等書籍，切中學生學習痛點及弱點，必將掀起大陸英文學習革命的新高潮。

劉毅老師與菁尚教育全體老師合影

劉毅老師親傳大弟子——Windy老師帶領30名「一口氣英語」代言學生帶來精采開場。"You always put me first, You make me feel so special." 《感恩父母之英文演講篇》的朗朗背誦聲震撼全場，小演說家們精準的發音、翩翩的台風、一氣呵成的現場演講，贏得聽眾們陣陣掌聲。

劉毅老師與Windy老師合影

　　重磅級嘉賓——劉毅老師的登台，更是把氛圍推向了高潮。為什麼學英文容易忘記，背了很多卻不能學以致用，單詞量總感覺不夠？劉毅老師獨創的「一口氣英語」學習法對症下藥，全面助力孩子提升英語成績。